BABY QUEEN

THE COURT BOOK THREE

SPECIAL EDITION

CHARLIE NOVAK

May there always be beautiful people who help us heal.

Love,
Charlie

Copyright © Charlie Novak 2024

Cover by Natasha Snow

Cover photography by Wander Aguiar

Editing by Jennifer Smith

Formatting by Pumpkin Author Services

All rights reserved. Charlie Novak asserts the moral right to be identified as the author of this work.

This novel is entirely a work of fiction. Names, characters, places, and incidents are the products of the author's imagination or are used fictitiously. Any resemblance to actual events, locales, organizations or persons, living or dead, is entirely coincidental.

A NOTE FROM THE AUTHOR

Many drag performers use different pronouns in and out of drag, depending on their style of drag and their personal gender identity, and the performers in this book do the same.

To help you get to know them, here's a list of *Baby Queen*'s drag stars and their pronouns in and out of drag.

Barbie Summers, drag queen: she/her in drag, he/him out of it.
Sugar Pill, drag queen: she/her in drag, he/him out of it.
Bitch Fit, drag queen: she/her in drag, he/him out of it.
Bubblegum Galaxy, drag queen: she/her in drag, he/him out of it.
Eva Nessence, drag queen: she/her in drag, he/him out of it.
Peachy Keen, drag queen: she/her in drag, he/him out of it.
Legs Luthor, drag queen: she/her in drag, he/they out of it.
Violet Bucket, drag queen: she/her in drag, he/him out of it.

Ginger Biscuits, drag queen: she/her in drag, he/they out of it.
Moxxie Toxxic, drag king: they/them in and out of drag.
Incubussy, drag king: he/him in drag, she/her out of it.

Like many artists, musicians, writers, and performers, you'll also find many of the drag artists in this novel are referred to by their drag name, or a variation, while out of drag as well as in it.

*For all of us who've blamed ourselves for something that wasn't our fault.
Please forgive yourself.*

CHAPTER ONE

Barbie Summers

If one more person tried to tell me that everything happened for a reason, I swore I would scream. Because in what world would I choose to be broke, single, and homeless after winning one of the biggest drag shows in the world?

The answer was none.

There was no universe in which I'd prefer dragging whatever was left of my worldly possessions back into my childhood bedroom and flopping down onto my old squeaky, saggy single bed over living in my cosy London flat and selling out club tours up and down the UK.

Unfortunately, that was the hell I was living in and I was still adjusting to the fact I'd ended up here.

I groaned as I reached for one of the nearby pillows and pulled it over my face, muffling my frustrated scream. At least I had somewhere to come back to—that was what I kept telling myself. At least Mum hadn't been against me moving back in. In fact, she'd been delighted and I'd added a new dimension to my guilt and self-loathing when I'd realised I'd barely seen her since I'd moved to London four years ago.

I could add being a terrible son to the long list of my other failures.

A hollow chuckle slipped from my lips as I wondered what my fans would think if they knew the truth: Barbie Summers, the UK's hottest drag superstar, was a broke-ass whiny bitch. And sure, I had about twenty grand's worth of drag to my name, but I couldn't exactly use that to put a deposit down on a flat.

I had considered selling some of it, but so far I'd held off because there was no way to sell things quietly without some fan or other getting wind of it and plastering it all over social media. And while I could say I was clearing out my wardrobe to make space for new looks, I couldn't sell half my outfits because they technically were owned by *Drag Stars* and therefore nobody else could ever wear them. Plus if I said I was making room for new shit, people would expect to see new shit. And that wasn't happening.

It'd been made painfully obvious to everyone who'd watched my season of *Drag Stars UK* that I couldn't sew beyond a basic running stitch, so I wouldn't be magically conjuring up couture drag looks any time soon, especially not on my budget.

"Knock knock. Anthony?" The knocks on the bedroom doorframe were accompanied by Mum's warm voice, and I pulled the pillow off my face and hugged it to my chest before I responded.

"Yeah?"

"Can I come in?"

"Yeah," I said, hauling myself into a sitting position as the bed squeaked again. "If you can get in." The room was full of black bin bags, old cardboard boxes I'd scavenged from the Tesco Express down the road from my old flat, a couple of cheap plastic tubs I'd picked up from a bargain store a couple of years ago that were now held together with duct tape, and two battered suitcases. At some point I'd have to unpack everything, but that was a problem for another day.

Or when I actually needed something that wasn't resting on top of a box or bag.

The door was shoved open, catching slightly on the threadbare carpet, and Mum's face appeared around it. Her dark blonde hair was scraped back into a messy bun and she looked more tired than I remembered. I knew she'd said work had been more stressful lately due to the local council's hiring freeze and budget cuts, but I wondered if it was more than that. I'd hate to think I was the reason she looked so exhausted.

Come on, Anthony. Not everything revolves around you.

Ah, the old adage of my ex-boyfriend. It was like being haunted by the ghost of douchebags past. What on earth I'd ever seen in him was a mystery I'd never solve. And why the fuck I'd gone back to him time and time again was another.

This time would probably be permanent, though. Especially since he couldn't use me to get anything.

Who knew that losing everything was the fastest way to get rid of leeches?

"Is he still sulking?" another voice called from over Mum's shoulder. It was bolder and brighter and just the sound of it made me smile.

"I'm not sulking. Piss off, Maddi," I said as Mum forced the door further open, shoving one of my boxes of shoes against the wall, which was still the pale lavender I'd painted it at fifteen. She slid through the door and looked around at the chaos, her expression saying everything her mouth wasn't.

"You've retreated to your room and... oh, for fuck's sake, you're hugging a pillow. Could you be any more overdramatic?" asked Maddi, my best friend in the entire world, as she stepped into the room alongside Mum, brushing her black cherry hair out of her face and looking around with disapproval.

Maddi did not like mess and I doubted she approved of me wallowing in self-pity when I could've been unpacking. But surely I deserved a little bit of time to wallow in my misery first?

Maddi, or Madam Mercy to the general population, was a drag queen I'd met through *Drag Stars UK*. We hadn't competed on the same season but we'd connected through social media when she'd tagged me in some posts cheering me on. I'd sent her a message to fangirl and she'd decided to adopt me as her friend. She made my life a million times better and while she'd never been afraid to call out my self-pitying ass, she was also the first to offer me a hug while she tried to fix my problems.

We talked every single day and shared everything, big and small.

I'd been one of the first people Maddi had come out as trans to at the end of last year, and it was a moment I'd treasure forever. If there was such a thing as platonic soulmates, Maddi would be mine. And I loved her even when she was determined to drag my life into shape by hook or by crook.

"Oh, come on, babe, can't I even get a little bit of sympathy?" I asked, fluttering my eyelashes in a way I hoped made me look cute.

"No." Maddi folded her arms. "I love you, honey, but you've done nothing but whine for the last three months. And I know this is all fucked-up dogshit but you can't keep moping around and expect the world to fucking fix everything for you." She glanced at my mum and winced. "Sorry, Sarah."

"It's fine," Mum said with a warm smile. "I've heard worse. And you've got a point." She folded her arms and looked at me. "I know this isn't want you wanted, Anthony, but doing this isn't going to help."

"Not you too," I said with a groan as I flopped back down on the bed, which moaned loudly like a stereotypical horde of cartoon ghosts, and pulled the pillow back over my face. They had a point—sort of—but did they have to be so mean about it? My entire life had fallen apart and now they were expecting me to pick up and carry on like nothing had happened. I knew I had to get back in the saddle at some point, but their continued insistence was making my brain dig its heels in like a stubborn toddler ready to scream and throw itself on the ground in an epic tantrum.

One of them sighed—probably Maddi—and then I heard boxes and bags being moved as they crossed the room. The bed dipped next to me and a hand patted my thigh. "I'm sorry," Maddi said gently.

I lifted the pillow slightly and looked at her, well aware I looked like a sulking teenager but unwilling to admit it or apologise for it. Maddi rubbed my thigh before continuing. "This whole situation is bollocks and I'm so angry for you… and I think… I just want everything to be okay. And I think that's why I'm pushing you, because if things get back to normal, I might feel less inclined to commit rampant and bloody murder on Caesar fucking Hurst and his entire organisation."

"Get in line, babe," I said. "I get first dibs. But I need to get paid first."

"Money first, then murder. Got it."

I chuckled and shoved the pillow under my head, realising Mum had left Maddi and me alone. I'd have to apologise to her later because she didn't deserve to have me bitch at her, not when she was only trying to help.

"I don't think things can ever go back to normal, Mads," I said quietly, staring up at the ceiling where a few glow-in-the-dark stars still clung to the paint. It made something warm flicker in my chest because while I might be completely lost at sea, I still had a safe place to call home. And while it might be small and filled with remnants of my teenage dreams, from vintage Barbie posters on the wall to the bookshelves filled with old copies of *Vogue* dating back to the nineties, it was mine and nobody could touch me here. "Everything is too different."

"Yeah, I know," she said, flopping down next to me. The bed was a bit small for both of us and I had to wiggle across as far as I could, lying on my side facing her and pressing my butt against the wall. "Maybe things can be better, though? Maybe all this change will be good for you."

I had to admire her unrelenting optimism but for Maddi there wasn't another choice, and that was part of why I loved her. "Maybe. Who knows."

She grinned. "I'll take it."

We lay in comfortable silence for a moment, our fingers interlaced on the bed between us. "I appreciate you getting me in with your friend, though," I said. When I'd told Maddi I was having to move back to Newark in the East Midlands, she'd immediately asked me where it was near and when I'd mentioned Lincoln, she'd squealed that she knew someone there. I hadn't thought much of it, which in hindsight had been a rookie move on my part because two days later Maddi had called me out of the blue while I'd been making the most of my soon-to-be-ending gym membership to tell me she'd found me something.

Apparently, a drag friend she'd toured with, Bitch Fit, was from Lincoln and knew a club I might be able to perform at but, more interestingly, was looking to put together the area's first drag pantomime and would kill to have me involved. She'd given me Bitch's email and I'd said yes without a second thought.

I'd had no details about the money, the contract, the

dates, anything, but it was a job and one I desperately needed.

Afterwards I'd cursed myself for not asking for more details, because that was how I'd gotten into this mess in the first place, but luckily Maddi was not me and it turned out Bitch Fit had a law degree, so I hoped I was in safe hands. But still, I had gotten a loving bollocking from Maddi for not thinking things through. Which was why I now had a list of questions pinned to the notes section in my phone to ask everyone who wanted to book me.

Fool me once, shame on you. Fool me multiple times and never pay me for my work... well, that made you a bastard and me a naïve, ignorant twit.

"Of course, babe," Maddi said. "I promise, you're going to love everyone at The Court. And they're going to love you."

"Did you tell them?"

"About what happened?" Maddi asked with a gentle frown. I nodded. "God no. They just know whatever you've told them."

"Okay, good." I'd kept my reasons for moving home vague and hopefully nobody would press me further. And if they did... well, I guessed I'd need to come up with a couple of convincing lies. "I'm going up on Saturday to say hi to everyone. I wish you could come."

"Me too, but it's gonna be awesome. I promise."

I nodded, hoping that Maddi was right.

The only problem was, I'd been burned too many times to have hope anymore.

CHAPTER TWO

Colin

I LOOKED at my reflection in the mirror, scrutinising every detail of my carefully made-up face.

My eyebrows were good, the eye shadow was definitely better, the liner… well, hopefully nobody would be looking at it that closely. And the less said about my contour, the better. I liked this lip colour on me, though—it wasn't too dark against my pale skin and didn't make me look like an extra in some slutty vampire fantasy.

Not that there was anything wrong with slutty vampire fantasies, it was what made up half my bookshelf, but it wasn't quite the look I was going for.

At least, I didn't think it was.

I grabbed my phone off my desk, which was doubling as a vanity table, and took a few quick selfies, trying to capture as much detail as possible before picking up the nearby bottle of make-up remover and pouring some on my fingers. My skin still wasn't on board with this whole wanting-to-do-drag thing. Or maybe it was more the "starting a PhD in maths at a Russell Group university in a completely new city where I knew nobody" thing, especially because it came with an added side of dealing with a clingy, controlling ex-boyfriend who refused to accept we'd broken up. Who, despite the fact I'd blocked him on every platform and number possible, kept finding ways to leave me endless voice messages. I needed to just suck it up and change my number.

Whatever it was, it was making me break out and half my money this month had gone on a ton of new skincare that at least five different websites all swore would help. I wasn't completely convinced but I'd spent the money now, so it felt like a waste not to use it.

After I'd carefully removed all traces of my make-up, I picked up my phone to take a quick break before I attempted another look. As soon as I opened Instagram, a new post from the drag queen Bubblegum Galaxy appeared at the top of my feed and I gazed in awe at the gorgeous baby blue and pink outfit she was wearing, complete with a perfectly painted face. She even had little pink rhinestones dotted around her eyes.

It was everything I wanted to be able to do, and while I knew we all had to start somewhere, looking at Bubblegum's photos made my stomach sink like it was full of lead because there was no way I was ever going to be able to do anything like that.

No. I wasn't going to think like that. I had to be positive.

If Elle Woods could get a 179 on her LSAT and get into

Harvard Law School, then I could become a drag queen. Because in the words of Elle herself, "What, like it's hard?"

And it wasn't like I was completely on my own. I'd been offered help. I simply hadn't plucked up the courage to reach out yet.

Rhys, one of the guys I did pole with, knew a couple of local drag artists and had promised me Bubblegum would be happy to help if I had questions. I wasn't even sure *how* Rhys had known I wanted to start drag since I'd never said anything, but he'd simply popped up at pole one day and said if it was something I was interested in, then he knew people who could help.

I'd thought he'd been volunteering his boyfriend, Evan, who was also a drag queen, but since Evan was recovering from burnout, Rhys had smartly insisted he did less stuff rather than adding more to his plate.

It was what also made the offer of help feel so overwhelming, because Rhys had gone out of his way for me—a person he barely knew—on the off chance drag was something I was interested in.

My finger hovered over Bubblegum's photo and before I could think it through, I tapped onto her profile and clicked message.

The blank screen stared up at me and I was filled with overwhelming dread as I realised I actually had to write something.

Would "hey" sound too casual? "Hello" would probably be too formal—I wasn't messaging one of my lecturers.

Why was writing a simple message so fucking hard?

Eventually, after writing and rewriting everything, I had

something I was vaguely happy with, even if my stomach was churning at the idea of sending it.

> **Colin**
> Hi! I hope it's okay for me to message you. My name is Colin and Rhys told me I could drop you a line if I had any questions about drag? Sorry if that's not the case. Thanks.

I wondered if I should mention that Rhys was Evan's boyfriend, but hopefully Bubblegum would know who I was talking about. And if not, we'd cross that awkward bridge when we came to it.

"You can do it," I said, trying to psych myself up enough to hit send. "It's not hard to send a message."

I stared at the screen for another minute before I finally tapped the button, then slammed my phone face down on the desk so I couldn't read anything that popped up. My heart was thundering and I rubbed my chest absent-mindedly in the hope it might soothe my anxiety or at least convince me to stop holding my breath.

It wasn't like I was expecting a response and I doubted I'd even get one, so I didn't know why I was worrying. Bubblegum definitely had better things to do on a Thursday night than message some random stranger who'd popped into her inbox. Because while I knew her from Instagram, TikTok, and her performances at The Court in Lincoln, I was nothing more than a wannabe with terrible eyeliner and no idea where my own cheekbones were.

To distract myself I selected my other eye shadow

palette, since I only owned two, picked up my concealer, and started working on my eyes again. I wanted to go for something bright and bold but still soft. In my head I could picture exactly what I wanted it to look like. The only issue was transferring it to my face.

I'd watched countless tutorials on blending eye shadow and creating perfect cut creases, and in principle it hadn't seemed that difficult. But the reality was proving to be the complete opposite. How was this more complicated than my PhD? I spent most of my days dealing with mathematical modelling, clinical data, and computational analysis, and that was still easier. Maybe it was because numbers had always made sense to me—maths and science were complicated, sure, but they'd never confused me in the same way creative work did. I loved being creative, which was why I adored pole dance and drag, but the idea of studying it and writing endless pieces of literary analysis made me shudder.

"This is hopeless," I muttered to myself as I put my brushes down and turned my head from side to side, examining my reflection. I didn't like how it had turned out at all. Maybe the colours weren't right for me... my bright red hair was beautiful but it did clash with things. Although maybe if I was wearing a wig, it would be different.

I glanced around my room, trying to remember where I'd put the two wigs I'd ordered from Amazon but hadn't actually had the courage to open.

My stomach twinged as I did, stopping me in my seat as I tried to remember the last time I'd had something to eat. My housemates had been in the kitchen when I'd gotten home from the university and I hadn't wanted to get in the way, so I'd said hi then come straight up to my room. And now it was nearly nine at night and I still hadn't had dinner.

Grabbing the make-up wipes I used for quick corrections, I quickly wiped the half-finished eye make-up off my face, shoved my phone in the pocket of my hoodie, and headed downstairs.

The house I rented a room in was an old town house not too far from the university but far enough away that most of our neighbours were other postgraduates or people in full-time work rather than undergraduates who spent half their time partying. The house wasn't in too bad a condition despite its age, and although the decor was drab and there was the odd spot of damp, it could have been a hell of a lot worse. The kitchen had obviously been refurbished in the past five or six years, and there was plenty of cupboard space for the four of us along with an enormous American-style fridge-freezer, which meant none of us had to cram our food onto half a shelf or into a small vegetable drawer.

And sharing with other PhD students meant we'd all grown out of the habit of nicking someone else's leftovers or drinking each other's milk. As someone with lactose intolerance I'd been safe from that for a few years, at least until almond milk had become popular and nobody else had wanted to pay for it. Luckily, here everyone was grown up and kept their sticky paws to themselves.

The only issue was that my other housemates all studied in the same school and had clearly known each other for several years, and while they'd tried their best to make me feel welcome, it was still hard not to feel like the odd one out.

Maybe I needed to make more of an effort.

I opened the fridge and stared inside, hoping dinner would leap fully formed out of it. But no such luck. I didn't even have that much in. Pasta and grated cheese it was then.

Since it would be faster to use boiling water for the pasta, I stuck the kettle on while I rummaged around for a saucepan, putting it on the hob and pouring a decent amount of pasta into it. Once the kettle had boiled I filled the pan with water, sprinkled some salt in, and flicked the burner on. I didn't want to leave it unsupervised because there was a good chance I'd forget about it until the fire alarm went off or one of my housemates came to ask why there was a burnt saucepan of pasta on the hob. I'd lost more than a couple of saucepans that way over the years.

I leant against the counter while I waited, pulling my phone out of my hoodie to pass the time. But when I unlocked it, I was surprised to see a message notification from Instagram.

Bubblegum Galaxy had replied to me.

With shaking fingers, I opened her message.

> **Bubblegum Galaxy**
> Hi!! Rhys told me and Bitch Fit all about you and I'm so glad you reached out! What can I help you with? Are you just getting into drag? What sort of stage are you at? <3

Colin
Hey, thanks for getting back to me! I'm just getting started and still playing around with looks and make-up (definitely finding it harder than I anticipated) but I'd like to know more about getting started, where to go from here etc. Thanks.

Bubblegum Galaxy
Okay that's perfect! Don't worry, we all have to start somewhere and your make-up will improve the more you practice and there are so many good tutorials out there for basics (sorry if you're already doing that). Do you have a drag name yet? Or an idea of style? Don't worry if not because that'll come with time too. Most of us start out as a bit of a hot mess!

Bubblegum Galaxy
What are you doing on Saturday? Why don't you come to The Court and maybe meet a few of us? I'm sure we'll be able to give you some pointers! You've come to the shows with Rhys before, right? So you know where we are. It'd be so nice to meet you <3

I stared at her message, her generosity truly flooring me. Rhys had said Bubblegum was sweeter than candyfloss, but he'd said it almost as a joke. There was no denying the sweetness in her words, though. I'd been expecting a few tips at most but inviting me to meet her and some of the other artists at The Court wasn't something I'd ever imagined happening. And even if I only got five minutes with them, every second of it would be worthwhile.

> **Colin**
> Thank you, it would be amazing to meet you all too! Are you sure that's okay?

> **Bubblegum Galaxy**
> Of course, babe! Come along at about six-ish, you don't need to be in drag, and just ask someone at the bar to let me know you're there.

> **Colin**
> Thank you so much, I really appreciate it.

> **Bubblegum Galaxy**
> No worries! Can't wait to meet you <3

An achingly bright smile split my face as I bounced on the spot. I was one step closer to making my drag dreams a reality.

Now all I had to do was not fuck it up.

CHAPTER THREE

Barbie Summers

Despite the fact that I felt like a craptastic piece of shit, there was no way in hell I was letting it show on my face. Barbie Summers didn't do depression. Anthony could do that on his own fucking time when making a good impression wasn't at stake.

I'd initially asked Bitch Fit whether I needed to turn up at The Court in drag or whether street clothes would be fine, and since she'd said it was totally up to me and whatever I felt most comfortable in, I'd been planning to just turn up in jeans and a tank top. But as the clock ticked down towards five, which was when I needed to leave, I'd felt panic rising in my stomach at the idea of people actually seeing me for who I was.

They were expecting Barbie, polished, pageant-ready, and serving pussy. The queen who'd won an impressive four challenges on her season of *Drag Stars UK* before sweeping the crown, who'd never been in the bottom two, and whose final lip-sync had already reached iconic status in the fandom. The winner with sparkle and panache, who'd done sold-out tours, appeared on fucking *BBC Breakfast* and *The One Show*, and had nearly two hundred and fifty thousand followers on Instagram.

The one with her fucking life together.

Going as Anthony was no longer an option.

Which meant I spent a chaotic hour pulling things out of boxes, trying to work out where the hell I'd put my tits, attempting not to put holes in my tights, and painting my face to the level of perfection I'd come to expect of myself. And despite the stress, it was good to get back into drag again—with the chaos of the move, my break-up, and being fucked over by the tour company who'd promised me everything, I hadn't felt like being Barbie.

Maybe that had been part of the problem—I'd pulled away from the part of me that had always made me feel accomplished, that had allowed me to put myself out there to be loved and applauded, and it had left me open to emptiness and despair.

Once I was fully dragged up, I'd only ended up leaving fifteen minutes late and since I'd given myself more time than I'd needed, I found myself arriving at The Court at five past six in my favourite pair of seven-inch heels.

I hadn't been here for years because even in my early drag days I'd drifted more towards the Nottingham scene than Lincoln, but just walking into the small lobby with its wooden floor, neon rainbows in different pride flags, and camp, retro decor made a warm feeling of comfort settle in my gut. It wasn't quite a sense of home but more a sense of belonging.

"Hey! You can only be Barbie Summers," said a bright, bouncing voice from behind me. I turned to see a handsome man with softly curling brown hair swept into a pompadour and eyes that sparkled with mischief strolling out from a small door to the left, which I assumed led backstage. He was wearing a loose band T-shirt and a pair of black jeans with holes in the knees, and I vaguely recognised him from Instagram. "I'm Bitch Fit. Thanks for coming."

"Nice to meet you," I said as Bitch Fit walked over to me and shook my hand. "Thanks for having me."

"My pleasure, seriously, I'm so fucking glad you're here." He beamed at me, his eyes roaming over me. "God, you really are stunning. Mercy said you were gorgeous but I think she undersold you."

I perked up at his words. Egotistical as it was, I'd always loved it when people complimented me. Out of drag I was pretty hot, but in drag I looked fucking stunning. And sure, half of it was padding and the rest was make-up, but I was sexy and I knew it. It was sweet of Maddi to say so too.

"Thanks," I said, giving him my perfected-for-TV smile and a little shimmy. "I couldn't resist getting a little dressed up. It's been a while, especially with the move, and I needed to get everything out of boxes."

"God, moving is such a fucking nightmare," Bitch said. "I don't know what's worse—the packing or unpacking."

"I'm going with unpacking. Mostly because I can't remember where I put half of my stuff. At the end, I was just shoving things in boxes and telling myself I'd find it later."

"This is why I'm never moving house again," Bitch said, beckoning me to follow him towards the stage door. "I'm simply going to..." He trailed off, glancing over my shoulder as a door behind me swung open. I turned, my gaze following Bitch's to see another man stepping through The Court's front door. He wasn't in drag, and there was an air of nervousness clinging to him.

But fuck me, he was the most gorgeous man I'd ever seen.

He had waist-length red hair that was the colour of fire and rippled as he moved, soft doe eyes, a sweet, puckered mouth, and high cheekbones that could cut glass. The pinstripe trousers he was wearing looked tailor-made for his willowy frame, and the black waist corset over a white shirt highlighted his narrow waist. He almost looked like a haute couture model crossed with a baby deer, and I was instantly obsessed with him. If he was one of the drag artists who performed here regularly, then I'd be begging for a spot on their roster.

"Hey," Bitch called, giving the man a wave. "Can I help you?"

"Yes, hi, sorry I'm late. I'm Colin. Er, Bubblegum Galaxy said I could pop down to meet people and maybe get some pointers. On starting drag." He smiled awkwardly as he spoke, sounding so formal it was like he was here for a job interview. It made him even cuter.

"Oh, the baby queen! Come in! Sparkles said you were coming down. You're Rhys's friend?"

"Yes, we do pole dancing together."

"Awesome." Bitch beamed and stepped around me to shepherd Colin towards the stage door like he was a lost duckling. "I'm Bitch Fit. This beautiful babe is Barbie Summers. Come with me, and we'll head backstage."

There was a flash of recognition in Colin's eyes, but he stifled it quickly and smiled instead. "Hello," he said softly as Bitch ushered us through the door.

"Hey," I said as charmingly as I could manage. I might be the queen of hot messes, but I was a charismatic one. "Don't worry, I promise we're not that scary. I'm not, at least. I can't speak for the rest of them. They might all be a bunch of psychopaths. Or people who put milk in their tea first."

Colin let out a snort of laughter, then bit his lip to stifle the sound. "Does that make me a heathen then since I don't put milk in my tea? Just lemon."

"Lemon?"

"Yeah." A candyfloss-coloured blush spread across his nose. It was the cutest thing I'd seen in years. "I'm lactose intolerant and I don't like soy milk, and my granny used to have tea with lemon, so I started copying her. Now it's just a habit."

"I've never tried tea with lemon," I said as Bitch opened the stage door and gestured us through. He was clearly listening by the smile on his face but seemed to have decided not to interrupt. Maybe he could also sense that Colin was nervous, and the best way to distract him was to get him talking. "But I have tried peppermint tea with milk and sugar. My uncle insists it tastes like After Eights but I think it tastes like weirdly sweet mint water."

"Surely if it was going to taste like After Eights, there'd be chocolate involved?" Colin asked, tilting his head to the side as he spoke, his hair rippling.

"As charming as this conversation is," Bitch said with a grin as he shut the door, "and I *definitely* have opinions about mint tea with milk—would you like a quick tour of backstage? Then, Barbie, I'll steal you to discuss the panto and, Colin, I'll leave you with Sparkles. Eva's there too, but I promise her bark is worse than her bite."

"A tour sounds great," I said, finally taking in my surroundings. Like all backstage areas, The Court's was pretty stripped back with the brick walls plastered over and painted white and a concrete floor that rang with our footsteps. There were pictures on the walls of performers throughout the years and the casts of various variety shows, and it was nice to see that the drag artists were at least somewhat valued here.

"Perfect," Bitch said as he clapped his hands together. "Okay, I'll keep this short since I'm sure neither of you wants a history lesson, but basically our lovely Phil, or Violet Bucket as she's known on stage, bought this place back in… I don't know… maybe ten years, fuck no, it's longer than that now… How old am I? Wait, ignore that. Anyway, Phil bought it when it was horribly neglected and turned it into this fabulous establishment where we host drag shows, variety performances—and we'll do special themed ones for special occasions like Christmas, Halloween, Pride, Valentine's, that sort of thing—plus fun things like karaoke, drag bingo, club nights, all the good shit."

He beckoned us to follow him, leading us to the side of the stage where we could peek out into the club, which was currently doubling as a bar. It wasn't the biggest venue I'd ever played, not by a long shot, but like the foyer, there was something intimate and welcoming about the club's speakeasy vibe, with its lamp-lit round tables and the stage's heavy red velvet curtains and polished boards.

I could see myself feeling at home here, which surprised me. I hadn't ever expected to take to a place so quickly.

In London, I'd had a number of clubs, bars, restaurants, and theatres on my rotation and while I'd enjoyed playing some more than others, none of them had given me the same feeling as standing in the wings of The Court. Maybe I was feeling vulnerable, or maybe it was sentimentality at getting back in drag again. Because surely I shouldn't feel like this from a quick glance?

I shook my head, attempting to snap myself out of whatever place I'd gotten stuck in, and instead looked over at Colin. His eyes were wide and his mouth was slightly open as he stared in wonder at the stage, his whole body exuding reverence, awe, and just the tiniest bit of pants-wetting terror. Which was a pretty good summary of what it was like walking on stage for the first time.

Bitch was saying something about the sound and lighting, and I nodded politely. I wasn't listening, though. I was too busy looking at the baby drag queen stood next to me, waiting to blossom into someone beautiful. I'd never considered having a drag daughter before—someone I could guide and mentor through the wilds of the drag world, helping them to learn the art of drag and transforming them into the queen they could be.

And as appealing as the idea was, it wasn't a commitment I could take on lightly.

Not only would it involve my reputation, but it would mean inviting someone into my life, and while I could keep a drag daughter at arm's length, keeping my life a secret from her kind of felt like a dick move. Because how could I promise someone the earth knowing how that dream had betrayed me? I couldn't send them out naïve and unprepared like I'd been, and that would mean telling them my secrets.

Secrets I wasn't ready to reveal to anyone but Maddi. And, if I was being honest, some of those secrets were things I didn't even want to admit to myself.

So no matter how much I loved the idea of the House of Summers, that dream would have to wait for another day.

When I wasn't a disaster in disguise.

CHAPTER FOUR

Colin

STANDING in the wings of The Court's stage and looking out at the velvet curtains and well-trodden boards as my body thrummed with excitement was one of those rare, beautiful moments where everything in my life suddenly snapped into place with a deep, calm feeling of clarity.

I wanted this.

I wanted to be out on that stage, made up, dressed up, and living my drag queen dreams while the audience looked on and cheered. I didn't know what my act would be or even if I'd be any good at it, but the burning need inside me wasn't going to be quashed by such petty fears. Not tonight at least. Those were for two o'clock tomorrow morning when I woke up in a cold sweat, my heart racing in terror as my nightmares of failure and public humiliation closed in around me.

But for now, I would live and smile and dream of rapturous applause.

"You want to be out there," Barbie said quietly, looking up at me with a warm smile. She was still shorter than me, even in heels. There was no judgement in her expression, and her words were a statement, not a question. She knew what I was feeling, perhaps better than anyone else in my life, and that was comforting in a way I didn't know how to voice.

"Yeah," I said with a nod as I gave the stage one final longing look before turning away. "One day."

"Hold on to that feeling. You'll need it." Barbie was still smiling, but for a second it seemed like something else flashed across her face. Sadness, perhaps. Or anger. But a moment later it was gone, and I was left wondering if it'd been a trick of the light.

After all, why would someone like Barbie Summers be sad?

I shook the thought out of my head as Bitch beckoned the two of us to follow him backstage where he showed us some of the dressing rooms and introduced us to some of the artists who were getting ready. I hung back shyly, introducing myself with a little wave and a "hello" when Bitch told them who I was, but everyone was much more interested in Barbie than me—quite rightly so considering who she was.

When I'd seen her standing in the foyer, I'd thought it was a dream, but apparently this was very, very real. And she was so nice. Not that I was expecting her to be otherwise, but there were always stories about celebrities. And she'd won *Drag Stars*, so it wasn't as if she needed to bother with someone like me.

But she had. And now every time I looked at her, my stomach flipped.

There was no doubting that Barbie was gorgeous, with her long, curling blonde hair with an enormous wave at the front, highly stylised sixties make-up with hot pink accents, large pastel rainbow earrings, and brightly patterned dress. It almost looked like someone had put Barbie, Brigitte Bardot, Twiggy, and a young Dolly Parton in a blender with a healthy dollop of drag fabulousness, and she was the incredible result. I'd always been in awe of her looks but seeing her up close and in person stole my breath.

If I could be even a fraction as fabulous, then I'd be a very happy drag queen.

"Okay," Bitch said as he led us up some stairs. "To my room. Colin, I'll leave you here with Sparkles while I steal Barbie for a bit. That's assuming Sparkles doesn't pass out from excitement." He shot Barbie an apologetic smile over his shoulder. "Bubblegum Galaxy is a fan of yours and she's a bit… enthusiastic. We love her to pieces but she's like a glittery squirrel on crack. She's promised to be on her best behaviour but if the screaming gets too much, let me know and we'll gag her. I'm sure Eva's got a ball gag or something in her bag—she's got everything in there."

Barbie chuckled. "What else are giant handbags for?"

"See, I prefer those comically tiny ones that I can maybe fit a lipstick in. And my phone if I'm lucky. I need us to go back to the early noughties so I can have one of those Razr flip phones again."

"Oh my God, my mum had one of those," Barbie said. "I wanted it so fucking much. Maddi… er, Madam Mercy has got one of those new Samsung ones. I don't know how fucking much she paid for it, but she's put phone charms on it and everything."

"Fuck, I need it," Bitch said. "I'll have to ask her about it. And then work out which organ I can sell to get one."

I listened quietly to their conversation, not wanting to interject because I didn't have anything to add. I was very content to simply listen and study how they interacted with each other. Despite Barbie's fame, Bitch acted like they'd known each other forever, and I was in awe of his casual confidence. It didn't feel overwhelming, though, more like he simply wanted to befriend everyone he met—superstar or not.

I followed them up the stairs and towards a door, which had a brass number tacked onto it. Bitch knocked loudly then cracked the door open without waiting for a response, yelling, "Get your shit together, hoes. We have guests."

From behind the door another voice, which was slightly deeper and more acerbic, said, "Get your own shit together. Neither of us happens to look like we've been dragged through a hedge backwards."

"Aha, I love you too," Bitch said as he threw the door open wide and ushered us inside. There were three people, two seated at the long make-up counter and one standing by a rack of clothes wearing a loose pair of shorts with a pile of garments in hand. They all looked at us, and I immediately recognised one of the two sitting at the counter as Bubblegum Galaxy, who was currently very pink in the face and looked like she was trying very hard not to pass out. Or start screaming.

"Okay, in here we have our sparkling squirrel who should never be allowed to drink Red Bull, Bubblegum Galaxy, our beautiful little gothic nightmare, Eva Nessence, and our very own non-binary, rhinestoned cowboy, Moxxie Toxxic." Bitch gestured to them all in turn before pointing at Barbie and me. "Darlings, this is our brand-new baby queen, Colin, who wants to pick your brains about starting drag, and the sickeningly talented Barbie Summers, winner of *Drag Stars UK* season five and gorgeously cunty bitch."

"Hey, it's so nice to meet you," Barbie said with the same achingly charming smile she'd been wearing all evening.

"Nice to meet you too," Eva said with a little nod, a small smile on her blood-red lips. She made me think of one of those fantasy dark fairy queens—the ones who'd steal your heart and your soul with a single kiss. I'd met her out of drag once when she'd picked Rhys up from pole but she'd been a lot less terrifying then. She twisted in her seat slightly and beckoned me forward with a long, sharp nail. "Come in, Colin, I promise we won't bite. Bubbles would invite you herself, but she's currently..." Eva chuckled and snapped her fingers in front of Bubblegum's face. "Earth to Sparkles."

"I'm here," Bubblegum squeaked. "Hi! It's, er, it's... hey."

"Charismatic as always then," Eva said with a fond shake of her head.

"Bless her, she'll come down to earth in a minute," Moxxie said, tipping their head to Barbie and me. "Nice to meet you both. Sorry I'm not more presentable but *someone* didn't mention we'd have company." They raised an eyebrow at Bubblegum, whose blush went from hot pink to virtually scarlet.

"I did! It's not my fault that you didn't believe me." She picked up a make-up sponge and threw it vaguely in Moxxie's direction. Then she let out a deep breath and sat up straighter in her seat, turning more towards me and adding, "Eva's right, Colin. Come on in and grab a seat." She gestured at the armchair in the corner, which had a few bits of clothing draped across the arms and thrown over the back.

I glanced at Barbie and Bitch, and Bitch gave me an encouraging nod and gently put his hand on my back like he was steering a lost child. "Have fun," he said like a parent dropping their kid off for their first day of school. Although as far as I could remember, my mum had been the one crying, not me. "We'll be back in a bit. You lot be nice. Don't scare the baby off before he's even put on his first pair of heels!"

Bubblegum scoffed, throwing a top that had been on the chair in the direction of the door. "Thank God you're not staying then. Otherwise he'd run screaming."

I bit back a snort as Bubblegum finished clearing the chair and I carefully slid across the room to seat myself in the corner. The dressing room wasn't as large as it had looked from the door, or maybe that was because of all the stuff strewn everywhere. I could hardly take my eyes off the numerous wigs, endless pairs of shoes, overflowing racks of clothes, and stacks of make-up covering the counter in front of the large make-up lights.

The three of them were watching me closely, but Eva was the first to speak, shooting me a kind smile. "How're you doing, Colin? Are you still breathing?"

"I think so," I said, hoping my voice didn't come out too breathlessly. "It's, er, it's a bit more overwhelming than I thought. But the stage is amazing, and everyone's been so nice."

"They're a pretty good bunch," Eva said. She crossed one long leg over the other and rested her hands on top of her knee. It was only then that I realised she was wearing a pair of fluffy black slippers instead of heels. "Rhys said he thought you might want to start drag."

"Yeah." I nodded. "I've been practising make-up at home when I get a minute, and I got a few cheap wigs to play around with. And clothes… I'm struggling a little actually. I need to look at brands for tall women because all the dresses I've tried won't even cover my bum." I'd always been tall and willowy, so getting clothes to fit me had been an issue since I was ten and suddenly five foot two. Eventually I'd found clothes that fit both me and my developing style, but now I had to start the search all over again.

"How tall are you?" Bubblegum asked, looking me up and down with a frown. "Six three?"

"Six four. And a half, technically."

Moxxie whistled. "Impressive."

"Thanks," I said. "Although it's not all it's cracked up to be. I hit my head on doorframes a lot. And ceilings. My granny and granddad live in this tiny cottage and I can't stand up properly inside."

"West does that," Bubblegum said, smiling fondly. "My boyfriend—he's a rugby player, so he's tall and broad. He's useful for getting stuff off the top of cupboards, though."

"That's my one skill. Well, that and mental maths but somehow I doubt anyone wants to see me do that on stage."

"You can pole dance," Eva said. "That's another skill. How's your heel work?"

I waved my hand from side to side sheepishly. "So-so. I've been trying to practice and I've done a few heel workshops at pole, but I always feel like Bambi."

"Okay, first tip," Bubblegum said as she stood and walked over to some shoes piled on a shelf. "You definitely don't have to wear skyscraper heels! Wear whatever is comfortable for you as long as they look pretty and match your aesthetic. No boring shoes or club kid boots. What size shoes do you wear?"

"Twelve."

"I can work with that." She picked up a pair of slightly battered, sparkling red shoes with a small heel, a strap across the ankle, and a bow on the front. They reminded me a little of Dorothy's ruby slippers from *The Wizard of Oz*. "Try these. I'm not sure where they came from, but they should fit."

She handed me the shoes with an encouraging nod. I reached down to slip off my boots, wondering if I needed some tights or pop socks instead of my actual socks, but nobody said anything, so I slowly slid my feet into the shoes, doing the strap up across the nerdy maths socks my mum had gotten me for Christmas.

"In terms of clothes, try somewhere like ASOS," Moxxie said as they finished pulling on a pair of fringed trousers and buckling up their belt, which had an enormous glittering buckle in the shape of an M. "They'll have a women's tall section with plenty of variety, and you'll probably be able to get shit that's reasonably priced. You don't need to spend a fortune, especially not when you're starting out and discovering your style."

"And you can always alter things," Bubblegum said. "Hemming it to make it shorter, taking it in. Things like that. Depends on the look you want to go for."

"I, er, I don't know how to sew," I said as I put my feet on the wooden floor, flexing them inside the shoes. They felt good. Right.

"Don't worry about that," Bubblegum said with a dismissive wave of her manicured hand. "I can teach you. Or do it for you."

"She's pretty good," Eva said.

"From you that's a compliment and I'll take it," Bubblegum said, laughing. "How are the shoes? Stand up, have a walk around."

Pushing my nerves aside, I stood slowly and waited for my centre of balance to disintegrate in the same way it usually did. But it didn't. Sure, I didn't feel totally secure but I didn't feel like I was about to go flying and break something—in either me or the room. "They feel good," I said, taking a tentative step forward. "Really good."

A smile broke out on my face as Bubblegum clapped with delight, saying something about taking them home to practice in.

I looked down at my very own ruby slippers and began to wonder what adventures they'd take me on.

CHAPTER FIVE

Barbie Summers

I CLICKED out of the temp agency website with a frustrated sigh, doing my best not to scream silently into the void. Or maybe some screaming would do me some good—clear my lungs and get some of my anger out. Did Lincoln or Nottingham have one of those rage rooms where I could go and smash some shit? That would be very fucking cathartic about now.

I looked around my room at the mess, wondering if unpacking would serve as a good distraction. I'd made a start… I just hadn't finished, and as a result there was stuff strewn around everywhere. I'd opened boxes and bags searching for wigs, make-up, and my ring light so I could film some content for YouTube and social media but I'd not actually found a place for things to go afterwards.

Now I'd thought about my content, I realised I should be editing instead of skimming through job websites in the vain hope of finding something remote, part-time, and not completely and utterly soul destroying.

I'd have better luck trying to win the lottery.

My videos for YouTube and TikTok were more likely to make me money anyway, especially since I'd been approached about doing a couple of ads and some sponsored content. They'd all asked for the details of my agent or manager, and I'd had to say I didn't have one at the moment, which I was really hoping wasn't going to throw a spanner in the works.

I'd *had* a manager. Emphasis on *had*.

I'd signed up with Andi as soon as the first episode of my season of *Drag Stars UK* had aired, when she'd approached me and promised me the world. I'd been stupidly awestruck and said yes without reading everything through, and it was only afterwards that I realised she'd been part of the scam.

She'd said all the right things, offered me a package with the tour company—which she'd promised was very reputable and would do a great job—and then pocketed my earnings and disappeared with them along with the company owner, Caesar Hurst. I wasn't sure if she was his girlfriend, sister, or partner, but whatever she was, she was part of the reason I was in this mess.

She'd played me for a fool. A poor, stupid, naïve fool. And I'd been burned hard.

I was sure I couldn't be the only one, because Candy Club had put loads of queens on tour over the past few years, but I was terrified of opening that can of worms and reaching out to anyone else in case I was.

Maybe everyone else had been paid. Maybe it was only me who'd been taken for a ride. And if I spoke out about that, people would see me for the fool I was and my career would be over. After all, who'd want to work with an artist who'd allowed themselves to be taken advantage of like that?

And even though Candy Club wasn't associated with *Drag Stars*, maybe the production company would consider me speaking out to be damaging to their brand, and I couldn't afford a lawsuit.

It was better to keep my head down, pretend everything was fine, and try and dig myself out of the deep, dark hole I'd found myself in.

Which meant I needed to get my ass to work.

I grabbed my headphones, pulled up my video editing software, and began working on the edits for YouTube and TikTok. Way before *Drag Stars* and my drag career, I'd trained as a make-up artist and had made a nice little business of make-up tutorials and prom and wedding make-up, and I'd been smart enough to keep those skills up while I was in London trying to make it as a drag queen.

My content had pivoted over the years to keep up with trends, not only in the cosmetics industry but in social media and my own career, but I still had a decent following looking for tips, tricks, and recommendations.

I'd made a nice little niche for myself doing drag and costume make-up tutorials, which were perfect for new queens and cosplayers wanting a more dramatic, exaggerated look for characters. And while I hadn't exactly been feeling creative lately, I'd forced myself to do a few bits to keep me ticking over, including a few puff promo pieces of products I'd been sent.

That reminded me that I needed to do a ton of fucking admin and update all my bloody details with people. Otherwise all my PR packages would sit languishing in London. Or, more likely, be nicked as soon as someone realised I wasn't going to collect them.

I reached for my phone to make a note to myself and quickly realised how much admin I needed to do. It wasn't just the PR lists that needed my new details but things like my driving licence, phone, credit cards, bank accounts, and all the other things required for me to exist. The idea of doing any admin was galling and I quickly distracted myself by opening Instagram and starting to scroll leisurely through.

There were a few posts from artists I knew, so I left appropriately excited comments about their work before scrolling on, but it wasn't until I was a few minutes deep before something really caught my eye.

It was a video of Colin hanging upside down on a metal pole by what looked like one knee, his inner thigh, and sheer force of will. His hair was bound up in some sort of plaited crown, and he was only wearing a tiny pair of mint green shorts that showed off miles of creamy skin and toned muscle. The pole was spinning leisurely, allowing me to admire him from all angles. There was music playing too, but I was too busy staring at Colin to do more than register it.

I didn't know how many times I watched the clip. I wasn't even counting.

Colin had utterly intrigued me on Saturday night with his sweet smile, anxious determination, and stunning cheekbones. I wished we'd been able to spend more time together, but once I'd been whisked off by Bitch it had been hard to get away, especially once we'd started talking about the panto. I'd gone into the whole thing with trepidation, not really sure what to expect, but as soon as Bitch had begun walking me through the details, I'd been totally suckered in and we'd ended up chatting for hours.

For the first time since the end of my last tour, I'd felt the flickering flames of excitement in my gut.

The panto might not have been my first choice, but the more we'd talked about it, the more I wanted to do it. Not only did it sound well thought out and well written, but it also sounded like a lot of fun, which was something I'd sorely been missing in my life.

I wasn't going to admit that the "everything happens for a reason" crowd were right—no fucking way—but maybe the panto wasn't the sinking black hole I'd originally imagined.

I watched Colin spin around on the pole again, admiring his long legs, before tapping on his profile to see if he had any more pole clips. I'd followed him on Saturday night, having quickly grabbed his details before he'd left, but I hadn't done more than quickly glance at his page until now. That'd been a mistake because fuck, the man was talented.

There were hundreds of photos and videos of him doing pole with everything from what appeared to be fairly simple poses all the way through to complex routines. Not that I could even do the simple shit.

One of the videos of him near the top of the page started with him sitting on the floor, legs spread with his back to the pole, one hand above his head. As I watched, he rolled up onto the balls of his feet, slowly rolling and thrusting his hips before lifting and sweeping his feet in some sort of fan motion—I couldn't totally follow it—but all I knew was Colin suddenly had his back to the camera and his ass in the air. I couldn't stop staring at his legs, wondering what they might feel like wrapped around me.

Fuck. No. Absolutely not.

I was not going there.

Colin didn't need me perving over him.

So why the fuck was I still watching?

He'd climbed onto the pole now, hanging gracefully off it like it was the most natural thing in the world. I didn't even know how this shit was physically possible.

Before I'd completely thought it through, I tapped the little message button.

> **Barbie**
> You didn't tell me you were so talented. How the fuck is any of that physically possible?
>
> **Barbie**
> I know it has to be, but you make it look so easy. Doesn't it hurt?

I wasn't expecting a response. Colin would probably think I was rude for even asking. I tried to go back to editing, hoping to lose myself in the process, but every so often I glanced at my phone in the vague hope I'd hear back.

Maybe he was busy. His bio said he was doing a PhD, which was almost as impressive as hanging upside down by one knee, so maybe he was working. Or in the library. I didn't even know what a PhD involved—I'd never been particularly academic and the idea of spending hours in a library pouring over stacks of books made me want to cry.

Eventually, I managed to focus long enough to get two videos and an assortment of TikToks edited and ready for posting, and by then I was starving and in desperate need of snacks. I grabbed my phone and headed downstairs, noticing it was nearly half five according to the kitsch clock on the kitchen wall. It was in the shape of a flamingo and my mum had bought it when she'd taken me to Disney World in Florida when I was ten.

That holiday was one of my favourite memories, and I still had all the tickets in a box along with a T-shirt she'd bought me that I'd worn for years until I'd finally had to admit I'd grown out of it. One day I wanted to save up and take her back so we could relive all those memories while getting drunk together.

Since it was getting on and Mum still wasn't back from work, I decided to kill two birds with one stone and make us something for dinner. There was a pack of mince in the fridge and I was feeling vaguely indulgent, so lasagna it was. There was nothing in the world better than meat, pasta, and a ton of cheese sauce.

I connected my phone to the small Bluetooth speaker perched on the windowsill behind the sink and as I did, I realised I had a message from Colin. And not just a quick three-word reply either. It was a two-minute voice note.

I hit play and turned the volume on the speaker all the way up so I could listen as I started to find everything I'd need for dinner.

"Hey, sorry I didn't get back to you earlier. I've been in a lab all afternoon looking at sperm… which sounds really fucking weird out of context. Fuck, sorry, you must think I'm an absolute weirdo." He laughed breathlessly and I wondered if he was blushing.

"It's for my PhD. I'm building mathematical models to study how sperm use their tails and swim so we can basically study them and work out how to identify the best sperm—because I guess that's the best way to say it. Anyway, the hope is eventually to develop clinical tools to help with male infertility. So I spend half my time analysing swimming sperm, which doesn't sound any less weird when I say it that way. And I'm walking down the street while I record this, so now everyone in Nottingham knows I like jizz. Which I do, but that's not the point."

I chuckled to myself, shaking my head. I'd never heard cum talked about in such a sweet and scientific way. It was cute.

"Anyway, er, you asked me a question… what was… oh, pole! It does hurt, at least some of it, but I don't really notice it as much? Either that or I've just killed all the nerves on my inner thighs, knees, and elbows. And yes, it does take a lot of practice but I'm kind of obsessed, so I practice about four or five times a week at the moment. Or maybe it's because I have no friends and no other hobbies.

Sorry, you must think I'm such a twat. I'm just rambling at you now. I hope you're having a good day so far!"

His voice note ended and I felt my stomach flip. Colin might have thought he'd come off badly by admitting he was lonely, but it made me feel more connected to him. Everyone around here already seemed to know each other, but we were both new, both lost, and both searching for something. Although what I was searching for beyond revenge and a bucketload of cash wasn't completely clear.

I put the knife I'd been holding down and grabbed my phone to respond, pressing the record button to leave my own little voice note.

"You know, I thought you were interesting before but I have to say I'm even more intrigued by the fact you're studying cum. I have no fucking clue about mathematical modelling but the whole infertility thing is cool as fuck. Look at you changing the world! Also I want to say I don't get doing a hobby that causes you physical pain, but I regularly shove my nuts back into my body, reshape my waist, and wear ridiculous shoes—like the amount of fucking scars on my feet I've got from where shoes have rubbed is insane. I don't think anyone would want to buy feet pics from me now. And as for my day... it's been pretty boring, to be honest. I need to finish unpacking but I'm lazy, so I've been trying to edit videos and now I'm making lasagna."

I sent the message, hoping it made him smile, and went back to chopping an onion. By the time I'd finished and started to brown the mince, Colin had responded.

"You're making lasagna? Oh, that sounds so good! I think it's a sign you've got your life pretty together if you can make a good lasagna. I really want some now... although I can't have, like, proper lasagna because I'm lactose intolerant, so I have to make it with lactose-free stuff. I mean, I *could* have ordinary lasagna if I take Lactaid. If not I'll suffer for like, two days afterwards, but sometimes it's worth it. It's like, sometimes it's worth the suffering to eat pizza. Also, yes, unpacking is the worst and I actually ended up getting rid of a load of my stuff before I moved so I didn't have to schlep it all the way to Nottingham. Although now I've kinda replaced it with wigs and skin-care, so it's not like I've achieved much."

I chuckled to myself as I listened because I'd had the intention of getting rid of a load of shit too, but in the end I'd left it too late, had been unable to decide what to bin, and had shoved everything in boxes instead.

"Also," Colin continued in a second message. "This, er, this might be weird and forward, so you can, like, a hundred percent tell me to sod off, but I didn't know if you fancied meeting up at some point? It's absolutely fine if not, but I just thought since we're both kinda new here it might be nice? Although I'm sure you already have a ton of friends. Yeah, I'm going to end this now before I totally put my foot in it."

My stomach did a little kick-flip as he spoke and I heard the embarrassment in his voice. I'd told myself getting involved with Colin would be trouble, but he wasn't suggesting anything more than a friendly drink and what was the harm in that?

"Sure," I said, holding the button again. "I'd love that. What are you doing on Friday?"

CHAPTER SIX

Colin

I ANXIOUSLY CHECKED my watch again as I strode through Nottingham, half walking, half running, as I tried to make it to the restaurant on time. I'd thought I'd have time to go home after work and change, but the bus had gotten stuck in traffic and I'd barely had time to dump my laptop before I'd needed to head out again.

I really hoped I didn't look too much of a mess or too boring, but I usually just wore T-shirts and jeans to university because it was easier. There wasn't exactly anyone to dress up for.

Not that I needed to dress up for tonight, though. It wasn't a date. It was just two people hanging out, getting some food, maybe a drink, and chatting about drag.

I didn't even know Barbie's real name, and I wasn't going to ask unless he offered it because I didn't want to make him uncomfortable. There was a whole social etiquette of drag and I was still trying to get to grips with it. Some of it seemed to be unspoken, but I wasn't sure if I could ask someone to explain how things worked to me.

Would that also be considered rude? Was I supposed to know some of this stuff already? I'd always been socially awkward, but it wasn't as if society came with a manual. Even just thinking about it was giving me a headache.

I turned down another side street and saw the neon sign for Papaya, the Thai street food restaurant we'd agreed to meet at, ahead of me. There was nobody else waiting on the street, but that wasn't calming because Barbie could easily have been waiting inside. Or worse, decided that my being late wasn't worth hanging around for. I was only six minutes late, but that felt like forever to me.

"Colin!" A warm voice called from my right as I approached the door and saw Barbie bounding down the street, grinning wildly. It suddenly felt like someone had grabbed me around the waist and pulled me to a stop while I'd been running flat out, leaving my midriff far behind the rest of my body. Almost like Wile E. Coyote in those old Road Runner cartoons.

I'd seen photos of Barbie in boy mode after all the confessionals on *Drag Stars* were filmed with the contestants out of drag, but nothing had prepared me for seeing him up close.

He was shorter than I'd imagined—although that wasn't hard when you were standing next to me—but he definitely had to look up at me and the top of his head seemed like it would only reach my chin. His hair skimmed his strong jaw in a gorgeously messy style that almost looked wet, and I wanted to run my hands through it. It was blond at the end but darker at the roots, like he was growing the colour out, and while on someone else it might have looked odd or out of place, on him it simply looked charming. He had a broader body than I'd been expecting too, and it highlighted just how good his drag skills were that he could make himself look so completely different. If I'd passed him on the street, I'd never have known who he was.

A black T-shirt hugged his shoulders and chest before loosely skimming over his stomach, and his slightly holey, stonewashed jeans looked more high fashion and artful than battered, although I suspected they were more of the latter than the former. Barbie simply had a way of wearing clothes that made it look like an art form. He could probably have made a bin bag look like high fashion.

"Hey," he said. "I thought it was you! Sorry I'm late. I got lost." He laughed self-deprecatingly and shook his head. "How the fuck I managed that on the way from the train station I'll never know. It's not like it's far. My only defence is I haven't been to Nottingham in fucking forever and everything's changed."

"You're not late. I've only just gotten here too. My bus got stuck in traffic this afternoon and it's... well, it's been a mess."

"Story of my life." He grinned and nodded his head in the direction of the restaurant's large front door. "Want to go in and see if they've got a table?"

"Sure."

"I know it's why we're here, but I wanted to check in

case you've taken one look at me and decided to run screaming."

I snorted as we headed inside. "First of all, I'd absolutely never tell you that. I'm so socially awkward that I'd sit through dinner with my worst enemy or, like, someone who chewed really loudly rather than leave. Just in case they thought I was rude. Not that I think you're my worst enemy but…"

I trailed off, feeling even more awkward than ever, but Barbie smiled cheerfully and nudged me playfully as we waited for someone to spot us. "Ah, another member of the 'boundaries are for other people' club," he said. "I'm the same. I'd rather torture myself than even think about upsetting someone else."

I winced because that felt horribly familiar. "At least I'm not the only one."

"Definitely not. Maddi keeps telling me I need to not let people walk all over me, but that's what I have Maddi for. She'd literally kill for me."

"Those friends are the best. I don't think I've ever had anyone like that."

"Oh, don't worry. If you ever meet Maddi, you'll have one. She has a tendency to just adopt people, and you don't always get a choice." There was a fond look on his face and I wondered if that was how he'd met Maddi in the first place.

I imagined it would be nice to have a friend like that. Although I'd sort of experienced that since Rhys and his twin brother, Ianto, from pole had both decided they were going to be my friends and seemed determined to go through with their plan, even though I'd insisted they didn't have to.

I didn't want to be an inconvenience but apparently, like Barbie, I didn't get a say.

A petite waitress approached us and was happy to lead us through the busy restaurant towards one of the booths on the far wall, which were built to resemble brightly coloured tuktuks with padded seats that were colour-coordinated to match the outside. Ours was bright green. In fact, the whole restaurant was brightly coloured, with metal signs and neon lights hanging from the ceiling, giving it a street food market feel.

From my seat on the far side of the covered booth I could see into the large open-plan kitchen where people thronged around metal benches and burners. Woks and large pans clacked and clanged, mixing with the loud hum of chatter around us in a way that would have been overwhelming if we'd been sat at one of the small tables dotted around the rest of the restaurant. The scents wafting out of the kitchen were delicious and my mouth watered as I watched a waiter walk past with two brightly coloured plates piled high with noodles.

"You know," Barbie said, glancing up from the large paper menu on the wooden table between us. There was a sly smile on his lips, but it didn't look mischievous. Just inquisitive and... flirty. No. That couldn't be it. Why the hell would he be flirting with me? "You said first of all earlier... first of all, you'd never run screaming because you're too awkward. What're the other reasons?"

"Oh... I..." I rolled my lips together and tried to think of a way to avoid the question. But I couldn't. "I'd never take one look at you and run screaming because... well, second of all you're Barbie Summers, and you're amazing! And third, you're, er, you're gorgeous. Sorry, I shouldn't have said that."

"Hey," Barbie said with a warm firmness that seemed designed to stop me getting lost in my thoughts. "Compliments are always allowed." He winked at me dramatically. "And you're pretty fucking cute yourself. I'm kind of obsessed with your hair."

"Thank you." I smiled and brushed my fingers through it lazily. I'd spent all day with it tied up and I'd missed having it there to play with. "I've been growing it for years. It can be a pain in the butt to maintain, but I love it."

"It's gorgeous. Also, if we're going to be friends, you can call me Anthony."

"Are you sure?"

"Yeah. I'll answer to Barbie, though, but yeah, you can use my name. Just don't go spreading it around."

"I won't, promise." I drew a little cross over my heart, which was racing at the level of trust that Barbie... Anthony, had suddenly thrust at me. I had so many things I wanted to ask him about, but I wasn't even sure where to start. I didn't want him to think I *only* wanted to talk about his drag expertise too. I'd hate for him to feel used. "Can I ask you a question? I'm not sure if it's too personal, though."

"Fire away," he said. "Just don't go posting the answers on Reddit or some shit."

I stared, eyes agog and feeling utterly stunned. "I'd never… do people actually do that?"

Barbie laughed hollowly and pursed his lips. "My ex tried. Luckily, the mods flagged it and one of them reached out to me to let me know. They booted him out and they've been pretty watchful in case he tries it again. I know he's tried TikTok but apparently some of my fans tore him to shreds. He's a bit of a cunt to be honest. I don't know what I ever saw in him. It wasn't like his ass was that good!"

I bit back a laugh and looked down at the menu. "I can't judge you because my ex was kind of the same. Less expose you online, though, and more just gaslight the fuck out of you. He's part of the reason I applied for this PhD, because I needed a fresh start and he's far too lazy to get on a train and drag his ass up to Nottingham."

"Laziness, the easiest way to escape shitty exes."

"Is that why you moved?" I asked as our waitress appeared to take our orders. We hadn't even looked at the food but we did order some drinks and promised to be ready when she returned with them. I looked back to Barbie, who was staring out across the restaurant and looked lost in thought. I suddenly wondered if I'd touched on a sore spot. "Sorry, I didn't mean to pry. You don't have to tell me."

"No, it's fine." He flashed me a smile but this one didn't quite stretch to his eyes. "It was part of the reason. Probably a bigger part than I'd want to admit. Feels like I'm letting him win if I say that, like he fucking chased me out. It was my fucking flat too."

I winced. "I'm sorry, that sounds shit."

"It really is," he said with a laugh. "Not that I don't love my mum, but I really didn't think I'd be back living at home again. Especially because my bed is shit. I'm going to have to order a new mattress. And set the old one on fucking fire. Wait, does cum burn? The number of times I jerked off as a teenager on that bed, there's probably a ton of the stuff soaked into the fibres."

"Sadly that sounds like a biohazard, so yes, it will burn, but you'll need to have it collected by the council. And I doubt any bonfire you build would reach the temperature you'd need."

Anthony leant on the table and smiled at me in a way that made my stomach flip. "That's what petrol is for."

I snorted. "I think that'll just get you arrested."

"I'd get off. The police are too busy to deal with that. I'd just say it was an accident." He flipped his hair and winked. "I'm sure I can play a blond himbo and pretend I had no idea. I mean, I won my acting challenge, so I can't be *that* terrible. Although my competition wasn't exactly fierce, so maybe we won't use that as a bar of comparison."

"You were definitely the best," I said, trying to ignore the way his wink made me feel. I wasn't supposed to be getting butterflies. "I've never done much acting."

"Don't worry about it. Drag artists mostly just need to be good performers and that's a skill which comes with practice. Like doing your make-up. How're you getting on with that?"

"Better?"

"You don't sound convinced."

"I'm not," I said. "Sometimes I think it's getting better

but then when I look at the pictures I've taken, it just looks worse. I'm not sure if I'm noticing more things I want to change, or whether I'm too critical, or if I really do look like a clown."

"Hey, some people are proud of being clowns," Anthony said with a smile that shouldn't have made me want to swoon. "Can I see your pics? Also, what do you want to eat because I think we're going to piss the waitress off if we take forever to decide."

Our conversation quickly turned to food and whether we wanted to get any sides to share. I'd remembered to ask for an allergen menu, and my choices were slightly more limited than I'd imagined but we settled on ordering some steamed prawn dumplings and steamed buns filled with roasted red pork, which were my absolute favourites, to share and I decided to get myself some Pad Thai because I really wanted noodles.

Once the waitress had arrived with our drinks and we'd ordered, I dug my phone out of my jacket pocket and opened my gallery. Nerves made my stomach bubble and I hesitated. What if Anthony thought they were terrible? What if he took one look at them and told me I should never be a drag queen?

Logically, I knew everyone had to start somewhere, but that didn't mean I was applying that to myself. I'd always expected things of myself that weren't reasonable, even if nobody else had.

"They're not great," I said, twisting my phone in my hand. "I'm still not sure what I'm doing most of the time. And I'm struggling to get my eyes right. I think I know what I want to do, but I'm not there yet and I keep getting frustrated, which I think is making it worse. Also, I don't have a lot of palettes and stuff yet, so it's not—"

"It's okay," Anthony said. His voice had softened and it soothed the anxious scratching in my soul that was threatening to unravel me. "You don't have to have a ton of stuff or know exactly how to do a smoky eye or killer contour. You definitely don't have to be perfect. All you have to do is be willing to try."

"But… what if I have to be perfect?" I asked with a half chuckle, trying to pretend I wasn't being serious.

"Well then, sorry, sugar, but I have bad news because you won't be. None of us are."

"But you—"

"Still have days where I look like a hot mess. I've just learned how to carry it off," he said. "Besides, nobody expects a baby queen to be perfect. That's like expecting a toddler to do Olympic-level gymnastics." He held out his hand. "Now stop stalling and show me your pics."

Reluctantly, I handed my phone over, my hands suddenly feeling sticky and clammy.

Anthony studied the photo carefully. "Can I scroll?"

"Yeah. There's a few more of that look on there."

"Thanks." He scrolled through the photos while I watched, waiting to hear my fate. I'd never been so terrified of getting results. After this, my PhD viva was going to feel like a walk in the park. "Don't look so worried," he said. "I'm not about to summon a guillotine or ban you from doing drag."

"That's a start." One that didn't quite ease the anxiety in my chest.

"And it's not as bad as you think either. Smile, sugar, you're making a good start." His soft smile was back and it made my heart flutter. "Also, you should know I'm a trained make-up artist and I've been doing this shit for years." He turned the phone around so I could see the screen. "It might be your lighting but I think your foundation might not be quite right for you—it's making you slightly orange. Correct me if I'm talking shit, but I don't think that's the vibe you're going for."

"No… definitely not."

"Okay, we can look at some different options. Your eyeliner is better than you think it is, and you have the most gorgeous cheekbones, so if you want to highlight them, we absolutely can. The most important thing is that *you* love it and you feel comfortable. And happy. Your drag persona should be… well, everyone's different, and how they find them is different, but they're a part of you. You want to love being them."

"Do you love being Barbie?" I asked as I sipped my Fanta Lemon through a black and white paper straw.

"I do." He glanced away for a second, smiling into the distance. He was so gorgeous and it caught me off guard. I nearly found myself staring. "She's… she's been there for me through a lot. Barbie is my armour on bad days and half the reason I'm still standing. She's why I'm where I am, in good and bad ways, I guess. Most of all… I don't want to look back at my life and say, 'what if,' and Barbie will be the reason I won't do that."

I didn't want that either. I didn't want to live in the shadows, in the grip of my anxiety and my past mistakes. I wanted to live with stage lights on my skin, applause in my ears. Because I'd always regret it if I didn't get up on stage.

"Will you... will you help me? Please? I could really do with some pointers," I said, flexing my foot hard so I didn't tap it nervously on the floor. Asking for help had never been my strongest skill, but asking for help from someone I didn't just admire but was starting to feel something—was it friendship?—for was more terrifying than the worst horror movie jump scare.

Anthony looked at me, tilting his head, his eyes sparkling. He thought for a second and then he smiled. "Sure. I'll help you."

CHAPTER SEVEN

Barbie Summers

"You know I said the other day that I'd finished unpacking? Well, I lied. It's still a mess," I said as I shoved the door to my bedroom open and gestured for Colin to step inside, suddenly wishing I'd gotten off my ass and at least made an attempt to tidy up.

It wasn't like I hadn't had time in the last few days since I'd offered to help Colin over dinner at Papaya and, really, the only reason I had to explain myself was that I couldn't be bothered.

My mum would kill me when she found out. It'd always been the rule growing up in our house that my friends, and later boyfriends, could only come round if my bedroom wasn't a complete tip, and looking at the state of it now, Colin wouldn't have been allowed within ten feet of the house.

I might've been twenty-six now, but I wasn't exactly doing the best job of proving I was a responsible adult.

Or an adult at all.

"Don't worry about it," Colin said, neatly sidestepping an overflowing box of dresses that I really needed to hang up. "I won't judge you. Besides, it sounds like you've had to cram your entire flat into one room, so I'm not surprised you're struggling for space."

"Thanks. I appreciate it." I gestured to the bed, which I'd at least remembered to make with clean sheets. "Grab a seat. Just ignore the squeaking and the broken springs. I'm waiting for a new bed to be delivered." I glanced around the small room with its old lavender decor and teenage knick-knacks and chuckled dryly. "I'm not sure where half this shit is going to go when I try and cram a double bed in here, but fuck it, I'll deal with it then."

At least the bed I'd given in and ordered had storage underneath it so I could shove some of my possessions in there. Ideally, I needed another room to put my drag stuff in, but Mum's house only had two bedrooms and I didn't think she'd appreciate me taking over her living room. I supposed it was time for me to start shoving stuff in the attic and praying it didn't fall victim to mice or the damp.

"Well, if you need help moving or sorting anything, then let me know," Colin said as he sat on the bed, which groaned underneath him like the door to the creepy basement in a horror movie. Colin politely ignored it and simply put his backpack down next to him. "It's the least I can do."

"I might take you up on that." I grabbed a black bag of

wigs off the floor and dumped it on top of the dress box to create a nominal amount of extra space on the floor. "I think I might have to hit up IKEA too. There's still one in Nottingham, right?"

Colin nodded and smiled brightly. It was like a small beam of sunlight had erupted in the middle of my room. "Yeah, there's a huge one not far from the motorway. I went there not long after I'd moved up to see if I could find a mirror and some extra bookshelves. I may have also come out with some fake flowers, candles, a ton of chocolate, some ceramic cacti, and a lamp shaped like an owl, but that's beside the point."

I laughed and shoved another bag out of the way. "Sounds like a typical trip to IKEA then. I might have to try and go in the next few weeks. It'll depend on when I can borrow Mum's car."

Since I'd never needed a car in London and simply thinking about keeping one there would've bankrupted me, I'd sold my old banger before I'd moved. And now I barely had twenty quid to my name, I couldn't see myself buying another one any time soon.

"If you do want to go, I can always take you," Colin said. "My car's not very big but we can get a few things in there if we fold the back seats down, and at least you'll be able to see what they've got."

"Are you sure? I don't want to inconvenience you."

"You won't be. And it means I can get more Swedish chocolate, so it's a win-win."

"Cool, maybe next weekend then? I'm not performing much at the moment, so I've got a lot of time on my hands."

I could hear the bitterness in my voice but I didn't know how to get rid of it. I'd never been out of work this long and I hated every minute of it. I'd had some offers to go back to bars in London, but the obscene price of train tickets was putting me off because by the time I'd factored those in I'd barely be any better off.

Maybe it would be worth sucking it up and taking the hit just so I had content to post of myself at gigs and people didn't think there was something wrong. The last thing I wanted was for it to look like my career was in the toilet, even if it technically was.

"Sure," Colin said. "Are you not at The Court?"

"Er, maybe. I need to check," I said, trying to brush the question away. "Phil said he could maybe get me in for a few shows because they're doing a bunch of extra stuff for Pride month, but this stuff was all worked out months ago and I'm literally only getting in because they can use me for marketing. Having a *Drag Stars UK* winner on your list is pretty good publicity."

Colin frowned and pulled the corner of his bottom lip between his teeth. "You don't sound keen on that."

"It's fine. And I'd rather work than not." I shrugged, hoping to get away from this subject. The truth was I wasn't keen, but mostly because I was still holding on to enough grudges and resentment of seeing my name being used to make other people money to last a lifetime.

I'd debated telling Colin about the Candy Club debacle, but I didn't want to subject myself to another pity party. Besides, I wasn't the reason he was here and I didn't want to make everything about me for once. "Anyway, enough about my woes. Grab your make-up out. Let's see what you've got."

Colin rummaged in his backpack and pulled out a mint green make-up bag that matched his phone case. It was cute to see how well it matched and I wondered if more of his stuff was the same colour.

"I know you said my foundation wasn't quite the right shade but I brought it anyway. I was tempted to go to Boots and get a colour match done but time got away from me," he said.

"Don't worry about it," I said with a wave of my hand as I began grabbing various bottles and tubes out of my old desk drawers. I'd repurposed it into a make-up station and it was the only thing I'd organised. Excitement fizzed in my chest because this shit was what I lived for, and it had been too long since I'd been able to do a make-up deep dive with someone.

"You don't want an exact match, more like..." I tried to think how to explain what I meant. "I'll try not to make it too complex or you start getting into, like, colour theory, but for drag you're looking for more of a stage make-up approach. Now you don't want to look orange, unless that's your thing, but you also don't want to wash out under the stage lights or you'll look like a fucking ghost."

Colin nodded. "The videos I watched said you need to make sure it complements your skin tone but is maybe a shade or two darker."

"Pretty much, but you also need to make sure it still matches your undertones." I looked at Colin's face and then down at the bottles in my hand, instantly dismissing a couple of them. I didn't know if I'd have the exact shade that would work for him, but I was a bit of a cosmetics magpie and hoarded products like I was expecting some sort of make-up apocalypse. I was the sort of person who bought things in half the shade range just in case it came in useful.

At least, I had been. I couldn't exactly buy much on my budget.

Still, maybe now I'd use half the shit I had instead of opening it, testing the colour, and putting it in a drawer forever.

"Undertones?" Colin asked. "Like... cool, warm, neutral?"

"Exactly. It's not always easy to figure out but that's what you've got me for, sugar," I said, winking at him and loving the way that he flushed. "By the way, I guess I should've asked this first but what style of drag are you going for? What sort of drag artist are you? Who is your drag persona? Tell me all the good shit."

"Er... so." Colin sat up straighter with his hands in his lap like he was about to give some sort of presentation. It was so fucking adorable I nearly melted and it was only a stern voice in my head, which sounded strongly like Maddi, that stopped me from throwing myself at him. "I've been trying lots of styles but I'm not sure I'm very... pageanty? I want to be pretty, but I'm not sparkly or the next Miss World. I'm not super alternative either. I mean Eva is stunning, but I don't think her style is for me. I kinda want soft... floral... but not too floral... like..."

"Have you got any pictures? Inspiration?"

"Yes!" He pulled his phone out of the side pocket of his backpack and started tapping the screen. "I made a Pinterest board and saved a few things on Instagram."

"Perfect." I sat down on the bed next to him, ignoring the springs complaining about having to put up with both of us. I still had a couple of bottles of foundation in my hand. "You can draw from anything that inspires you—music, art, photos, books, films, celebrities, anything really."

Colin turned his head and I suddenly realised how close we were. His eyes were a soft greenish brown that reminded me of a forest in spring, when winter was fading and everything was bursting into life. "What inspires you?" he asked softly and as my eyes drifted down to his mouth, I noticed his nose was dusted with freckles.

I swallowed, trying to think of an answer. It wasn't a hard question. I'd been asked it dozens of times before. But I couldn't remember what I'd said.

"Lots of things." I coughed and felt my brain suddenly jump-start. "I love kitsch, camp things, vintage Barbies, sixties fashion—everything from psychedelic patterns to mod style, Dolly girls, and bright colours, but putting my own spin on it. For me, it's about taking things I love, whether that's clothes, colours, or even just... a feeling, like summer days... and like, beach holidays as a kid, all the brightness and joy, and channelling those things into my art."

"That's beautiful," Colin said. "I love that. It's so... real."

"Thanks." I smiled at him. His words had done more to

brighten my mood than anything else I'd tried. There was something about his sweet earnestness that made me feel like I'd been drenched in sunshine.

It made me want to try again.

"Don't overthink it," I continued, the words fumbling out of my mouth. "I mean, you can if that works for you, if you like doing deep dives into things. But also, it doesn't have to be complicated if you don't want it to be. Your drag doesn't have to be like anyone else's, and there's no rules either. You don't have to follow any arbitrary guidelines about what 'good drag' is because, frankly, they're all bollocks. Just do what makes *you* happy."

Colin nodded. "I think… that might be some of my problem. I keep trying so many different things because I'm not sure if it's good or not. I like things with rules because it helps me understand things—it's why I like maths. It makes sense to me. But with drag… if there are no rules, that almost scares me."

"I get that," I said, reaching out and putting my hand on top of his where it was resting on the bed between us. The back of his hand was warm and soft. It was nothing more than a comforting touch—at least, that was my intention—so why was it making my heart race like I was up in front of the *Drag Stars* judges?

"Rules can be comforting. But maybe… view this as a chance to make your own rules? Create something that speaks to you and that you want to present to the world. And then you perfect it. That's what good drag is, I suppose, if you really wanted to define it. It's not certain ideals or looks or styles, but perfecting and elevating your drag to the best version it can be. Does that help?"

"It does. Thank you."

"So if I said, what inspires you, Colin? Where does your drag come from? What would you say?"

He thought for a second, a slight wrinkle forming in his nose as he scrunched it up. "Nature, spring flowers, vintage glamour, old-fashioned sweets and sugar mice, china dolls—the ones with the big eyes that are almost a bit terrifying but still kinda cute—pop stars like Kylie and Madonna but also like Kate Bush and Enya. Thunderstorms. Dance, but I like it when people take something classical and reimagine it, like Matthew Bourne's ballets—I love his version of *Sleeping Beauty*—and obviously pole dancing because of the freedom it gives me to just be. Things that are beautiful and powerful and a little bit wild. I don't know if any of that makes sense."

"It does," I said, gently wrapping my fingers around his hand and squeezing. "And I think it's beautiful."

This man was gorgeous, inside and out, and I could see the artist inside of him, just waiting to blossom. I wanted to be the one who helped him realise his dreams because his vision was too interesting to be left inside and forgotten. He just needed a bit of guidance to make it a reality.

"Really?"

"Yeah."

"I was thinking..." Colin glanced away for a second, his gaze seeming to scan my make-up table. "You know those queens who draw their eyes bigger? I was thinking about trying that. And almost like a doll pout. Would that work?"

"I don't see why the fuck not," I said with a grin, my inner make-up artist practically squealing with joy. "I think it would be fabulous. But there's only one way to find out." I held out the bottle of foundation in my other hand. "Let's play with make-up!"

CHAPTER EIGHT

Colin

IT WAS weird how one simple conversation with Anthony had unlocked something inside me I hadn't even realised was there.

For months I'd been going around in circles, trying to figure out what I wanted and practising looks from YouTube that I thought would be right because it was the sort of make-up I'd seen on other queens and never truly asking myself the questions that mattered.

Until last weekend, I'd believed I was on the right path and everything would suddenly click into place once I'd picked up a few more skills. That everything would magically fall in line one day. And it had, in a way, but not in the way I'd expected.

Because Anthony's questions, and his own explanation, had made me realise that I was approaching things from completely the wrong direction—for me, at least. And now, thanks to him, I had a heading and a course.

It was exciting and terrifying all at once, but now that I knew what sort of artist I wanted to be, it was all I could think about.

Even at horrifically inopportune moments like this one, where I was supposed to be concentrating on the next section of choreography Connor, my pole dance instructor, was demonstrating for today's heels workshop.

I'd definitely missed something because Connor was now lying on his stomach on the floor, rolling his hips up and down, and the last I'd checked we were sitting on the pole…

"Okay," Connor said as he pulled himself into a sitting position and then gracefully climbed to his feet as if the eight-inch Pleasers he was wearing were nothing more than a natural extension of his legs. "Any questions? Does anyone want me to go over it again?"

"Would you mind doing it once more, please?" I asked. "I got slightly lost in the middle."

"Of course." He smiled brightly and climbed onto the pole into the position I remembered and began to demonstrate the small section again while I focused all my attention on his movements. Connor talked through every move and position as he did them, adding a few pointers and tips as he went, which I really appreciated since I was still afraid of my shoes.

I'd debated bringing my ruby slippers to wear, but they weren't really suitable for this workshop, so I was wearing my own pair of sparkling mint green Pleasers. The only upside was that they were boots and therefore had considerably more ankle support than the standard Pleasers with ankle straps, but I doubted it made me much more graceful.

Still, I'd only fallen over once today, so I supposed that was an improvement.

"Does that make sense?" Connor asked once he was lying on the floor again. "Do you want to give it a try? I can come round while you do, and once you've practised this section, make sure you try connecting it to the rest of the routine. We've only got one more part after this. Then we'll look at putting it all together with the music. And at the end if you want to record yourself, there'll be time for that too."

"How come Connor always looks so graceful and sexy when he humps the floor, and I just look like a dying fish?" Rhys asked from his spot next to me as he applied a little bit of liquid chalk to his hands to help with grip. Rhys was one of those people whose personality was like liquid sunshine and simply being near him was enough to brighten my day.

"You can't look any worse than me," I said as I adjusted my knee pads and prepared to pull myself onto the pole. "I don't think me and sexy have ever existed in the same sentence together."

Rhys scoffed loudly. "That's a bloody lie. You're gorgeous. Don't you think, Ianto?"

"What?" Ianto asked, turning to look at us from his spot on the pole behind Rhys. He and Rhys were identical twins, and the only reason I could ever tell them apart was by looking at their tattoos, because Ianto had a plaster tattooed on his left knee while Rhys's was on his right. Apparently, it was to match scars they both had from throwing themselves off the roof of a garden shed as kids.

"Colin is sexy, right? He thinks he's not and never has been."

"Well, that's a lie," Ianto said. "Look at you, bloody stunning."

"I... I'm not," I said as I felt myself flush, knowing that my embarrassment would show up all over my pale skin. "You don't have to lie."

"I'm not lying," Rhys said. "And neither's Ianto. You'd know if he was because he gets this funny twitch in his eyebrow."

"No, I don't!" Ianto laughed and threw his pole cleaning cloth at his brother's head before pulling himself onto the pole and neatly crossing his legs over. His boots were black patent with a deep red platform, sole, and heel. "Anyway, Colin, whoever told you that you weren't sexy is a proper bastard because you're gorgeous."

"Even if you don't feel it," Rhys said, also climbing onto the pole and crossing his legs. "Fake it. Confidence isn't an overnight thing. Sometimes you just have to practice it."

"It's the same as everything else in life," Ianto said. "For some people it's natural, and for some, you have to work at it."

"I think I might be the second," I said.

"And there's nothing wrong with that," Rhys said. He grinned at me and then began to tilt himself back slightly before grabbing the pole in both hands, releasing his legs, and sliding down it with a casual sexiness that I couldn't even begin to fathom possessing.

He kicked his legs out behind him, making the toes of his shoes clack on the floor as he landed, then pivoted and drew his legs towards him, executing a perfect fan kick to spread them wide before sliding down to the floor like a popstar sliding down a wall in a music video.

I realised I needed to practice instead of just staring at Rhys, otherwise I'd be lost when we moved on. Technically the routine wasn't difficult, so I could do all the moves. The part I struggled with was executing them with grace and sex appeal.

But as the twins had said, sometimes you had to fake it until you made it. And this was one of those times.

I pulled myself up onto the pole, squeezing the metal between my thighs to hold myself in place as I ran through the moves in my head. Then I let out a slow breath and began to move, letting the flow sweep me away.

Before, I'd always kept my movements soft and conservative, aiming for grace and beauty above everything else. But now I wanted more. I wanted to be graceful, beautiful, *and* sexy.

I clacked my heels on the floor, drawing out my fan kick as I spread my legs, focusing on a random spot on the wall and imagining I was putting on a show for someone as I slid down to the floor until I was lying on my back with my hands just above my head, still on the pole. I lifted my legs and did some little twists and kicks before using my momentum, and my grip on the pole, to swing my legs up and over my head, clacking my heels on the floor behind me.

I wondered what it looked like from the audience's

perspective when I did that... whoever was watching would get an eyeful of my ass and my thighs.

My ex had always told me I was nothing special, that my thighs were too skinny and my bottom was too flat, because somehow he only wanted to date skinny men who had round, perky bums like porn stars or fitness influencers. And maybe my body wasn't what he'd wanted, but that didn't mean other men wouldn't like it.

My mind suddenly flashed to Anthony and his reaction.

Would he like what he saw?

I tightened my grip on the pole as I clacked my shoes on the floor again, the burst of noise forcing me to focus as I moved on to the final part of this section where I twisted gracefully onto my stomach and began to roll my hips. I moved my head too, letting my gaze fix on my imaginary viewer.

If it was Anthony, what would he do if I winked at him while I was like this, spread out on the floor and grinding my hips? Would he be turned on? Would he imagine being behind me... or underneath me? Would he stare open-mouthed as his cock grew hard, desperate to touch but not wanting to ruin the show?

Or would he be repulsed?

Fuck, I really hoped it wasn't the second.

Not that I should even be thinking about him in the first place. Anthony was my friend. He'd offered to mentor me. I shouldn't be dreaming about doing sexy dances for him in teeny tiny shorts and platform shoes that made my legs look even longer than they already were.

"Are you seriously going to tell me you're not sexy after

doing that?" Rhys asked, his words making my imaginary version of Anthony disappear in a puff of smoke. "Because that was hot."

"Agreed," Ianto said as he leant over his twin's shoulder. "Very sexy. Especially the slide."

"Really?" I rolled up into a kneeling position, very grateful for my knee pads, and tried not to impale my bottom on my heels. "You think so?"

"Yeah." Rhys grinned. "Were you thinking about someone?"

"No."

"Are you sure?" Ianto asked. "You don't sound it."

"It's nothing," I said, really hoping they'd drop it because I didn't even know what was going on in my head, let alone how to explain it. "I was just… trying to fake it."

"It's a very good start." Rhys nodded approvingly, but I wasn't sure if he believed me or not. "Do you ever take nudes of yourself?"

"Who the hell else is he going to take them of?" Ianto asked, jabbing his brother in the ribs. "If he's not seeing anyone, casually or seriously, who on earth would Colin take nudes of?"

"You know what I mean!" Rhys moved towards the pole and began wiping it with the cloth Ianto had thrown at him several minutes before. "My point was that if you look at yourself naked every day, then maybe you'll start finding things to love about yourself. I mean, it's got to be an active practice—you can't just stand starkers in front of the mirror or take photos of your butt and expect to feel better, but if you really look at yourself and find things to love, maybe you'll start feeling sexy and more confident in yourself."

"Oh, that's true," Ianto said with a nod. "A different sort of self-love—although a good wank also helps—but you've only got one body, so you have to learn to love it."

"O-Okay," I said, not sure if I was embarrassed by their directness or touched by the sweetness of their gesture. "I'll give it a try."

"Good. And you can always send nudes to us—not in a sexy way, but in like a friend way—and we'll always tell you you look hot, won't we, Ianto?"

Ianto nodded. "We will. If you can't send your best friends nudes, then why the fuck are you friends?"

I laughed because I supposed they had a point, even if I'd never had friends I was close enough with to even consider sending nude pictures.

Our class continued and Connor showed us the final section of the routine before giving us a chance to practice the whole thing together. Then he split the class in two so we could do a mini performance for the other half while also giving us the opportunity to record ourselves for posterity. And Instagram.

Ianto and I were in the same half while Rhys was stood on the sidelines. I'd assumed he was going to film for his brother, so I was surprised when Ianto propped his phone up against a stack of the yoga blocks we used for stretching and Rhys held out his hand for mine. "Go on," he said with a sly smile. "Be sexy. Think about that guy you definitely weren't thinking about earlier."

I rolled my eyes and tried to pretend Anthony's smile

and the way he looked at me when I spoke, like every word out of my mouth was the most interesting thing he'd ever heard, hadn't popped into my mind. Instead, I took my position just away from the pole because we had a few introductory steps to do first.

The song Connor had chosen today was Hozier's 'Eat Your Young', which had a slow, sensual beat and was perfect for what we were trying to achieve today. Now all I had to do was nail the choreography, try and look sexy, and not fall over… simple.

"Are we ready?" Connor asked, taking his position at the front of the class. "Lucy, can you do the music, please? Cheers."

I let out a slow breath as the first beats of the music hummed through the studio speakers, letting my fears melt away as I sank into concentration. This was something I loved doing, and nothing would change that. My distracted thoughts quieted as I began, the flow of the movements enveloping me.

I was still thinking about Anthony, though…

Imagining him standing beside Rhys, watching me with those beautiful eyes and pretty pout. It made me want to show off for him so he could see exactly what I was capable of. Even if I didn't think I was sexy, maybe he would. And if I couldn't be sexy for myself, maybe I could be for someone else.

As soon as we finished, the rest of the class burst into applause and I realised my chest was heaving, sweat beading on my skin from the exertion. I hadn't even noticed getting out of breath while I was dancing.

"Fucking hell!" Rhys exclaimed as he handed me my phone. "You looked amazing!"

"Thanks," I said, reaching for my water bottle and taking a few grateful swigs. "I really enjoyed that. Want me to film yours?"

"You sure? I can get Ianto to do it."

"It's fine." I held my hand out for his phone. "Now go make a sexy video for Evan."

He laughed. "He's on shift today… although I'm pretty sure he'd appreciate a distraction." His wicked smile suggested it wasn't necessarily the case but that Rhys was going to do it anyway. I chuckled and shook my head. I wasn't going to ask Rhys for more details and open a whole new can of worms.

But he had given me an idea.

While he was setting up, I opened my message thread with Anthony and fired off a quick message.

With a video attached.

CHAPTER NINE

Barbie Summers

CLEANING my make-up brushes could suck my dick as far as I was concerned. But considering it was either that or sort my room, I was going for the considerably less tedious of the tasks.

At least once I'd cleaned my brushes and left them to dry, I could move on to fun things like lying on my bed and mainlining whatever crafting reality show I could find on Mum's multitude of streaming services.

I'd never thought I'd be the sort of person to get addicted to *The Great British Sewing Bee* or *The Great Pottery Throw Down*, but I couldn't get enough and now I was the sort of person who had *opinions* about stitches and patterns and different types of glazes.

I'd thought being a contestant on a reality show would have destroyed my love of the whole genre because I'd seen behind the curtain and knew exactly how it worked, but thankfully it hadn't. In fact, it almost made it more entertaining because I could see when the producers were deliberately editing something to cause drama. Although considering these shows were nice, cosy British reality shows, it wasn't like there was a lot of drama to begin with.

Adding drag queens to something like the sewing bee would be hilarious. The shade would be legendary.

My phone buzzed from beside the plastic washing-up bowl filled with hot water and brush soap that was sat on my desk. I was sure there were better ways to clean my multitude of brushes and sponges, but tipping them into a bowl like this had always worked for me and it wasn't like I was using them on anyone else, so if I damaged the bristles or destroyed the handles, it didn't matter. Although I would have to buy replacements, so maybe I needed to be a bit more careful.

"Shit," I muttered as I pulled my hands out of the bowl and dripped water all over my joggers and phone while reaching for a towel. I quickly wiped my fingers and tapped my phone screen to see who I could blame for distracting me.

Colin's name flashed onto the screen and I felt a smile tug at the corner of my mouth as I opened our message thread, noticing the cover frame of the video attachment that showed a dance studio and a metal pole that stretched all the way to the ceiling.

> **Colin**
> [Sent a video] This is what we did in my heels workshop today! And I managed not to fall over =D

My smile widened and my interest perked up as I opened the video. If Colin had sent it to me, it was bound to be fabulous. I turned the volume up and heard the opening bars of Hozier's 'Eat Your Young' start playing in the background.

Okay… so maybe this was going to be sexier than I'd imagined. That whole song was about eating pussy for fuck's sake.

I stared at the screen as Colin strolled into view wearing nothing but a pair of tiny black shorts, black knee pads, and mint green ankle boots with platforms and spiked heels that must have made him close to seven feet tall and accentuated his gorgeously long, toned legs and the soft swell of his petite butt.

God, what the fuck would those legs feel like wrapped around my waist? What would it be like to have him behind me, driving his cock into me? With our height difference, he'd have to stand and I'd have to kneel on the bed, and fuck, I loved that idea.

Shit, I shouldn't have been thinking about sex. But it was really fucking hard not to when Colin was grinding on the pole and spinning around it with more grace in his entire body than I possessed in my little finger.

My cock throbbed, growing uncomfortably hard inside my boxers as Colin's eyes met the camera. The intense heat in his gaze made a funny knot form in my stomach, and I licked my lips as he kicked his legs out wide and slid down the pole. A shiver ran down my spine as he lifted his legs and cracked his shoes on the floor behind his head, unable to take my eyes off his ass.

I'd known Colin was flexible from all his previous work I'd seen, but this felt different.

It was like he was showing off for me, putting on a show for my eyes only.

I groaned as he rolled onto his front and began to slowly roll his hips up and down, my mind conjuring up filthy fantasies. My hand grabbed my crotch, massaging my aching dick through my joggers, and fuck, if I'd been hoping that would make me feel better, it didn't. It just turned my desire up to a hundred.

The video ended with Colin stood, one leg hooked around the pole as he tipped backwards, his chest heaving and a bright, eager smile on his face like he knew he'd done a good job. It was too fucking adorable for words.

I knew I shouldn't watch it again, especially not with my hand on my dick, but I'd never had much common sense. So I restarted the video and slid my hand past the waistband of my joggers, into my underwear, and wrapped my fingers around my rock-hard cock.

My movement was restricted by the material, but that only made me more desperate. I groaned as I rapidly pumped my shaft, my hips rolling as I humped up into my hand. My eyes were still fixed on Colin, drinking in every inch of his body as he danced. Did he know how beautiful he was? Had he known what this would do to me? I groaned as he writhed on the floor, his scantily clad ass bouncing up and down.

"Fuck!" I groaned as the video came to an end again but this time I didn't hit replay. Instead I lost myself in fantasies of Colin in my bed, kissing me, tasting me, spread out naked beneath me so I could ride his cock... lying on my stomach with my aching dick pressed into the mattress, my legs spread so Colin could lie between my thighs and fuck me slowly, his body draped over mine, enveloping me in him.

"S-Shit! Ugh... fuck!" I gasped loudly, glad I was home alone, as I chased my release. My orgasm was right there, burning under my skin like molten gold. I wished I'd moved to the bed so I could grab a dildo to shove in my ass, but it was too late for that now. I was at the mercy of my desire, and all I could do was hump my fucking fist like a desperate teenage boy who'd just discovered his dick.

What tipped me over the edge wasn't the thought of Colin fucking me. It was of him coming... whispering my name like a breathless prayer, soft and sweet and for my ears only.

Grunts and gasps filled the room as my release hit me, pleasure bursting under my skin and filling me with warmth as I pumped cum across my fingers and into my underwear. The sticky mess was fucking worth it, though.

I let myself catch my breath before I shoved my joggers and underwear down, wiping my hand on my boxers to get rid of the excess cum, before throwing them both in my washing basket in the corner. I was still riding the high of my orgasm, and it was only after I'd nipped to the bathroom to wash my hands that the full force of what I'd just done hit me.

Goddammit, could I have been any more of a stupid motherfucker?

Colin was my friend. Emphasis on *friend*. Not hook-up, not fuck buddy, not booty call, and definitely not boyfriend. Friend. And sure, getting off to hot things your friends sent you wasn't that unusual, but my friends weren't usually the subject of the hot videos.

I'd promised Colin I would help with drag. And while I'd told myself I wasn't taking on a drag daughter, it was pretty obvious that was where things were heading.

I needed someone to talk me off the ledge and make me see sense. And there was only one option for that.

As soon as I'd grabbed some clean joggers, I picked up my phone and messaged Maddi.

> **Barbie**
> I did something stupid

Maddi
Bitch! What did you do?

> **Barbie**
> Remember I told you about Colin?

Maddi
Yes...

Maddi
Please tell me you didn't fuck him?

> **Barbie**
> I didn't! But I may have just jerked off to a video he sent me of him doing a pole dance routine.

The phone rang almost as soon as I'd sent the message and I braced myself as I answered it. "Hey, Mads—"

"I'm sorry, bitch," she said, cutting through my weak-ass attempt to distract her. "You did what?"

"Colin sent me a video of himself from his heels workshop today and I…"

"You decided to wank over it?"

"Yes?"

"You can't answer my question with a question. Either you wanked or you didn't. There's no magical middle ground."

"Yes, I wanked over it but it was really fucking hot, Mads! And the way he was looking at the camera, God, it was like he was looking straight at me," I said, well aware I sounded like a pining, love-sick creep.

"He was performing, you dumb-ass!" Maddi's exasperation was clear and I didn't blame her. Thank fuck she was a hundred miles away or she'd have fucking smacked me. "Jesus fucking Christ, babe."

"I know. I shouldn't have done it."

"It's a bit bloody late for that now," she said. "You weren't planning on telling him, were you?"

"God no!"

"Thank fuck for small mercies then."

"Wait, did you seriously think I'd tell him?" I asked, flopping down on the bed, which gave its customary wail of sorrow. The new one couldn't arrive fast enough.

"Maybe? I don't know," Maddi said. She sighed. "I know you're lonely and feeling like shit and Colin sounds cute as fuck, but if you're mentoring him, there's a whole power dynamic there. And this isn't some bad student-teacher porn with a twink in a miniskirt and thong. This has actual consequences. For both of you."

"Firstly, I want to watch that," I said with a wry smile and Maddi chuckled.

"I'll send you a link."

"Secondly, I know there are consequences. Why the hell do you think I messaged you? I need you to talk me down."

Maddi sighed again, but this one was softer. Fonder. And I knew if she was here, she'd be ruffling my hair and pulling me in for a hug. I really missed her hugs. "Look, I know you want to help him because it's what you do. You can deny it all you want but you love helping new artists. It's your fucking jam. And I know you're jaded right now because of all the endless Candy Club shit, but maybe helping Colin will give you a bit of purpose again? Help remind you why you fell in love with drag in the first place. Plus, you'd be a killer drag mother. Do you know how many people would give their entire fucking right leg to be your drag daughter? Bitch, there'd be bloodshed. You have a chance to make a real difference in his life, and that's not a responsibility you should take lightly."

"You're right," I said, because she was and we both knew it. "He's got so much potential, Maddi. I can see it. He just needs a bit of a steer but once he gets going… it's going to be incredible. And his dedication, fuck, I wish I could bottle it. I just need to give him some confidence, but who doesn't need confidence when they first start?"

"He's in good hands," Maddi said and I could hear her smiling. "This is why you can't cross that line, Babs, no matter how much you want to. What's my one golden rule?"

"Never ask when the last time you washed your tights was?"

"The *other* golden rule."

"Don't share eye make-up?"

Maddi laughed. "Fuck you."

"What? The eye make-up thing is real. Do you want a fucking stye? Or an eye infection?" I always cringed when I saw queens sharing eyeliners and used lashes. It was the one thing that always made me shudder.

"No, but I never share that shit anyway, you know that," Maddi said. "Anyway, my rule about mentorship is…"

I sighed and stared up at the ceiling as I muttered, "Never fuck your drag daughter."

"I'm sorry, I didn't hear you."

"Never fuck your drag daughter!"

"Thank you," Maddi said. "It always leads to trouble. I don't care that you're both consenting adults. There's too much at stake and you have too much control over Colin's career to add sex into the mix."

"I'd never fuck him over, though," I said weakly. "You know that. And I don't think he'd ever consider using me to get a platform."

"I don't give a shit, babe. Don't fuck him."

Maddi was right. I knew it, she knew it, the whole world fucking knew it. And the point she'd made was an excellent one because we'd both seen too many young drag artists destroyed by petty and vindictive members of their drag family, and established artist's being flattered and used by newbies looking for a leg up.

But there was one problem I hadn't counted on.

Maddi had turned Colin into forbidden fruit.

And now I wanted him more than ever.

CHAPTER TEN

Colin

"I BOUGHT the two I showed you because I couldn't decide between them, and if they don't work, I can just send them back," I said as I picked up the ASOS bag on the floor and pulled out the two dresses I'd ordered during the week to show Anthony. They weren't perfect, but I didn't need them to be. I just wanted them to give me an idea of what shapes, cuts, and styles to use in my drag.

"I've also got some amazing bell-bottom jeans with embroidery and an orange panel that I found in a vintage thrift shop," I added, trying to remember where I'd put them. "I thought they'd be cute with some boots, a crop top, and a giant wig."

"Oh, I love that idea. Plus boots will give you more stability to move in," Anthony said with an approving nod. He was sat in the middle of my bed watching me with interest and I couldn't help smiling every time I looked at him.

When he'd suggested we get together to do more drag practice, I'd jumped at the chance but I wasn't sure if it was just because of the idea of getting advice from him or because I wanted us to spend more time together.

"That's what I was thinking," I said. "I saw a pair that were pink and baby blue with daisies on, and I thought they'd be perfect. You won't be able to see a lot of them under the jeans but it'd work for the overall look. Plus I'm sure I could find other things to wear them with."

"If you can't, I'll steal them," Anthony said with a laugh. "Wait, what shoe size are you?"

"Twelve."

"Damn, I'm only a ten." He shrugged. "I can wear thick socks."

"You can get those winter hiking ones," I said. "Your feet might melt a bit, though."

"Eh, I melt enough in drag anyway. And at least thick socks would stop me getting blisters or bleeding everywhere. I hope you're prepared for a little bit of pain, by the way. Drag isn't always comfortable."

"I think that's why I want to try jeans. Although I know I'll need to tuck underneath them. Or wear some really, really tight underwear."

"That depends," Anthony said and I swore he was looking at me with new heat in his gaze as his eyes travelled down my body.

"On what?"

He shook his head and suddenly looked over at my desk, which was piled high with textbooks and research papers. "Er, on a few things really. Some of it is personal comfort. You don't have to tuck if you don't want to—I know more and more queens who are choosing not to. Or if they do, it's only for specific looks. Depends on what look you're going for. It also depends on the cut of the jeans or the dress. I mean, if you're wearing a ball gown, it's not like anyone can see your dick anyway. Also, it kinda depends on the size of your dick in the first place. Like, if you're really packing, even soft, then it's going to be rough."

"That makes sense," I said, trying to keep my voice level. What was wrong with me? Anthony was offering some friendly and helpful advice and here I was wondering if he'd been checking out the front of my jeans.

"I… er… well, luckily, I don't think I'll have the latter issue. My dick is spectacularly average, but that's surprisingly helpful for pole—although I usually wear two pairs of shorts anyway to prevent accidentally flashing my genitals. And I've never had any complaints, even though I haven't topped for a while because my ex didn't like bottoming… I'm not sure he enjoyed fucking me at all, to be honest, considering how much he grumbled about my butt. Sorry, that's far too much oversharing. Please pretend I didn't say any of that."

"Oh, sugar, that's nothing, I promise," Anthony said with a wave of his hand and a cheeky smile that calmed my fears. "You should hear the shit that gets shared in dressing rooms—nothing is sacred. There was one queen I knew who literally told us all the ins and outs of her anal fissure."

I blinked in surprise, my eyes wide, and Anthony laughed. "Exactly! That was my reaction at first too. And then you kind of get used to it. You obviously don't have to share, but you should be aware that people do."

"That's good to know, I suppose."

"You'll get there." He winked. "Also I have a bone to pick with this bastard ex-boyfriend of yours. What the fuck was he complaining about? Your butt is gorgeous."

"T-Thanks," I said, giving it a little shake for good measure and feeling my stomach flip as Anthony grinned. "Apparently, it was too small, too flat, and very bony. And too tight, but also not tight enough—which I'm not really sure how to take but then again I'm not totally convinced he knew how anal muscles work."

"Another man defeated by basic biology. What a knob."

"Very much so." I smiled and it was the first time I'd done so while thinking about him since before we'd broken up. "I'm glad we're not together anymore. Once upon a time, I'd have hated that idea but now…"

Anthony nodded. "Change is hard, especially in relationships. You get comfortable. And even when you know things are shit, it can be hard to change things because you just kinda get used to it. Like Steve… he was a dickhead, like a proper loser who sponged off of everything I did and I knew he wasn't good for me, but it took some real shit going down for me to realise he was never going to be there for me. Like, I could give up my fucking kidney for him, and he'd bitch it wasn't both of them."

"Can I ask what happened?"

He ran his hand through his hair and tried to smile, but

it didn't reach his eyes. It must have been painful, and I didn't like that he was trying to play it off. But maybe it was easier for him this way. Everyone processed their emotions differently, even if sometimes I wished it was more straightforward than that.

"Just had some issues with the landlord," he said. "A few money problems too. Going on *Drag Stars* isn't cheap and it doesn't help when you can't work for three months while you film. You're basically locked in a hotel, and you can't tell anyone where you are or what you're doing."

"Is that legal?"

"Yeah, technically. And we all signed up for it. The amount of paperwork I had to sign would make you cry."

I chuckled and waved airily at my desk. "I read research papers for fun—I think that trumps all your paperwork hands down."

"Nope." He grinned and shuffled towards me, hanging his legs over the edge of the bed and tilting forwards, a sly smirk on his face. "You willingly chose to do that to yourself. My paperwork was literally just to get me on the show."

"Was it worth it?" I asked, stepping slightly closer. I wasn't sure what I wanted to achieve, only that I needed to be closer to him.

"Yeah, it was," he said softly. "Sometimes, I forget about all the good things that happened because of it. I only focus on the bad…"

I frowned. "The bad?"

"Yeah, just… falling out with Steve, the stress, the

exhaustion, the online negativity. Silly things really." He shrugged. "I want to focus on more of the good."

I smiled, inching a tiny bit closer until I was almost stood between his thighs. I was too close now, but he hadn't moved away. "Like? Give me some examples."

Anthony tilted his head up to look at me, his elbows resting on his spread knees, hands hanging loose. If I stepped half an inch closer, he could rest them on my thighs. "All my runway looks were on point, but my finale look really was spectacular. I'm so proud of that one, even if it cost me a fucking fortune."

"Don't focus on that." I put my hand out, aiming to push him playfully on the shoulder, but instead I just brushed his T-shirt and left my hand resting there. "Only the good things."

He grinned. "You mean putting myself in twenty grand's worth of debt isn't a good thing?"

"Twenty grand?" I stared at him, unable to quite process the sheer absurdity of what he was saying. I knew drag could be expensive and that competing on *Drag Stars* wasn't going to be cheap, but hearing him put a number to it was different. It made it tangible. "T-Twenty thousand pounds?"

"Give or take a few grand, yeah. It's not fucking cheap. But that's a story for another day. We're staying positive, remember?"

"If you're sure. We can talk about something else."

"No," he said quietly, lifting his hand, reaching out, and gently putting it on my hip like he was going to hold me in place if I tried to run away. "It's been a while since I thought about the good things."

"Okay... tell me."

"I made a lot of good friends, especially Maddi. I got a huge new platform and sure, it can be difficult to manage, but the love and joy is fucking infectious. I won... like, it's not as easy as I make it out to be, and that probably makes me sound like a proper stuck-up dickhead, but I *won*. I have a fucking crown and everything. And I'm proud of that."

"You should be." I slid a tiny bit closer so I was stood between his knees. "It's an incredible achievement."

"Thanks..." His hand tightened slightly on my hip. "The... the tours... knowing people came to see me... that they wanted to fucking meet me and take pictures. It's a whole new level of mind-fuck. Being told I was people's favourite drag artist, shit, I don't think I'll ever get over it."

"Does it really surprise you?"

"Yeah. It does."

"Why?"

"Because even though Barbie Summers is, like, this drag goddess, underneath her, I'm still this stubborn, mouthy brat from Newark—which half the country doesn't know exists. And now I'm supposed to be *someone*. It's everything I wanted, but I still can't believe it happened. Sometimes I wonder if it really did."

For a moment he looked almost sad, or maybe it was wistful. I couldn't imagine what that level of success was like. The pressure had to be immense.

"It did, but I... is it weird to say that I like that it hasn't gone to your head? I mean, it might have—I've only known you for a few weeks, so I suppose you could be a complete arsehole, but I don't think you are."

"You have Maddi to thank for that," he said with a chuckle. "Maddi would pop my ego like an overinflated balloon if I even thought about getting up myself."

"She sounds good for you."

"She'd agree with you."

We were still very close and his hand was like a brand on my hip. I half expected it to leave a mark there, like Castiel's handprint on Dean Winchester in *Supernatural*. If that happened, I'd take a photo of it to remember it forever. Or maybe do something stupidly extreme like getting it tattooed.

"I'm glad you don't think I'm a cunt, though," he said, tipping his head back even further as he gazed at me. It felt like I was under a spotlight, but it wasn't scary. It was beautiful. Like I was suddenly the centre of his universe.

"I don't think I'd ever think that."

"Really?"

"Yeah." I put my other hand on his shoulder. "I don't think you'd be helping me if you were a cunt. You'd have just told me to jog on. But I'm glad you didn't because meeting you has changed my life."

Anthony nodded, his smile fading for a second. He pulled his hand back and I wondered if I'd said something wrong. "I haven't done anything yet," he said. His smile was back and I wondered if I'd imagined the change in his expression. "Well, except for helping you with your make-up. But a drag artist isn't just their make-up, no matter what some people might say. Which is why we need to get you dressed." He sat back slightly and reached for one of the dresses I'd left on the bed.

"Time to see what sort of body you'll be serving me, sugar."

CHAPTER ELEVEN

Barbie Summers

THE MORE I told myself Colin was out of bounds, the more my brain wanted him.

No, it wasn't my brain at all.

It was my dick, closely followed by my heart, although I wasn't looking too closely at that because love was a fucking curse and I wasn't going to get within a thousand miles of it.

That was what I was telling myself anyway.

In all honesty this situation was a fucking mess, and if I was a sensible man, I'd be keeping Colin at arm's length, maybe even going as far as telling him that this whole mentorship situation wasn't going to work. But I wasn't sensible and I didn't fancy having to come up with a reason to push Colin away that wasn't "I think you're hot as balls, I really want us to bang, but if we do that, then I'll be breaking all sorts of boundaries and Maddi will be mad at me." And there was the whole "being responsible for his drag career" thing too.

I was in over my head and on the verge of drowning, but I couldn't bring myself to let go. I'd never thought of myself as jealous or possessive before, but thinking about someone else taking over my role... getting close to Colin and seeing that wondrous look in his eyes as things began to click, I wouldn't give that up for anything. And I'd stab any bastard who tried to take him away from me with my heels.

Colin was mine and I didn't give a damn if I ruined my life in the process of supporting him. It wasn't like there was much left to fucking ruin anyway. But if I could give him the things I'd always craved as a new performer, then it would be worth any suffering I inflicted upon myself along the way.

And if we happened to cross that thin line between friends and more, then I'd deal with the consequences. I knew the risks, turning them over in my head in the dead of night when I was awake and alone, staring up at my darkened ceiling and the faint outline of the ancient stars littered across the paint. And in that darkness I promised myself that I wouldn't let Colin's career suffer if things didn't work out. I wasn't going to become one of those petty, immature, selfish bastards who took revenge on their drag daughters for daring to be better or for whatever other imagined slight I could conjure up.

I knew relationships fell apart—it wasn't like I'd never experienced it myself—but I'd never felt so spiteful about another person that I wanted to ruin their life. Not even

Steve, and if anyone deserved to experience my wrath, it was him.

Besides, what was the likelihood that Colin felt the same? Sure, he'd been flirting with me, but that didn't mean anything. Plenty of guys had flirted with me in the past and not wanted anything more than my dick, my approval, or my Instagram following.

"Okay, Barbie, we're ready for you!" Bitch's voice sounded like he was shouting through a megaphone rather than standing on the other side of the small studio we were crammed into. Today was the first step on the winding road to the drag pantomime: taking head shots and promo photos of the cast to be used on everything from social media to programmes.

It seemed a little early to me because it was only June, but since Bitch was managing the production around touring, temp jobs, performing, and everyone else's schedules, this was apparently the easiest time to do it. Plus it allowed us to all get together and say hi before various people disappeared for the summer and the read-through didn't start until September.

"I'm here," I said with a wave, pulling myself off the plastic chair I'd been sprawled on in full drag. I had to do two shoots because I'd somehow scored the lead—thanks, *Drag Stars*—and we were doing *Cinderella*, so I had to do one in an initial Cinders look and one in full princess mode.

Luckily, I hadn't had to provide the costumes or the wigs. I'd just had to show up, paint my face, and smile prettily for the camera.

"Where do you want me?" I asked as I walked over to

the little set in the corner where Bitch and the photographer, Bastian, were waiting.

"Just in the middle, please," Bastian said with a welcoming smile as he looked up from adjusting his equipment. He wasn't a photographer I knew, and I'd heard on the grapevine while getting ready that he was a friend of a friend of Bitch's who usually did cosplay and weddings. "Perfect. I'm just going to adjust the lighting and then we'll get started. I know we're shooting you twice, so I'll try not to take too long so you've got time to change."

"Thanks," I said. "I appreciate that."

"No worries. It's not like we're in any rush."

Bitch chuckled from his seat, which was a little to one side, out of the way. "Slightly in a rush. We've only got the studio until five."

"It won't take me that long." Besides I had plans that evening with Colin and I didn't want to be late.

We'd started meeting up at least three or four times a week, usually a couple of evenings and then either all of Saturday or Sunday. We talked constantly too, even when Colin was supposed to be busy at university—I could tell when he was bored because he sent me every thought that popped into his head along with a stream of reels on Instagram.

Whatever they were, seeing the notifications pop up always made me smile. Because it meant he was thinking about me.

"Shortest I've ever done a full change, by myself, is just under ten minutes," I added. "But I'd rather not feel like a walking hot mess. Well, not any more than usual."

"You're definitely going to fit in here," Bitch said, gesturing in the direction of the rest of the main cast, who were either still getting ready or chatting happily with each other. "We're all a bit hot messy."

"Speak for yourself, honey," said Peachy Keen, a drop-dead gorgeous artist in drag and a stunningly handsome man outside it. I'd first met her at my first night at The Court where she'd immediately told me to call her Peaches and roped me into her summer holiday drag story hour extravaganza.

In the panto, she was playing one of my ugly sisters, although it was clear costuming was going to have its work fucking cut out to make Peaches look anything less than sickening. "I'm the furthest thing from a mess."

"Clearly, you're forgetting every single incident involving you and a bottle of tequila," said Incubussy, the drag king who was playing our Prince Charming. He was grinning at Peaches while buttoning up his white and gold coat that was so gaudy and camp I couldn't have pictured anything more perfect.

Peaches rolled her eyes as she focused on painting her lips. "Yes, thank you, babe. Your opinion wasn't wanted."

"Tough shit, you get it anyway."

I stifled my laughter as Eva, who was sitting quietly in the corner and tapping on her phone, looked up with a wicked smile on her darkly painted lips. She was going to make a fucking terrifying evil stepmother and I was so here for it. "I don't think I'm in the hot mess club either," Eva said. "Especially not if we're using Bitch as the baseline for comparison."

"Er, no," Bitch said, turning in his chair to look at Eva. "I'm sorry, babe, but bitches who had flu six weeks ago get zero say in this discussion."

Eva raised an eyebrow pointedly and while I couldn't see Bitch's expression, I got the feeling there was more going on here than I realised. Maybe I wasn't the only one with secrets. In fact, I could guarantee I wasn't. Every fucker had secrets, things they kept hidden just under the surface.

I idly wondered what Colin's secrets were. And whether he'd ever share them with me. I hadn't told him about the whole Candy Club fiasco and I didn't know if I ever would. As much as I was starting to trust him, I didn't know if I'd ever be willing to bare my deepest shame.

"Not even saying you're the baseline for comparison?" Eva asked, a little smile pulling at the corner of her mouth. "I saw that dress you were wearing last weekend."

"I... Bollocks, I can't even deny that." Bitch laughed. "In my defence—"

"You don't have a defence," Eva said.

"Agreed," Ink said. "Sorry, hun, but that dress was like the worst mashup of all the noughties fashions. Next thing you know you'll be wearing low-rise jeans with a lace thong and a rhinestone Playboy bunny hip tattoo."

I snorted, remembering Maddi ranting recently about the pain of trying to buy women's jeans. "Aren't low-rise jeans coming back?"

"I fucking well hope not," Ink said, pulling a face. "They were bad enough the first time around."

"You just wear dungarees all the time anyway," Peaches said with a laugh.

"Yeah, because I'm fucking scarred!"

"Low-rise jeans I get," said Ginger Biscuits, who was playing the other ugly sister. She was getting ready next to Peaches and I'd noticed the two of them had barely said a word to each other since they'd arrived. "But thongs are cute on the right person."

"You telling us something?" Peaches asked, the sweetness in her tone laced with ice.

Ginger smirked. "Are you asking?"

All of us were suddenly watching them and I could practically see the buckets of popcorn appearing on everyone's laps as we waited for the drama to explode. You could cut the tension with a knife.

Or an interruption from the sweet, dreamy photographer I'd almost forgotten was here. "Shall we get started?" Bastian asked. "I'm ready when you are."

"Yes! Sorry," I said, because it was the easiest thing to say. I softened my expression into a charming smile, the sort I imagined any Disney princess might wear. But this was me, so there was a sparkling edge to it too. Something that offered sass behind the sweetness.

It wasn't hard getting back in front of the camera and Bastian was very easy to shoot with, offering little suggestions and plenty of compliments. He stopped now and then to assess our progress, giving me a moment to breathe, and I realised how much I was enjoying myself. It had been a hot fucking minute since I'd felt this good. And I was determined to enjoy every minute of it.

"Looks amazing," Bastian said as he glanced up at me. "I think we're done with this look if you want to get changed. I'll shoot everyone else and then circle back to you, so like I said earlier, don't rush."

"If you need a hand with the dress, then just yell," Bitch said. "I think it's got a zip in the side but Edward will help you."

"I heard my name. What scheme are you involving me in now?" asked the tall, ethereal-looking man who'd provided many of the costumes for today and seemed to be the walking, talking version of a classic romantic vampire fantasy with waist-length white blond hair, an open ruffled shirt, and skin-tight black trousers. He was currently sipping tea out of a china teacup, although where it had come from I had no fucking clue.

"I'm not involving you with anything. Barbie's ready for her transformation, but if you want to be roped into schemes, I'm sure I can find something."

"Absolutely not, your brother would kill me if I added anything else to my calendar. Do you know when I mentioned this, he nearly went as pink as his hair?"

Bitch shrugged and beckoned Eva over. "That's because Lewis worries too much."

"I suggest you try telling him that yourself," Edward said, putting his tea down on a nearby table as I wandered over to him. Listening to their conversation made me realise that no matter how much I was starting to feel at home here, I was still an outsider. I didn't know these people, didn't have the connections they'd built up over the years. They'd come with time and effort, but today it carved out a hollow feeling in my chest, like I was the new kid at school clinging on to the desperate hope that people would like me.

Maybe that was why I'd gravitated to Colin so much. Despite our different levels of experience, we were both the new kids on the block.

Edward held out his hand graciously as I approached, leading me over into the corner where he'd set up his wares. "How are you doing, darling?" he asked as he walked over to a nearby railing and began to retrieve a truly astonishing number of petticoats. "Eli said you're rather new around here. And as experienced as you are, my brother-in-law is something not many people have ever had to deal with."

"Brother-in-law?" I asked with surprise as I began to strip off.

"Well, in a roundabout way. His brother Lewis is my PA and dearest friend, and we spend enough time together that we might as well be related at this point." He smiled wickedly and lowered his voice like he was sharing an inside joke with me and suddenly I felt like I was part of the secret.

"Besides, it annoys Eli no end and I've found I quite enjoy that. Although my beloved other half says it's because I enjoy being Lincoln's resident drama queen and I don't enjoy sharing that title. Anyway, enough of me, let's get you naked and into this dress. Now I will say it is a cosplay I made for myself, so it might not fit perfectly and we'll probably need to find you a box to stand on, but it's just for photos, so nobody will see."

I finished stripping off my first look then stepped into a giant hoop that Edward helped me pull up and tighten before he began to drag petticoats over my head. "Thanks for your help," I said. "I really appreciate it."

"Oh, it's quite all right, darling. It's what I do." He smiled at me. "And I cut you off before you could answer my question. How're you feeling? It must be strange being thrown in among a group of people who know each other so well—I imagine it's very similar to how I felt when I started cosplaying and realised half the community had already been friends for years. And being successful doesn't always help. I rather find it makes people reluctant to talk to you. Of course, that could just be me."

I bit back a laugh at the expression on his face, like the idea of his personality keeping people away was preposterous. "Yeah, the success bit is weird. Some people think I'm just a stuck-up prick now, some want to know what I can do for them, and some just run away screaming. I'm still the same person, though—a hot mess with big earrings and bigger hair."

Edward laughed softly as he began pulling the top layer of the skirt into place, which was a beautiful, glittering blue. "It's always the way. I'm sure some of this lot will be the same, but just be yourself. You'll make friends in no time. Eli will make sure of it—as much of a two-bit trash goblin as he is, he never wants anyone to be left out. You'll be rounded up like a lost duckling and adopted. And the rest of them… well, I think they'll surprise you. You might be famous now but give it a few weeks and you'll become part of the family, and they won't give a shit."

"Yeah? You think so?" I asked, wondering if I sounded as desperate as I felt. I wanted to feel at home here, to find friendships to replace the ones I'd lost and a community that wanted me and which I could support.

A place where I could belong.

"I know so," Edward said with a bright smile. "Now, tell me a little about yourself. I, terribly, haven't watched much *Drag Stars*, so I've been told you won but that's about it."

My heart filled with warmth at his kindness and for a moment, I felt less like Queen Barbie, drag superstar and icon, and more like just plain old Barbie Summers, drag queen, make-up lover, and collector of vintage fashion magazines.

As I talked about myself, I suddenly realised people were listening, and soon Eva chimed in about her favourite lipsticks and then Peaches asked about my favourite foundation brands, sending the conversation off on a tangent about their make-up horror stories. Someone mentioned jewellery, and Ink mentioned that his cousin made giant rainbow earrings from polymer clay.

By the time I'd been transformed into a princess, we were all chatting as if we'd known each other for years.

And from just beside me, I could see Edward smiling as he sipped his tea.

Maybe I wouldn't be as alone here as I'd first thought.

CHAPTER TWELVE

Colin

"How're things going with your mystery man?" Rhys asked, ambushing me with the question while I was pulling on my joggers after our class had finished. "Did you hook up yet?"

"Er… well…" I yanked my joggers over my knees and up my thighs because the faster I finished getting dressed, the faster I could run away from this conversation.

"Is my brother being a knob again?" Ianto asked from Rhys's other side. He was sat on the floor lacing his trainers, his head sticking out around his twin's shin. "You can tell him to sod off if he's being annoying."

"Like you're any better," Rhys said as he pulled his T-shirt on, the static making his hair stand up. "I know you were thinking it."

"I'm just not stupid enough to say it out loud, dipshit."

I bit my lip and tried not to laugh because that would

only encourage them. And as endearing as their concern was, this wasn't a conversation I really wanted to have. I grabbed my trainers out of the little cubby where we left our stuff during class and dropped them onto the floor. The cubby was really just one of those IKEA units with the square spaces, but it worked wonders for storage in the limited space of the studio.

It reminded me that I'd promised to take Anthony to IKEA and we still hadn't gotten around to making the trip. I'd have to see if he had a free weekend any time soon because he really needed some extra storage for his room. Every time I went over there it was getting a little tidier, but it would be impossible to completely sort the space without more storage options for his drag wardrobe.

"You don't have to tell us if you don't want," Ianto continued, shooting me a warm smile as he stood and reached for his hoodie, which was black and had the studio's logo emblazoned across the back in hot pink and his name embroidered on the front in the same colour. "But we're here if you want to talk about anything."

"We know this shit can be complicated," Rhys said as he grabbed his own hoodie, which was identical to his brother's, barring the name. "And we just don't want you to go through this on your own when we're here."

"Thanks." I genuinely appreciated their concern because it came from a good place, even if I wasn't sure how to begin talking to them about my crush. But maybe talking to someone neutral was exactly what I needed. Maybe then my heart would listen when they told me what a terrible idea this was. "I know it sounds cliché but things with Anthony are… complicated."

Rhys and Ianto nodded knowingly. "You want to go and get some ice cream?" Ianto asked as he grabbed his backpack and slung it over his shoulder.

"I'm sorry, I'm lactose intolerant and I don't have any pills with me," I said sadly. I'd have loved some ice cream but very few places did dairy-free alternatives or even something like fruit sorbets, which I'd never had a problem with.

I knew some people's intolerances were so bad that even the tiniest trace amounts of milk could make them vomit, but mine had—touch wood—never been that bad. I just got horribly gassy and painfully bloated to the point I wanted to curl up in bed and never move again.

I could take Lactaid pills beforehand to relieve the symptoms but I didn't have any in my dance bag. It was what I took whenever my cravings for decent pizza, ice cream, and mac and cheese got really bad.

"Fuck," Rhys said. "That sucks."

"If it helps, it's one of those dessert restaurants, so they'll do more than just ice cream," Ianto said.

I grinned. "Do you just really want ice cream?"

"Who wouldn't?"

"Sure," I said. "Why not?" If I was going to pour my heart out, I might as well do it over something sweet.

"Awesome!" Ianto beamed and glanced at Rhys. "You coming too?"

"Fuck yeah, I'm not turning down ice cream!"

I didn't know anywhere open this late that would serve

us pudding. The only place I could think of was McDonald's, but I was intrigued by the idea of a dessert restaurant, so I picked up my bag and followed the twins out onto the street.

Above The Barre was located about a ten-minute walk from Nottingham city centre and as we walked, the twins chatted happily about class, what muscles hurt most, where they expected to bruise tomorrow, and their plans to get up and go swimming first thing in the morning.

I was surprised they hadn't used the walk to continue our conversation about my situation, but instead they seemed content to keep it light and joke around. I knew it wasn't their intention, but it felt like I was being lulled into a false sense of security and by the time we reached the bright neon lighting of a late-night dessert restaurant in the middle of town, I felt even more nervous than before.

"Have you ever been here?" Rhys asked as the waitress led us upstairs to a padded booth by the window. Despite the time, the place was busier than I'd expected, with plenty of students, teenagers, and couples occupying the Formica tables, which had glitter laid into the black surface.

I shook my head as I slid into the booth. "No. I didn't even know this place existed." I glanced down at the large menu that had been placed in front of me, my eyes widening at the selection of sundaes, waffles, crepes, desserts, and milkshakes on offer. I didn't know how much of it I could actually eat without exploding, but luckily the waitress had also provided me a laminated allergen menu with a huge grid detailing exactly what was in each item.

"It's perfect if you want somewhere to hang out in the

evening that's not centred around alcohol," Ianto said from his seat opposite me. "And it offers pudding. What else could you want?"

"It does look pretty good," I said, my eyes landing on a couple of the sundae options. They had a bubblegum one, and a bubble of childish delight swelled in my chest, reminding me of the days my mum had made me my own screwballs at home since I could never get anything from the ice cream van that came round in the summer. She'd always drenched it in bubblegum sauce and put two or three bubblegum balls in the bottom of the glass.

To this day I didn't know where she'd gotten them from, but I had a sneaking suspicion she'd bought a box off the ice cream man just for me.

I knew I couldn't have the restaurant's version of the sundae, at least not today, but there was an option to build your own. And they had three different fruit sorbets as well as numerous sauces and toppings.

"You know, if you're looking for a cute date idea, you could bring Anthony here," Rhys said. He'd sat next to his twin and seeing them so close made me realise just how identical they were. It made me grateful they had names on their hoodies.

"Even as friends, if that's where you're still at," Ianto said, looking pointedly at his twin. "You said things are complicated?"

"Yeah... but maybe it's just me making it that way." I sighed and released my hair from its high ballet bun so I'd have something to play with while I talked. "Anthony is Barbie Summers... the drag queen... She won *Drag Stars* season five. I met him at The Court when I went up to see Eva and Bubblegum at the end of May and we kind of just hit it off. He's so sweet and he's helping me get into drag and his advice is amazing, truly amazing. But it's more than that." I twisted a thin strand of hair around my finger. "I really like him. And I don't think I can."

"Why not?" Ianto asked with a frown as our waitress approached the table to take our order.

"Is it because of the power dynamic thing?" Rhys asked once we'd ordered and were once again left alone. "He's your mentor. I think the correct term is drag mother—"

"Look at you with the lingo," Ianto teased and Rhys chuckled.

"I'm learning! I even know what fucking contour is now… haven't got a bloody clue how you apply it properly, but I know what it's for." He shook his head and fixed me with a knowing gaze. "Anyway, there's a whole power dynamic there, and not the sexy bedroom kind but more the 'student-teacher with massive real-world implications for your career' kind. Maybe it's more like master and apprentice, only without a battle that ends with one of you going up in flames."

"That's not helpful," Ianto said, elbowing his twin playfully.

"Why not? I'm making a good point here."

"He sort of is," I said. "It is this weird mix of student-teacher and master and apprentice. Because while I figured out the basics of drag for myself, I wouldn't be nearly as far down the path to figuring out who I want to be as an artist without him. And he knows so many people… he's got such a big platform… and I don't want him to help me because of who he is or what he can do for me, but…"

"But that sort of reach and influence is pretty hard to ignore," Rhys said softly. "I know you, Colin. I don't think you'd be capable of using him for his platform, but if someone like Barbie Summers chooses to take on a new drag queen, that's gonna be a pretty big fucking deal."

Ianto nodded in agreement. "I hadn't thought of that, but Rhys is right. That kind of connection is huge and I'm not surprised you're feeling a little hesitant."

"It's also…" I twisted my hair again as I tried to put my thoughts into words. "I don't want to put him in an awkward position either. Saying it out loud makes me realise just how much responsibility he has, at least that's how most people will see it, and I don't want to make things awkward."

I glanced around and leant across the table, lowering my voice and whispering my next thought. "I don't want anyone to think that I slept my way into Barbie's good graces either and the only reason he's helping me is because we had sex. Or are having sex… if we, if it happened I really wouldn't want it to only be a one-time thing."

The twins chuckled and Rhys opened his mouth to say something, only to be interrupted by the waitress with our drinks, closely followed by one of her colleagues bearing a tray laden with three enormous sundaes.

My eyes nearly popped out of my sockets as the one I'd built was placed down in front of me. The large glass dish was filled with scoops of brightly coloured mango, passion fruit, and raspberry sorbets and drenched with bubblegum and cherry sauce that dripped off the rim. Sprinkles covered half the surface and there was a wafer stuck jauntily in the top. Somewhere at the bottom there was also a ball of bubblegum. I just had to find it first.

Across from me, the twins were eyeing up their treats with hungry eyes. Ianto had gone for a cookies and cream sundae, which had crushed Oreos scattered across the top and was covered in chocolate syrup, while Rhys had opted for a strawberry cheesecake sundae that had slices of fresh strawberries and whipped cream piled on top of the various ice creams and gelatos as well as a heavy dusting of crushed digestives.

I picked up the wafer and snapped it in half, resisting the temptation to shove the whole thing in my mouth like a hamster.

"Do you really think Anthony would see it that way?" Ianto asked, using the long sundae spoon he'd been given to scoop up a mountain of ice cream and Oreos. "That you're using him? That any relationship you had would be you using sex to get what you want?"

"God no! At least, I hope not," I said before eating the rest of my wafer. "I'd never do anything like that. In fact, I'd rather give up his mentorship than give up him. Even if we can only be friends. I value what we have far more than his drag expertise."

It was the first time I'd said it out loud but as soon as I did, a sense of rightness filled me, settling deep into my bones like it belonged there. If I had to choose, I'd pick Anthony over Barbie every time. Because while Barbie was beautiful and wonderful in so many ways, she belonged to more than just one person. But Anthony... he was funny and endearing and cared so much it felt like he could fix any problem I'd ever have with a single smile.

We'd grown so close over the past couple of weeks and not a day went by when we didn't chat in some way. We were constantly sending each other messages and silly videos from the moment we woke up until we finally fell asleep.

We'd started hanging out more too and not always to talk about drag. We'd watch movies and TV shows, cook dinner together, talk about everything that popped into our heads, and play games on my Switch. We'd even started a co-op game of *Stardew Valley* together, which Anthony had never played before and had now become slightly obsessed with building the most extravagant chicken coop ever.

Our friendship might have started with the two of us gravitating towards each other simply out of necessity and loneliness, but we'd clicked in a way I'd never expected. He wasn't just my drag mentor; he was fast becoming my best friend, and I couldn't bear the idea of losing what we'd found.

If Barbie belonged to everyone, then Anthony belonged to nobody except himself, and sometimes it felt like he expected nobody else to want him.

But I did.

And if I had my way, I'd keep him too.

"I think that's your answer then," Rhys said, sucking a stray bit of sauce off the end of his spoon. "You're both adults, you're both aware of the risks, but ultimately it doesn't feel like this is about the drag, not really. It's about you as people, Colin and Anthony. And maybe that's the part you need to focus on first. The rest of it can come later."

I nodded and scooped up a spoonful of sorbet dripping in bubblegum sauce, the sweet smell so heavy in the air it felt like I could breathe in sugar.

Rhys was right—the rest could come later. There was no point rushing to the worst possible outcome when I didn't even know if Anthony wanted this with me.

I really hoped he did, though.

CHAPTER THIRTEEN

Barbie Summers

"I KNOW we said we'd do drag shit tonight, but how do you feel about sacking off and watching a movie instead?" I asked as I stepped inside Colin's front door, moving out of his way so he could shut it behind me while I kicked my shoes off.

I had some make-up and wig styling tools in my bag along with a cute top I'd found in a box that I thought would suit Colin's developing drag style, but it was Friday, I was tired, and I just wanted to do fuck all with the man I was trying, and failing, not to develop feelings for.

"Er, sure," Colin said, sounding a little thrown by the change of plans. "Everything okay? Did I—"

"You didn't do anything wrong," I said quickly. "And we can still do drag stuff if you want, but I was kinda hoping… maybe… to spend some time with you?"

Colin's expression broke into a bright, eager smile and

fucking hell, if I was supposed to be keeping away from him, then this was *not* going to help. That smile was like fucking oxygen. How had I existed for so long without knowing what that smile looked like? "That sounds fun. I'd like that. Do you know what you want to watch?"

"I have no fucking clue. I guess it depends what streaming services we've got between us. And if all else fails, I've got Maddi's Disney Plus login. As long as we don't interfere with her rewatch of *Grey's Anatomy* she won't mind us using it."

"I don't think I've ever watched *Grey's Anatomy*," Colin said as he beckoned me towards the stairs so we could head up to his room.

"Me neither, and it's like twenty-odd seasons now, so there's no fucking way I'm starting."

Our footsteps creaked on the stairs and from somewhere in the house I could hear voices chatting. I'd only met two of Colin's roommates in passing once when we'd been in the kitchen getting some drinks and the pair of them had come in to make dinner. They'd been polite enough but it was clear they weren't particularly interested in their housemate or his life, which was a bit fucking shitty, but I supposed it could have been worse.

At least they were tidy.

I kept meaning to ask Colin if he was planning on living here next year as well, but I hadn't gotten around to it. The idea of the two of us getting a place together had been floating around in my mind but that idea was probably more trouble than it was worth. Every time I toyed with bringing it up, I heard Maddi's splutter of disbelief in my head and it was enough to keep me from saying anything out loud.

"I have Netflix," Colin said as he opened his bedroom door. It wasn't much bigger than mine and only a basic rental beige, but he'd done a wonderful job of turning it into a cozy, slightly kitsch escape from the world, with fairy lights draped across the walls, cushions scattered across the bed, and a huge fluffy rug in the shape of an ice cream in the middle of the floor. "We could see what's on there? I've been watching that new period drama series, *Llewelyn*."

"Wait, is that the sexy gay one?" The name sounded vaguely familiar and I was sure I'd seen more than a few TikToks talking about it. At least, I had if it was the show with ruffled shirts, frock coats, and two beautiful men who seemed to fuck like bunnies. "With Jude Kane?"

"Yes! And Henry Lu. It's, er, yes, it's quite sexy." I put my bag down and glanced over at Colin, whose nose was an adorable shade of pink. "There's the one scene in episode four, no, wait, five… and er, well, you can see pretty much everything."

"Everything? Is there dick in this show?"

"No, sorry. Not that I've seen anyway. But there's a lot of nudity, including several lingering shots of Henry Lu's ass."

"Damn. I need to see that."

"Do you want to watch it now?" Colin asked. He wasn't quite meeting my eye but I didn't know if he was embarrassed or something more. "We could always order some food too? I haven't actually had dinner."

"If that's okay with you?" I stepped closer, putting my

hand out and brushing my fingers across his arm. I wanted to touch him, to pull him against me and trace the line of his jaw, but a knot in my stomach told me it would be too much. "We don't have to. I know watching smut with friends can be weird."

"It's not that." His eyes met mine and he smiled softly. "I promise."

"Are you sure?"

"Yeah, I am."

"Okay then, let's watch it." I moved half a step closer until there was barely any space between us. "And food sounds good. What do you fancy? You're lactose intolerant, right? So do you want to get Chinese?"

"Yeah." He nodded as he reached out with his fingers, lightly caressing my other hand as it hung down beside me. My body tensed and for a second it felt like both of us were holding our breath in the glow of the fairy lights. Without a word, I slid my fingers into his and exhaled. There were calluses on his long, slim fingers and his skin was cool despite the warm weather outside.

We stood there for a while, not speaking, barely breathing, our only point of connection being our interlinked hands. I wondered idly if I should say something and break the spell, but I couldn't bring myself to destroy this moment.

Colin looked at me from under his long lashes, which up close were a reddish blond that reminded me of ginger biscuits—something warm and familiar. There were a few freckles scattered across his nose and the bow in his lip seemed deeper this close up. The heady scents of mint and strawberries filled my senses, reminding me of fresh summer days and cocktails in the sun. It made me want to bury my face in his neck and drink in every drop until I was drowning in it.

"Anthony," he said quietly, whispering my name like saying it any louder would be a mistake. As if the universe would collapse in on itself if it knew what we were doing.

Maybe it would.

There was only one way to find out.

I lifted my other hand and cradled his jaw, sliding my fingers behind his ear and feeling his pulse in his neck as I stroked my thumb across his cheek. His skin was soft with only the first hints of new stubble beginning to break through. "Yes?"

"What are we… what is this?"

"I don't know," I said, because there was no other answer I could give. Or maybe there were a thousand, but I didn't have the sense to look for them. "Do you want me to stop?"

"No!" He tilted his face down and brought his forehead to rest against mine. "Don't go, please."

"I won't then."

The seconds stretched out around us, measured only in heartbeats.

"Can I kiss you?" Colin asked, the question shocking but so right all at once. I'd spent a lifetime waiting for it.

I didn't need words, but I used one anyway. "Yes." I tilted my head up as I drew him down to meet me, our height difference meaning I almost needed to stand on my toes.

The first touch of our lips was hesitant and in the back of my mind I could hear a voice screaming at me to stop, that there was no way back from this point. I ignored it, because fuck that. I needed Colin. Whatever this was, whatever we had—whether that was friendship or something more—it was the only thing keeping me afloat and if that disappeared, I'd drown before I even got the chance to tread water.

Colin softened against me and I felt myself relax as I was drawn into the kiss, which quickly gave way to another. And another. Colin's mouth was like candyfloss— sweet and delicious and impossible to only taste once. I pulled him closer and deepened the kiss, feeling the heat radiating off his body as I teased the seam of his lips with my tongue.

I groaned as Colin's mouth opened, his tongue slipping out to brush against my own. I couldn't remember the last time I'd revelled in kissing someone so much. My cock ached dully in the front of my jeans but I wasn't in a rush to do anything about it. For now, all I wanted was to keep kissing Colin until my lips were cracked and sore.

Colin's hand tightened on mine and he took a step backwards, then another, gently leading me towards his bed. I was tempted to make a bad joke about wanting to get me underneath him, but even for me that felt crass. Besides, talking would mean I'd have to stop kissing him and I didn't want that. Not even for a second.

All our ideas about watching *Llewelyn* and ordering Chinese had been forgotten, crumbled into dust at our feet, and I was happy to sweep them away in favour of wherever this new path took us.

There was a thump as Colin's legs hit the edge of his bed and he giggled against my lips as he wobbled in place. I tightened my grip on his neck and his hand, trying hard not to hurt him. "Maybe it's better if we lie down before we fucking fall down," I said in a low, rough voice.

"Sorry, I'm clumsy."

"Don't apologise, sugar," I said, feeling my way towards the edge of the bed and stopping when I felt my knee connect with the mattress. I was very damn grateful his bed didn't have a footboard. "And you're not clumsy."

Colin smiled and chuckled, pouring the sound into my mouth. "Agree to disagree." He released me reluctantly, a whimper sliding from between his lips as we parted. But I still kept hold of his hand because I couldn't fathom the idea of not touching him at all. I dropped onto the edge of the bed and shuffled further onto the mattress, pulling Colin along with me until we were stretched out together, his body pressed against mine.

Our legs tangled and I slid my free hand around his waist to rest it on his lower back, holding him gently in place as he kissed me again. His mouth was sweet and eager and I groaned as he pressed his tongue between my lips to tease my own. Colin's other hand grasped the front of my T-shirt, his hunger making my body thrum with need.

If he'd been any other man, I'd have wondered why we weren't fucking by now, but tonight I didn't feel the need to rush. There was no burning itch under my skin to get naked as fast as possible, no voice in my head whispering I couldn't be that attractive if they didn't want to be inside me or feel me inside them. Colin calmed all the rushing thoughts in my mind until they were a lazy river drifting slowly towards their destination.

Colin's knee pushed between my thighs, splitting them open as he rolled half on top of me. His hair cascaded around us like a curtain, eyes shining brightly as he looked down at me.

I didn't know where this was going to lead us and that should have scared me. Past experiences of going into things with my eyes closed had burned me but here I was, walking into another situation where I didn't know the parameters, the expectations, or the outcome. But I couldn't compare Colin to anyone or anything else. Yeah, there was a chance everything could go tits up tomorrow, but fuck it, I didn't care.

I'd rather things with Colin went to hell in a handcart than to never try.

And that was my last thought before I pulled him in for another kiss.

CHAPTER FOURTEEN

Colin

Kissing Anthony was like nothing I'd ever experienced in all the twenty-four years of my life.

The fantasy romances I spent my spare time devouring always made kissing sound like it could shake the very foundations of your life, but I'd always thought that was just part of the fantasy. Now I had to admit they might actually have been right.

Or maybe the only other two men I'd been with were absolutely rotten kissers.

Either way, kissing Anthony was a revelation I'd never recover from. If I could, I'd write my whole thesis on his mouth, detailing in equations and formulae and mathematical models what it was that made it so perfect.

His body radiated heat from underneath me and the gentle press of his fingers on my spine felt like they were blistering my skin. Would it ever not feel like he was branding me whenever we touched? I almost hoped not. I wanted him to mark me in some way, even if no one else could see it, so I could look at it in the mirror and know that I was his.

Which was probably a bit of an extreme reaction to a first kiss, but other men had done more for less.

I felt the press of his cock through his jeans, the hardness digging into my hip, and I couldn't resist sliding a little further on top of him to brush my own erection against his. I didn't know if he wanted to do more than make-out, but I wanted him to know I was open to the possibility.

Anthony groaned at the burst of friction and the sound drew a moan from my lips as he rolled his hips up, slowly grinding against me. I felt him smile as he kissed me and rolled his hips again, more deliberately this time. I gasped and pressed against him, desperately seeking some sort of relief.

His hand slid down my spine to graze the top of my ass, his fingers drifting over the waistband of my jeans like he was tempted to dip down underneath it. I wished he would and the next time he ground upwards, I rolled my hips in return and pushed back into his hand. I didn't know exactly what I wanted, but I knew I wanted *more*.

More kisses, more touches… more Anthony.

He hummed and gently pulled my bottom lip between his teeth, making me gasp. I deepened our next kiss, a surge of desperation rising in my chest and threatening to get the better of me. My mouth demanded more and Anthony seemed happy to oblige as our kisses turned messy and heated.

Our other hands had still been interlinked on the bed, but suddenly he released me and reached out to slide his fingers into my hair. I moaned because I'd always loved having my hair petted, played with, and pulled, and I tilted my head to lean into his touch, hoping he'd get the gist of what I wanted.

"Fuck," Anthony said with a moan as he broke our endless stream of kisses. "What do... can I?"

"Yes," I said, kissing across his jaw and licking down the side of his neck. Anthony smelt like something summery and spicy and it was making me almost feral. "Yes, anything."

"That's... mmm, that's not an answer, sugar."

I groaned and ground against him because the way he called me sugar... I'd never had a pet name I liked before—they'd always sounded sarcastic—but coming from his lips, it felt like pure affection. "You didn't ask a question."

"I suppose I didn't." He gently tugged my hair and pulled me away from his neck where I'd been debating sucking a mark into the soft skin. I huffed and groaned in frustration, my mouth settling into a sullen pout as I sat back on my knees, straddling one of his thighs. Anthony chuckled as he let go of my hair to run his thumb across my bottom lip. "You look so cute like this."

"Horny and pouting, you mean?"

"Yeah." He grinned and finally dipped his other hand under the waistband of my jeans and into my underwear. "What do you want, Colin?" His question threw me for a second because I hadn't been expecting him to ask. "You don't look sure."

"I'm not," I said, resisting the urge to glance away. "Both of my exes were a bit more… take charge? I mean, they made a lot of the decisions. And I didn't mind but…"

Anthony frowned and I saw something that almost looked like anger flit across his expression. "Did you not get a say at all?"

"No, I did! But… sorry, I'm ruining everything."

"You're not ruining anything, I promise," he said. "But I do want you to tell me what you want. You must have some idea." He smiled wickedly and winked as he gently caressed my ass, squeezing one of my tiny butt cheeks and making me brush against his erection. "Come on, I promise there are no bad ideas and no silly suggestions, and if I don't like something, I'll say."

"I want to keep kissing you," I said, swallowing down my fears about saying the wrong thing. "And I want… can I take your shirt off? Please?"

"Of course, as long as I can take yours off too."

"Yes."

"What else?" He was still squeezing my ass and encouraging me to slowly roll my hips, humping against him as we talked, which made it a thousand times harder to think of what to say, let alone get any words out. "Are there things you don't want?"

"I don't want to have sex," I said. "Sorry, is that weird? You must think that's odd."

He raised an eyebrow. "No? Why the fuck would I think that?"

"I just... I know I'm an anomaly compared to a lot of men. I've only been with two people and my ex—"

"Let me stop you there," Anthony said. "Whatever that cunt said, I want you to forget it. I fucking mean it. There's no right or wrong number of partners to have. You can have as many as you want. Whether that's two or two hundred, I don't give a fuck either way. You are fucking perfect, Colin. And I mean that too."

"But... are you sure?" I couldn't shake Kyle's words from my head, when he'd told me I was boring for only having one partner before him. That I was so lucky I'd found him because nobody else would be willing to fuck someone so dull.

In hindsight, I could see how poisonous his words had been, but it was only time and separation that had given me that power. Sometimes I wondered how I'd found the strength to leave when my veins had been overflowing with his poison. Wherever it had come from, I was grateful.

"Of course I'm sure." He smiled up at me as he caressed my jaw. "So you don't want to fuck. Is that all forms of sex off the table or just penetration? I'm not trying to find a loophole—I just want to know *exactly* what you want, love."

"No penetration, but I... mmm, I want..." I groaned as I rolled my hips again, heat simmering under my skin from the delicious bursts of friction. "Can I touch you? Can I use my hands?"

"Yeah, you can do that. Want to jack us off together? Can I touch you too?"

"Please. I'll be really disappointed if you don't."

"Thank you," Anthony said, leaning up on one arm and drawing me down for a kiss. "Fuck, I could kiss you all night."

"You can," I whispered, my lips still pressed against his.

"Are you saying I have to stay here until you let me go then?"

"Maybe... yes?" I let out a breathless laugh of embarrassment because it sounded so ridiculous when I said it out loud. But that didn't make my desires any less real. "Stay for a while, at least. Please."

"How long is a while?"

"How long is a piece of string?"

Anthony chuckled and kissed me fiercely. "God, you're so fucking adorable."

I groaned and tipped forward, eager to devour him. My palms landed on either side of his head and for a moment I forgot all about stripping him down and getting my hands on the rest of him. He moaned and bucked up against me, and I was powerless to resist. Our kisses were greedy and messy as we ground our cocks together, dry humping eagerly like we'd combust if we didn't keep moving.

Anthony's fingers reached for the bottom of my T-shirt, teasing it slowly up my torso, every tiny brush of his hands on my skin making me shiver. I had to sit up slightly to allow him to pull it over my head and our eyes met as he chucked the thin piece of fabric somewhere onto the floor. "Wow," Anthony said as he traced a finger down my chest while his other hand cupped my waist. "You're so fucking beautiful."

"Yeah?" I asked, hating how doubtful I sounded. I

didn't know why him seeing me shirtless felt like such a big deal; it wasn't like he hadn't seen it before on Instagram or when I'd gotten changed in front of him. Maybe it had something to do with the amount of pure desire radiating from his gaze.

"Yeah." He nodded, the hand on my chest drifting up to catch my chin as I considered looking away. "Don't be embarrassed, please. You're gorgeous, Colin."

"Thanks." I grinned and reached for the hem of his vest top. "This feels very one-sided, though."

"Fair's fair, I guess."

He pulled himself into a sitting position and smoothly tugged his top over his head, ruffling his blond hair as he did and giving himself the most gorgeous fucked-out, fluffy style that made me want to sink my hands into it while we kissed. But that wasn't the only part of him attracting my notice.

I'd seen Anthony shirtless before on TV when Barbie had been getting in and out of drag, but I'd never been able to appreciate how stunning his body was until we were this close.

Blond stubble dusted his chest where he hadn't shaved or waxed it recently, and while he had some muscles, there was a beautiful softness to him too. My gaze trailed down his torso and my fingers itched to reach out and touch.

"Take your jeans off," I said, shuffling back down his hips and then realising that wouldn't give him enough room. "Take all of it off, please."

He grinned at me, putting a hand out to gently tip me

onto the bed. "Only if you do the same, baby. I want to see everything."

He didn't need to ask me twice.

I grabbed the button on my jeans and yanked them open, tugging them down so hard it hurt. I kicked them onto the floor and reached for my underwear as my eyes trailed over to where Anthony was doing the same.

My movements slowed as I watched him tug his boxers over his hard cock, swallowing as I looked at his fat shaft, wondering what it would feel like in my hand... between my lips, on my tongue... and inside my ass.

His cock wasn't huge, which I was glad about because the thought of taking something massive almost scared me —I'd never been a size queen—but it was thick and beautiful, and fuck, I wanted it.

"Wow," I said, finally tugging my boxers off. "You... fuck, Anthony..." Lust surged through me and I practically threw myself at him, the pair of us giggling like teenagers as we landed in a heap on the bed, our limbs intertwined.

I'd never felt anything like this rush of need before. It was like my body had turned my desire up to ten and then discovered there were another ten notches beyond that.

Our mouths met in another series of messy kisses as we desperately rolled our hips, rutting and frotting together. Our cocks ground together, the heat and friction only soothed by a burst of precum from one of us, and a shiver of pleasure ran down my spine at the sudden addition.

My body was on fire, desire igniting every fibre of my being and making me burn white hot. Everything was too much and not enough. I needed more, craved it, but I didn't know how to do anything else with my mouth except keep kissing the incredible man underneath me.

He groaned as his tongue tangled with mine, thrusting his hips up again and again as we chased our release.

"Co-Colin," he growled and I melted, heat and pressure building inside me.

"Yes," I said, the word practically a moan. "I'm so close!"

Anthony groaned, his body shaking as he nipped my lip and kissed me feverishly, his cock pulsing against mine as he drenched me in his cum. It made me gasp and I frantically rocked my hips harder, desperate to reach my own release.

My orgasm caught me by surprise, hitting me with an unparalleled force that shook me all the way down to my soul. I moaned into Anthony's mouth as my cum mixed with his, hyper-aware of the feeling of his hands on my body, caressing my spine and stroking my hair as the last of my orgasm faded away.

I didn't know what any of this meant or what it would do to our friendship, let alone our drag relationship and him mentoring me.

But I couldn't find it in me to care.

Because this moment was far too perfect to waste on worry, and I wanted to remember every second of it.

Just in case it changed everything.

CHAPTER FIFTEEN

Barbie Summers

"Hypothetically, if I had done something stupid *but* it wasn't something I regretted, how mad would you be about it?" I asked casually as I lay on my bed with my phone held above my face so I was in frame.

I wasn't looking at the screen, though.

Instead, I was gazing up at my ceiling and letting my eyes trail lazily over the dull neon stars above me. Since it was lunchtime, they were lit by the late June sunshine streaming in through the window and I kinda hoped the old stars had enough juice to pick up some of the bright light and save it up for later.

There was a pause on the other end of the call, and then Maddi said, "You slept with Colin, didn't you?"

"Um…"

"Don't try and deny it, dumb-ass! You just admitted you'd done something stupid."

"Okay, but it could have been something else."

"Oh yeah? Like what?" Maddi asked and when I glanced at the screen, I saw her patented unimpressed eyebrow raise.

"I don't know, bought a new wig? Signed up for a tour with a company I don't know?"

"You're a twat, but you're not that foolish. Not about business shit, at least."

"Yeah," I said bitterly. "I've learnt that lesson already." I finally let my eyes meet the camera and saw Maddi looking at me expectantly. She wasn't going to let me get away with assumptions—she wanted a full explanation. "I went to his house on Friday. We were just going to watch something on Netflix, maybe order some food, but then we got chatting and he kissed me and… well, there was a lot of making out and some messy frotting, but… I thought I'd feel bad about it but fuck, Mads, I feel calmer than I have in fucking months."

She sipped an iced coffee and gestured for me to continue. I noticed she'd had her nails done since we'd last spoken and now she had some impressive neon green spikes on the ends of her fingers. "Keep talking."

"I like your nails," I said, smiling at her. I'd seen Mads wearing nails like that plenty of times in drag but this was the first time I'd seen her with them in her everyday life. "They suit you."

She grinned and glanced away for a second. "You think so? They're not too much?"

"Nah, they're perfect. They say don't fuck with me, bitch, or I will end you. And the colour is perfection."

"Cheers, babe. But we're not talking about me."

"Why not? You're gorgeous and worth celebrating."

"Okay, now you're being a proper twat." She laughed and sipped her coffee again. "Come on, spill the tea. You got off with Colin and now you feel calm. Do you think you just needed a good wank? How often have you been getting off lately? Orgasms are good for you—both mentally and physically—and you could do with something to make you feel better."

"Often enough," I said. "I don't think that's it. Like, surely if a good orgasm was the solution, I'd have felt the benefits before now. I've got enough porn saved to keep me amused. I really think it's because Colin's involved."

"Even though we talked about why doing that was a bad idea," Maddi said, pursing her lips around her straw. "Do you ever listen to me?"

"Most of the time. But Colin's different, Mads. I know there's a whole power dynamic thing between us, but I don't think he's using me for that."

"How do you mean?"

I looked back up at the ceiling, trying to think of a way to put my gut instinct into words. Telling Maddi that I "just had a feeling" wasn't going to cut it. "Okay, so, he hasn't asked me once about getting him gigs or announcing him on socials or promoting him in any way. Fuck, I don't know if he's got any drag social accounts yet. I need to get on that." I ran my hand through the top of my hair.

Maddi was frowning in disbelief. "Seriously? He's not even asked once?"

"Nope. It's like he doesn't want to be pushy or something."

"Bloody hell! How the fuck did you find the only non-pushy baby queen in the country? She's going to have to grow a nice shiny spine if she wants to make it because she's going to have to fucking push and shove if she wants to get out there. We can pretend we're all friends in this industry but we both know that's a damn lie. We all have to claw and shove our way through, even if it's just onto our local scenes."

"That's why you've always had long nails then?" I asked with a grin.

"How else am I supposed to get these other bitches out of my way? Use my elbows?"

I laughed because the thought of anyone daring to get in Maddi's way was absurd. She had carved out her niche and stuck to it, winning herself fans across the globe. Sure, she had her haters too—we all did—but Maddi had managed to rise above the noise with grace, poise, and sheer bloody-minded stubbornness.

"In all seriousness, though, babe, you know I'm right," she continued. "Your baby queen is going to have to leave the nest at some point, and if she can't stand on her own two feet at that point, then she's fucked."

"I know." Maddi had a good point and I made a mental note to start prodding Colin out into the wider world. "I'll give him a nudge. I'm still not sure how he'll feel about me offering more help than I have been, though. I could probably get him a couple of gigs, but I don't know if that'd be overstepping."

"What kind of drag mother would you be if you didn't lovingly shove him in front of an audience? This is why you need the separation of church and state. Or in this case, drag and your dick."

"Even if he's the only thing keeping me afloat?" I asked quietly, my eyes once again drifting off into the middle distance. The feeling of peace I got from being around Colin had only increased after Friday night, and for the first time in months it hadn't felt like I was losing myself. I didn't know what it was about Colin that made me feel that way. All I knew was he felt like steady ground after months on rocky seas.

"I know I shouldn't be relying on him so much to make me feel like myself," I continued. "But when I'm with him… it's like I can forget all my mistakes, forget how much I've fucked up over the past couple of years, and focus on me. He makes me believe in myself, Mads. Fuck, the way he looks at me? It makes me want to be the person he thinks I am."

"You already are, babe."

"I don't feel like it. I'm a fucked-up loser, Maddi. I'm the one who's supposed to have everything but instead I got scammed by both the manager and the tour company who promised to support me, got dumped by my boyfriend—"

"That's not a bad thing," Maddi interjected. "Steve was a prick. He tried to turn fans against you, he got you kicked out of your flat by never paying the fucking rent, and he used you as a magical money tree while he did nothing but sit on his ass all day getting high and letting anyone who took his fancy fuck him. Or had you forgotten about the cheating?"

I winced. "No… I was just trying not to think about it." I'd always known Steve wasn't the monogamous sort, and if he'd wanted an open relationship, I'd have been happy to talk about it. Instead he'd kept telling me that I was his one and only while dicking down everyone in a two-mile radius. I'd known as soon as I walked in to find him in bed with two guys for the fourth time I should have called it quits, but I'd been so desperate to be needed that I'd have let him pin a series of brutal bloody murders on me without saying a word.

It was funny in a way because Colin needed me too. But the two situations felt so wildly different I'd never want to compare them.

Steve had taken. Colin asked.

"Strike Steve the Absolute Knob dumping you off the list of bad things that happened to you then," Maddi said.

"Fine, but he is part of the reason I had to leave London since, you know, he took all the rent money I gave him and spent it on designer clothes and coke."

"I'll give you that one."

"Thanks."

"But it's still not your fault," Maddi continued, fixing me with a glare. "None of this is."

"The Candy Club thing kinda is," I argued. "I should've actually read the fucking fine print, or you know… been more insistent."

"You didn't know, babe. They promised you all this shit, they gave you what looked like a proper contract, and then they fucked off with the money. They had other queens from the show on their roster. You weren't to know they'd do this to you. From your perspective, they looked like a legitimate business."

Maddi had a point, but that didn't make me feel better. No matter what way we sliced it, the Candy Club thing was always going to feel like my fault.

"Have you talked to anyone else they worked with?" Maddi asked, the ice in her cup of coffee rattling loudly as she shook it. "To see if it happened to any of them?"

"No," I said as I ran my fingers through my hair again. "It sounds ridiculous but I don't want to admit it. Because what if I'm the only one? And I don't want anyone else to think less of me."

Maddi muttered something into her straw about men being twats and then sighed. "Have you at least thought about talking to a lawyer? Maybe they could help you get some of it back?"

I hummed because that wasn't actually a bad suggestion. There was just one glaring issue. "Where the fuck am I going to get the money to pay for a lawyer? I'd have to sell a bloody kidney, and I'm saving those for emergencies."

Maddi waved a hand. "I don't know. Don't most of them do, like, pro bone work?"

I snorted. "Pro bono?"

"That's it! Like this shit is for the public good. You're poor—they should help you."

"I don't think it's that simple," I said. Maddi made it sound easy, but it really couldn't be that simple, could it? I added the idea to my mental to-do list, knowing I'd probably never get around to it. But at least this way I could tell Maddi I was thinking about it. "But I'll have a look."

"Good," Maddi said with a pleased smile. "Now, back to Colin."

I groaned and let my arm flop over my face. "Do we have to?"

"Yes, because I want to know something."

"That doesn't sound good," I said with a huff. Why did Maddi have to keep pushing?

"You said Colin makes you believe in yourself again, that he doesn't think you're the loser you're so determined to believe you are."

"Yes..." I didn't like where this was going and my stomach dropped into the mattress.

"Have you told him about any of this?" Maddi asked gently.

"No," I said, still hiding under my arm. This was exactly where I'd seen this conversation heading and I didn't like it one bit. "And I'm not planning to either."

"Why not? Don't you think he deserves to know?"

I huffed, suddenly tempted to end the call or drop my phone onto the bed so Maddi's voice was muffled. I loved her, but did she have to ask so many bloody awkward questions? And why did she have to zero in on all my fucking weak spots and worries like a damn laser? "Probably, but that doesn't mean I'm going to tell him. And you're not either."

"And again I'm gonna ask you why the hell not?"

I lifted my arm and looked at her from underneath it. "Firstly, because he's the one person who doesn't think I'm a total fucking twat and I'd like to keep it that way. I mean, what kind of drag mother would I be with that kind of fuck up in my life?"

"A relatable one," Maddi said with a fixed glare and I knew she was wishing she could reach through the screen to shake some sense into me.

"And secondly," I continued, ignoring her point, "you're not going to tell him because you love me, and if you tell him, I'll file for divorce."

"I didn't know we were married."

I shrugged. "We practically are. You're like my drag wife."

Maddi laughed. "I suppose so. In which case, if we get divorced I want support payments."

"Good fucking luck with that," I said. "I'm flat broke."

"Damn, I guess we'll just have to stay married then."

"I guess so."

"So as your wife," Maddi said with renewed glee, "I'm telling you that you *have* to tell Colin everything. From everything you've told me about him, I know he'll understand. And even if you don't want to tell him as his drag mother, tell him as your friend… as your boyfriend."

"Boyfriend?" I repeated the word in surprise as I threw my arm off my face and nearly dropped my phone onto myself.

"Oh please, babe, if you're that hung up about Colin, then you're more than just friends," Maddi said like it was somehow really fucking obvious. Maybe it was to her, but I'd never have gone that far. Even if I'd wanted to. "And if you're not going to talk to him about everything that happened, at least tell him that you fancy the pants off him. Literally, given today's confession."

"Fine. I'll talk to him."

"Soon. Not at some point in the distant future. Don't try and get around me like that—I know you too well."

I chuckled. I wanted to say I couldn't believe she was bullying me into this, but that would be a lie. "Fine, I'll talk to him at some point in the next few weeks. By the middle of July. Happy now?"

"Not entirely, but it's a start." Maddi grinned victoriously as she sipped the last of her iced coffee. "I love you."

"I suppose I love you too," I said.

Despite the blatant pushing and shoving, I was glad I'd told Maddi. It made everything feel so much more real.

And maybe if I followed her advice, my dreams about Colin would exist in reality too.

CHAPTER SIXTEEN

Barbie Summers

A TRIP to IKEA was not high on my list of fun things to do but at least going with Colin would make the whole thing less of a tedious shitshow. Especially if I could find something cute to buy him, both as a thank you for bringing me and because I wanted to see him smile.

There was something about Colin's smile that made even the worst days seem brighter, like my life wasn't dreary, overcast, and perpetually waiting for a fresh storm to hit.

We hadn't really talked about the whole "making out and getting off together" thing, but since nothing between us seemed to have changed, I didn't see the need to bring it up. I'd promised Maddi I'd talk to him by the middle of July. Which was far fucking closer than I'd thought when I'd originally suggested it, but I still had time.

At this rate I could make a career out of burying my

head in the sand about important shit, but sadly I didn't think anyone would pay me for that skill.

"Okay, where do you want to start?" Colin asked as we walked through IKEA's revolving front door. At least coming on a Tuesday night meant it was much quieter than a Saturday afternoon when the whole place would be packed with screaming kids and stressed-out parents. "Did you make a list in the end or did you just want to get some ideas?"

"I made a bit of a list," I said vaguely, waving my phone. "But I'm happy to have a wander, see what takes my fancy. I'm gonna grab a trolley, though, in case I see anything on the way round."

The corner of Colin's mouth turned up in a knowing smile. "Why do I get the feeling that you're going to be a nightmare when we get to the market hall at the end?"

"I'm not the one who came out last time with some cacti, chocolate, and an owl lamp."

"That wasn't my fault," Colin said as I grabbed a small trolley and the pair of us began to wander towards the showrooms. "They were too cute to resist."

"Exactly, so I get to buy whatever I want. Except don't let me do that because otherwise someone will turn up from the bank and shred my credit card on my doorstep."

"Are you going to be okay buying stuff today?" Colin asked softly as we walked between a display kitchen and kids' bedroom, both laden with signs pointing out what was new. I paused by a stack of scented candles, debating whether to put some in the trolley now or wait until the end.

"Yeah, I should be," I said, an uncomfortable feeling of embarrassment bubbling up through my intestines. For all my jokes about my financial situation, it was difficult to discuss the details. "I got a payout from my YouTube channel and I did an ad on Instagram and TikTok, which paid out too."

"That's awesome!"

"I'm not sure I'd go that far," I said, picking up a couple of candles and sniffing them. "But it helps." I fought back the urge to run away from this entire conversation, but since I'd started it, I figured I owed Colin a nugget of something. "Most of it goes on my credit cards to pay back my *Drag Stars* debts, plus I have to make a loan payment each month, and I'm paying rent to my mum too. She tried to tell me it wasn't necessary but I couldn't not give her anything. But you have to be proud of me because this month I actually sat down and worked out what I could put aside to buy shit."

"I'm impressed," Colin said. He'd moved beside me and gently nudged my thigh with his fingers as he continued. "Seriously, budgeting is hard. And I'm still getting my head around the whole twenty-grand cost to go on *Drag Stars*. Is that just for your looks?"

I put two candles in the trolley and continued walking. "Pretty much. We have to provide a truly ridiculous number of outfits, half of which won't even get used because the producers think it's fun to keep us guessing what the challenges will be."

"But... that doesn't make any sense. Why not tell you the correct challenges up front? Especially if they're not providing you with any kind of budget or stipend? Which I'm assuming they don't given your debts."

"God no, how will the judges criticise us for looking cheap if they actually pay for our wardrobes? And as for the rest… I don't know. Makes for good television I guess."

We wandered through the displays of armchairs and coffee tables, pausing to stick our heads into one of the small display rooms. "I think they're trying to make this look cute and cosy," I said as I wandered inside, glancing at the packed shelving running all the way around the top. "But it just feels cramped. And dark."

Colin nodded as he slipped in alongside me. "I don't like that armchair either. It looks really uncomfortable."

"It kinda looks like the bastard child of a rocking chair and one of those padded plastic garden chairs," I said as I looked at the chair in the corner with a wooden frame and beige upholstery. "Maybe it's because it's beige. I fucking hate beige."

"Same," Colin said. "I've lived in boring rented rooms for so long that I really hate magnolia too. I know it's practical, but why are landlords so opposed to a pop of colour?"

"It's because they're all soulless bastards," I said, ducking back out of the room, Colin close behind me. There was another set of display rooms across the walkway, this time arranged as an entire petite flat. And the living room had pastel blue walls and bright cushions scattered on the blush-coloured sofa. "What about this one? Too bright?"

"No… it's lovely." He trailed his finger across the back of the sofa, smiling wistfully. "I don't think I could do vibrant colours but this is… comforting. That's probably a strange way to put it."

"No, I get it." I closed the gap between us and slid my hand into his. "It's actually cosy rather than minimalist cosy."

"I don't think all those shelves in the other one count as minimalist."

"I couldn't be a minimalist," I said. "I like stuff."

Colin chuckled and squeezed my hand, looking down at me with a fondness I'd rarely experienced from partners. Fuck, Colin wasn't even my boyfriend and here we were making goo-goo eyes at each other in the middle of fucking IKEA while comparing our tastes in home decor. I couldn't decide if that made me desperate or just gay. After all, half of my friends in settled relationships had ended up there by going the whole "sex first, moving in together second, and finally going on something resembling a first date after about six months" thing.

"I don't think any drag artist could be a minimalist. Surely you all have enough wigs and clothes to kit out a whole theatre of performers."

"Sugar, I could probably dress all five seasons of *Drag Stars* and still have clothes left over."

"Exactly my point," Colin said with a cheeky smile. "And I've seen your room."

"Hey, you said it yourself. I'm cramming a whole fucking flat in there." I pulled him close to me and tilted my head up to beg for a kiss. Colin obliged with a happy hum and I felt my whole body relax at the press of his lips. I could've kept kissing him for fucking hours, but the staff would probably get pissed off if we kept doing it here. "Which is why you're gonna help me find some more fucking furniture. And in return, I'll buy you as much Swedish chocolate as you want."

Colin brushed his nose against mine. "I'm warning you now, the limits of my desires don't exist."

"Oh?"

"For chocolate, I mean," he said quickly and I kept hold of his hand to keep him close to me. I didn't want him running away.

"Good to know," I said, kissing him again.

I'd buy Colin as much chocolate as he wanted at this rate. Fuck it, I'd buy him a whole fucking truckload if it made him smile. He didn't know it, and I'd never tell him, but without him, I probably wouldn't have done anything for the last few weeks. I'd have stayed in bed, rotting away and lamenting my life choices.

Maddi kept telling me none of this was my fault, but my brain was struggling to believe her and in the depths of the night when it was just me alone with my thoughts, I replayed memories over in my head in slow motion. The one that I always got stuck on was the moment I realised that Caesar Hurst had disappeared and my money was gone. It was like watching a pin drop as the realisation swept my feet out from under me and sent me crashing to the ground.

And no matter how many times I relived it in my dreams, it never got any easier.

I was used to waking up in a cold sweat now, tears dripping down my face and my heart thumping to a panicked beat. Maybe one day it would get better, but until then I'd be trapped in a never-ending cycle of my own mistakes and living nightmares.

"Anthony?" Colin asked. His voice was soft but concerned and I realised I'd let my brain follow the rabbit, my body tightening in anticipation of the horrors to come. "Are you okay?"

"Sorry, just… thinking about something else." I shook my head and tried to smile at him.

"Do you want to talk about it?"

"Not really," I said. "It's silly." I licked my lips as my brain whirred. "I just… sometimes I just get stuck on all my financial woes and work. I need to stop dwelling on this shit."

"It's okay," he said, squeezing my hand and gently leading me out of the tiny flat towards the trolley we'd abandoned. "It must be stressful. Especially because winning *Drag Stars* is supposed to be a dream come true. But I suppose for you it's both a dream and a nightmare."

"Something like that." I plastered a smile onto my lips, terrified Colin was going to ask about the tour. My mind spun in free fall as it desperately searched for another topic of conversation to latch on to. "Oh, I meant to ask you. What are you doing on Saturday?"

"This Saturday?" Colin frowned as he thought for a second. "Nothing, why?"

My fake smile melted into a real one as my nerves eased off. "How do you feel about going out in drag for the first time?"

"Really? Where? Are you sure I'm ready?"

"Honestly, there's never a perfect time," I said as I grabbed the trolley with my free hand, still holding Colin's hand in the other, and began to walk further into the store. "You can have all the preparation time in the world but nothing really compares to getting out there for the first time. And this won't be performing or anything—I'm doing a surprise lip-sync at The Court during Saturday's Pride Variety Night, and I thought you might like to come with me and meet everyone again, only this time in drag."

"Y-Yeah. Okay. That sounds… fun."

"You don't sound sure," I said, glancing over at Colin, who'd gone a little green around the edges. "If you're not ready, you don't have to come. But if you want to be a drag queen, you're going to get out at some point and this is a pretty low-stakes way for you to do that."

"No, I'm sure." He drew himself up taller and nodded. "I'm going to do it."

"Fucking awesome." I grinned. "You can come to mine and get ready. Then we'll go up together. And you can stay at mine if you want. My new bed is coming tomorrow, so there should be room."

"As long as you can get it in," he said, that cheeky grin coming back onto his face. I couldn't wait for everyone to see him in drag. They were going to be as blown away as I was by Colin's beauty.

"Yeah, yeah, I've got the fucking hint." I bumped my hip against his. "Let's go and find some fucking furniture. Do you think the restaurant's still open? If so, do you want to get some meatballs? I'm fucking starving."

CHAPTER SEVENTEEN

Colin

"Well?" Anthony asked as he stepped away from me, leaving me to stare at myself in the full-length mirror propped up against his bedroom wall. "What do you think? How do you feel?"

It was Saturday afternoon and I'd spent the last two hours getting myself into full drag for the first time, and now I was finally getting to see the results of all my hard work. And Anthony's.

None of this would have been possible without him.

"I… it's… wow…" My fingers trailed over the large bow on the front of the cropped V-neck blouse with pretty flounce sleeves that was a bright, warm orange—almost like something akin to a sunset. It highlighted my newly acquired set of boobs, which were courtesy of a spare breastplate Anthony had found in one of his suitcases and some carefully applied bronzer.

I let my gaze run down my body, past my exposed midriff, which I wasn't as self-conscious about as I'd expected, to the high-rise, wide leg trousers with a brightly coloured wave print in orange, cream, soft pink, deep red, and pastel blue. The trousers had an elasticated waist, which helped because Anthony had suggested I use a little bit of hip padding to accentuate my shape and the elastic had made it so much easier to get them on.

I'd found a pair of cute seventies-style cream boots online that had enough heel to look good but weren't high enough to send me sprawling as soon as I tried to walk. They looked perfect under the trousers, and I'd never seen my legs look so long.

On top of that, I'd added some chunky bangles and a large dangly necklace and a pair of orange clip-on earrings in the shape of daisies, all of which I'd found in the back of a thrift store in Nottingham before pole one afternoon. I'd never thought I was much of a jewellery person, and I still wasn't one hundred percent convinced about the earrings, but I liked the heaviness of the bangles on my wrists and the way they clacked as I moved. It was strangely soothing and not overwhelming like I'd always imagined.

Lastly, there was a pair of massive rhinestoned sunglasses that screamed dramatic bitch and a huge sun hat with an almost obscene brim which I could use to cover my face by gently angling it. It made me think of vintage film stars on the French Riviera, hiding from the paparazzi. It was gorgeously over the top and camp in a way I hadn't anticipated loving.

In fact, this whole look wasn't quite the wild and

dramatic vibes I'd expected to gravitate towards but as soon as I'd seen the trousers online, I'd had to have them and everything had just fallen into place around them.

But the outfit and accessories were only part of the overall look.

The hair currently falling around my shoulders was a deep honey blonde and blown out into huge waves that moved before I did. It was another gift from Anthony—an older wig that he no longer used, which we'd washed and restyled ourselves one evening while attempting to watch *Llewelyn*.

Trying to do both at the same time hadn't gone well and had resulted in me stabbing myself multiple times with wig pins and Anthony nearly burning himself with the hot end of a hair dryer. Eventually we'd given up trying to be clever and do two things at once, so we'd finished the wig and then gone back to the start of the episode, watching it together sprawled out on my bed with Anthony's arm thrown lazily across my waist.

The press of his arm and the heat of his skin against mine had been all I'd been able to focus on, and afterwards I hadn't been able to remember what on earth had happened in the episode. I'd had to watch it again the next day with the ghost of Anthony's arm wrapped around me.

And finally, to complete my transformation, there was the make-up.

It was simultaneously soft and pretty but bold enough to make someone take notice. I finally had a foundation that matched and had spent hours practising my contour to show off my sharp cheekbones and soften out my jaw. My eyes were exaggerated and over-lined underneath, making them bigger and rounder, almost like a doll's. I'd drawn eyelashes on the bottom of the fake lower-lash line and paired them with a big, fluffy pair of fake lashes that were so heavy it felt like I was having to strain to keep my eyes open.

My eye shadow was the same pastel blue as the trousers and it blended out to orange in the corners with a healthy dollop of glitter on the lid. It wasn't the cleanest blend of eye shadow I'd ever seen, but I was hoping nobody would look close enough to notice how messy it truly was. If not, I could hide behind my sunglasses, although every time I blinked, my fake lashes brushed against the lenses, which became a sensory nightmare after about two minutes.

Hopefully, being a baby queen would give me a bit of leeway with how polished and prepared I was supposed to look. Even if I expected myself to look perfect right from the off.

I'd added some freckles across my nose and my lips had a deep, accentuated bow and softer lined sides, inspired by the iconic lip looks of the nineteen twenties.

The whole look was the perfect blend of time periods, camp fashion, and snappy style with just a little bit of sugar to sweeten out the edges.

"It's perfect," I said as I turned my head to smile at Anthony, whose beaming expression was bursting with pride. "I feel amazing. I feel… I feel like a drag queen."

"You look like one too," he said. "Shit, if this is just your first attempt, I can't wait to see where you go."

"Really?"

"Yeah. I'm serious, sugar. You're fucking incredible." He walked back over to me and put his arm around my waist, standing on tiptoes to kiss my cheek. "Are you okay to wait while I finish getting ready? Then we can go."

"Of course," I said, leaning down to press a quick kiss to his lips. We still hadn't talked about whatever we were doing, but I couldn't resist giving him one kiss. After all, it wasn't like a single kiss was going to destroy the world.

Even if the sum of each individual kiss added up to far more than I could keep track of. But I loved the addition of kisses to our interactions, so I wasn't about to open my mouth and complain in case it changed something. I knew he was my mentor—my drag mother—and that could make things so much trickier if we weren't careful, but we were adults and I didn't want to have to choose which part of Anthony to have in my life.

Anthony and Barbie were two halves of a whole, and I couldn't imagine having to pretend one part didn't exist so I could have a relationship with the other.

Anthony hummed softly, his fingers squeezing my waist for a second before he released me and strolled over to the bed where he'd laid out his outfit for the evening. Given that Barbie's appearance was supposed to be a surprise, we were heading down to The Court before the doors opened so we could sneak in the side door and hide. Phil, The Court's owner, had offered up a dressing room for the evening so we could get ready there, but Anthony had still insisted we get ready beforehand.

Reading between the lines, I got the feeling that

Anthony *needed* to be Barbie before we even set foot out of the house. But for the life of me I couldn't think why.

I tried not to dwell on it too much and instead focused on the fact that the clock was rapidly ticking down to my public drag debut. It was supposed to be a fun, low-stakes, low-stress outing.

At least, that was the theory.

It could have been worse, though. Anthony could have organised for me to perform.

"I meant to ask you," he said as he began to strip off, throwing his loose vest top onto the bed and dumping his shorts and boxers onto the floor. I tried very hard not to stare at his dick and focus on his words instead, even if it was really fucking difficult to concentrate when all I wanted to do was drop to my knees. "And I probably should have asked you this ages ago—trust me to get it all arse-backwards—drag name? Have you got one? Also, social media? I know you've got a personal Instagram, but have you got a drag one? I was going to look through my followers list, but then I realised that would take me fucking forever."

He grabbed a different pair of pants, ones with little doughnuts all over them, off the bed and pulled them on, shoving his hand down the front to adjust the position of his dick before he reached for a pair of tights. "If you don't have a drag insta, you should probably set one up before we go out. 'Cos everyone will want to follow you, or you should at least follow everyone who's there tonight. It'd be good for you to start building a network up."

"Oh, I... er, I actually set one up a few weeks ago," I

said, gently brushing my hair over my shoulder and trying to resist the temptation to start twirling it around my fingers. "Mostly so I could keep track of my progress."

"Did you follow me?"

I shook my head as my stomach squirmed. "No. I didn't want to make things awkward. I made sure not to post any photos of you there either, and I haven't tagged or mentioned you. I wasn't sure if you'd be okay with that and I didn't know how to ask. And I've barely got like, twenty followers, so it's not like it's a big deal."

"Okay, you have to share your account with me so I can follow you and tag you because you're fabulous as fuck and I want to introduce you to the entire goddamn world," he said, his footsteps heavy on the old carpet as he closed the gap between us. He slid his arm around my waist and rested his head on my arm, the height difference between us exaggerated by my boots. "You're amazing, sugar." He kissed the nearest patch of skin, just under the bottom of my sleeve. "Is there a reason you didn't tell me?"

"I don't know... I don't want you to be embarrassed of me."

He tutted disapprovingly. "Not going to happen."

"And I guess if I told you, it would all be real," I said. My stomach was still bubbling but it was tempered by the weight of Anthony's body against mine. "I've wanted this for so long and this feels like such a big step. Sorry, this must sound so whiny to you. I mean, what's—"

"Nope." He bumped me with his hip and lightly tickled the bare skin of my waist, making me shriek and squirm in his arm like an eel. "You never forget your first time. It's like sex—kinda awkward, a bit messy and unsure, maybe a bit uncomfortable, but still fun and leaves you wanting to do it again afterwards. That's why your first times should always be with people you trust. You want to have good experiences."

"Was that what it was like for you? As Barbie."

"Yeah," he said with a fond smile. "I was twenty and I'd been practising drag on my own for months and this bar in Nottingham I went to loads had like, an open mic night for new drag performers, so I decided fuck it and went along with a couple of people I knew. I've got some fucking pictures somewhere—my wig was so amateur and my dress looked like I was going to a sixties fancy dress party, but you can see the baby Barbie in there. And as soon as I got out there, I knew it was something I wanted to do for the rest of my life."

He kissed my arm again, squeezing me tightly. "You're going to smash it tonight, but whatever happens, just enjoy it."

"I'll try."

"Good." He leant up and tilted my head down so he could lightly kiss my cheek. "Now, drag name. Who am I introducing you as, my beautiful little queen?"

I looked at myself in the mirror again, a smile caressing my lips. "Sugar Pill."

"Sugar Pill..." Anthony turned the name over on his tongue. "I like it. But with one slight alteration?"

"Oh?"

"Sugar Pill Summers. You're my drag daughter, darling. You have to carry on the family name."

My heart flipped and my insides tightened. There was something about the idea of belonging to him, to Barbie… to the two of us being something, that delighted me in a way I wasn't quite ready to admit. I'd never wanted to be with anyone possessive before, but with Anthony the idea was starting to turn me on.

And I did *not* have time to deal with that now. Not when we had to leave in less than an hour and Anthony wasn't made up and was wearing nothing but a tiny pair of boxers and some tights.

If I survived tonight, then I'd definitely do something about it.

"Sugar Pill Summers," I said with a nod. "It's perfect."

CHAPTER EIGHTEEN

Sugar Pill

"Oh my God! Look at you! Bitch, you look amazing," Bubblegum cried, throwing her arms around me and squeezing all the breath from my lungs. Bitch had dragged me up to their dressing room as soon as I'd arrived, almost as excited to show me off as Barbie, who'd been hurriedly shepherded away for a quick technical check behind the curtains while the bar began to fill up.

"Sparkles, put her down before she passes out," Eva said from beside us, where she was pulling a long, dark wig into place. "I'm not on duty and I'm not teaching you how to do mouth-to-mouth either."

"Jokes on you, I'm first aid trained," Bubblegum said as she released me, allowing all the air to flood back into my lungs leaving me feeling a little light-headed. "Dad made me go on a course a couple of years ago. I don't think he trusts me or Christopher not to do something stupid on a job site."

"What do you do?" I asked. This time around I was determined to take a more active role in the conversation and not sit quietly in the corner like a scared mouse. Colin might be nervous and socially awkward, but Sugar wasn't. Or at least, she was less so. I was hoping more confidence would come with time.

"I'm an electrician," Bubblegum said with a beaming smile, the rhinestones on her face sparkling in the lights of the large make-up mirror on the wall. "It's a little different from what most people expect but I really enjoy it. And I work for my dad, which means it's pretty flexible!"

"And I'm a paramedic," Eva said as she straightened her wig. "In Nottingham actually, I'm based out of the QMC. But I've recently gone part time to try and get a bit more of a work-life balance."

"And we're so proud of you," Bubblegum said, bouncing over to kiss Eva's cheek.

"That's where my lab is," I said, trying not to giggle at the look on Bubblegum's face when she realised she'd plastered bright pink lipstick onto Eva's pale cheek. "You'd need a map to find it, and if I'm half-asleep I still walk straight past it."

"Lab?" Bubblegum asked as she grabbed a make-up wipe and began dabbing at Eva's face. "That sounds cool. What do you do there?"

"You're doing a PhD, right?" Eva asked, taking the wipe out of Bubblegum's hand and shooing her away. The lip print on her face was still very prominent. "For fuck's sake, Sparkles, what's in this lipstick?"

"It's just a Sophie Lush one. Same as I normally wear. Oh, but I did use a new gloss today! It's got glitter in and this plumping effect."

"That's probably why it's so fucking sticky then," Eva muttered as she scrubbed her face. "No more kissing people, Sparkles. Not unless you want to permanently brand them."

Bubblegum smirked. "I'm definitely trying it on West later. I'll make sure nobody sees, though."

"Unless he gets naked in the showers at the club."

"They're on summer break," Bubblegum said. "Anyway, it'd just make them all wish they were getting their dick sucked as good as West is."

"Anyway," Eva said, grabbing another wipe out of the packet and turning around to face me. "PhD. Doing it on anything fun?"

"Semen," I said with a laugh, enjoying the shocked looks on their faces. "I'm studying sperm swimming patterns and tail movement to build mathematical models which will, hopefully, help treat male infertility. But I spend a lot of time looking at samples of jizz and watching sperm."

"Seriously?" Bubblegum stared at me like she was trying to work out whether I was telling the truth or pulling her leg.

"Seriously. It sounds made up, but it really is the topic of my research for the next three years. I should probably lead with the whole 'using maths to solve male infertility' thing but..."

"No, definitely lead with the cum thing," Eva said. "It's a good way to see people's reactions. And I appreciate the shock value."

I chuckled, slightly shifting my position because, despite my heels not being high, they were already starting to make my feet ache. "Thanks. I don't always describe it that way, but yeah, it's quite fun to see how people react."

"Sugar Pill Summers: Drag Queen and Cum Expert," Bubblegum said with a giggle. "You should put that on a business card."

The three of us laughed and Eva gestured to one of the nearby stools at the make-up counter. "Grab a seat or you won't be able to walk tomorrow. And you, Madam Sparkle Butt, pass me more of those wipes. That fucking lipstick has practically tattooed itself onto my face and I'm not going on stage with it all over me."

"How're you getting on?" Barbie asked when she came up to the dressing room a bit later and found me deep in conversation about social media with Eva, Bubblegum, and Moxxie, who'd arrived shortly after me.

I hadn't been expecting the three of them to be so free with their advice, but they'd all been happy to hand out tips and tricks while making it clear I didn't have to do everything all at once and to focus on what worked best for me.

It was nice to know I didn't have to become an expert in creating content overnight.

"Good," I said, smiling up at her from my seat on the stool next to Eva. "My earrings were pulling a bit, so I've taken them off for now." I pointed at the chunky daisies, which were resting on the counter behind me. "I think I need to practice wearing them more. How was your technical check?"

"Fine, we're all good to go. I had a quick chat with Phil too and talked through the introduction and stuff. He said we can watch the show from the side of the stage as long as we don't get in the way."

"That would be fun! I'd love to see everyone."

"Yeah, me too," Barbie said, her fingers grazing against my hand as she spoke. I wasn't sure if it was deliberate or because of how close we were, but either way it made my breath hitch. "Especially since it's a variety show. It'll give you a bit of inspiration too."

I glanced around the room, looking at Bubblegum and Moxxie, who were practising a few steps together for their Barbie and Ken duet. Both of them were dressed in hot pink with enough rhinestones and glitter to power a unicorn army.

Meanwhile, Eva was leaning against the door, which was now propped open, chatting to two identical drag queens who were holding hands and dressed in what could only be described as rainbow horror core, with glittering blood in every colour of the rainbow splattered on their hands and dripping down their faces.

The technical aspect fascinated me and I wondered if

they were wearing gloves or if they'd actually stuck glitter to their skin. Maybe, if I got a chance, I'd try and ask.

"I hope so," I said. "Everyone here is so talented."

"Hey, baby steps," Barbie said, sliding her little finger around mine and squeezing it. "That's all it is. One step at a time."

"Thank you." I tightened my grip on her finger and wished I could kiss her. But we hadn't talked about the boundaries between whatever personal and professional relationships we had, and since I was here as Barbie's drag daughter, I didn't think it would be appropriate to suddenly start kissing her.

And I didn't want to cause another lipstick fiasco.

"How're you feeling?" I asked. "Is this the first time you've gotten on stage since you moved back?"

"Yeah," Barbie said. There was a shocked edge to her tone, as if this was the first time she'd realised it. "I'm actually looking forward to it."

"You sound surprised."

"I am. It's been a while but I don't think I realised how long it's actually been. Until May, I was on stage four or five nights a week and since I moved… nothing. It's like I've been on some forced fucking holiday." She pulled a face. "I'm just hoping I can remember what the fuck I'm doing. At least I'm only doing the short medley I used to close each tour date with—I could probably sing it in my fucking sleep."

"You're going to be amazing," I said. "You *are* amazing. And not to sound like a broken record but you're *the* Barbie Summers. You're an icon—not only to me, but to so many of the performers here and people in the audience."

Barbie grinned and leant against me, lightly resting our heads together. Although she felt further away than usual simply due to the size of her enormous beehive wig. "You have to say that—you're my drag daughter. It's practically the law."

"I'll remember that. Rule one, stroke Barbie's ego."

Barbie snorted. "Behave."

"Or what?" I asked, smirking up at her. "Are you going to take away my phone or something?"

"Or something," she said. "I am your mother. You have to listen to me."

"Babe, I don't even listen to my own mother. Although that might be because she insists on telling me how fucking lonely my ex is and wouldn't it be nice if we got back together because he's such a 'nice boy.'" I shuddered. "Oh, and I shouldn't have moved so far away because now she never gets to see me. Even though she could easily get on a train, but I'm the one who abandoned her, so... Sorry, that got darker than I expected."

"Hey, which one of us doesn't have some sort of massive parental issues?" Barbie nudged me gently, which I knew was a sign of affection. "And no offence, but your mum can do one. You don't need that dickhead—you're fucking thriving here. You should be proud of yourself. I'm proud of you."

"Thanks." I smiled as her words warmed my chest, giving me a little boost and reminding me just how far I'd come in the last six months alone.

We people watched for a few more minutes, chatting quietly, before it was time to head down to the side of the stage to watch the show. I tried not to get in anyone's way or distract them because they all had plenty to concentrate on.

The host for the evening was The Court's owner, Phil, as the ever-fabulous Violet Bucket, whose homage to *Keeping Up Appearances* had made me giggle so hard I'd nearly doubled over. Her wig was a towering meringue of mint green and pastel pink to match her dress, and her loving snark reminded me of all those fabulous aunts I'd seen on television.

Barbie and I tucked ourselves into a corner of the wings, which gave us a perfect view of the stage, and as soon as the show began I forgot everything else going on around me.

Since it was a variety performance, it was a medley of shorter acts that included everything from dance, singing, comedy, lip-sync, burlesque, a queen in cosplay doing the most incredible routine inspired by *Arcane*, and a drag king using a giant Cyr wheel. Every single one of them was breathtaking and my body itched to join them.

I could easily get a freestanding pole, and while it would move a little more than the fixed ones in the studio, it wouldn't be hard to get used to. And I could swap my trousers for some tiny shorts and a crop top… maybe even have them underneath and pop the trousers, or dress, as part of the routine. I was sure Connor or Levi, who owned Above the Barre, could help me put something together.

"Wish me luck," Barbie said as the show began to draw

to a close and Violet walked onto the stage to announce their surprise guest.

"Good luck," I said, taking both her hands in mine and squeezing them tightly. "You've got this."

"Thanks." Barbie let out a breath as she took a microphone from a nearby crew member, and I watched her sink into full performance mode. She wasn't just Barbie anymore —she was Barbie fucking Summers: drag icon, superstar, and all-around goddess.

I couldn't have been prouder.

"Now," Violet was saying, "I know that should be the end of the show but I have decided to spoil you with one final surprise, not that you ungrateful lot have done anything to deserve it." There was a mixture of cheering and laughter from the audience. "Our guest star this evening is someone rather special. Not only is she a local queen but over the past few years she's become something of an icon with her legendary lip-syncs, sold-out tours, and spectacular runways. Darlings of The Court, I give you the winner of *Drag Stars* season five, the one, the only, Barbie Summers!"

The screaming that went up from the audience was almost deafening and it felt like the walls and floor were shaking from the noise. Barbie beamed as she strutted onto the stage and waved at the crowd like she was queen of the motherfucking universe. She didn't even speak but raised her microphone as the opening notes of Dolly Parton's iconic 'Dumb Blonde' filled the room.

She had the whole world in the palm of her hand, and we were just grateful to be in her presence.

CHAPTER NINETEEN

Barbie Summers

I REVELLED in the high of performing all the way back to my house, the cheers and applause echoing in my ears and washing away some of the hurt and pain that had etched itself into my skin over the past few weeks.

However I felt inside, to the crowd I had still been Barbie Summers and that was all that mattered.

"You were incredible tonight," Colin said as he sat on the bed to peel his boots off, a slightly pained look on his face as he wiggled his toes and flexed his feet. "Truly incredible. I've never seen anything like it."

"Thanks, sugar," I said as I undid my own boots and then reached for my wig, which had passed from heavy into crushingly uncomfortable about two hours ago. "I have to admit, it was nice to get back out there. I've missed it."

"Hopefully, you'll be able to do it again soon. I'm sure

Violet would love to have you back, especially considering the reaction."

"Fingers crossed." I set my wig carefully on the wig head next to my desk, then took off my earrings and put them on the desk. I could still hear the roar of the crowd and see their faces in my mind's eye. One boy at the front had even cried. I'd be riding the high for days. "It would be good to have some more gigs again. It would help if I actually got out there and looked for shit."

Colin, who was tentatively tugging at the edge of the sprayed-down lace front of his wig, hummed. "You've been very busy, though, what with your tour finishing and then the move. Taking time off can be good for you, especially if you don't want to burn out."

"I suppose," I said as I walked over to him and gently helped him lift the wig up and off. I always set mine with hairspray instead of wig glue because it made them so much easier to peel off at the end of the night but there was an art to getting wigs off without damaging the lace or your skin. "But I'm bored now. I need to get back on stage. If I'd thought about it, I'd have seen if I could've gotten a summer gig in Europe. There's tons of drag bars in Ibiza and Ayia Napa. They don't always pay the best, but I'd kill for some proper sunshine. Plus I've still got contacts from when I did a couple summers out there."

"I'm not sure if that sounds fun or not," Colin said as I balanced his wig on top of mine, making a mental note to sort them out in the morning when I wasn't quite as knackered. I hadn't expected one short medley lip-sync to take it out of me this much, but after being on edge all day, the emotional strain on my body was clearly starting to show. "I've never really been much of a party person."

"The work is fun and I hooked up with a ton of guys, but there's also a lot of loud music and drunk assholes. Although you get them here too."

"That's true. I guess I've just never been much for nights out—which might be counterintuitive to drag, but they feel like different things," Colin continued as he moved on to removing his jewellery and I paused to watch him. He'd done so well tonight and I didn't think I could've been prouder of my baby queen. Everyone I'd spoken to at The Court had been impressed with both his appearance and his confidence, and Violet had said to me afterwards that if Sugar hadn't mentioned it was her first time out and about in drag, she wouldn't have known.

I wanted to tell Colin all of this, but I needed to be out of drag to do it. Because I didn't think I could tell him how fucking incredible he'd been without kissing him, and doing that while we were in drag felt like crossing more boundaries than I should be comfortable with.

"They are, because one is work and one is, well, partying." I reached for the zip on the back of my dress and tugged it down, my eyes not leaving Colin.

"True," he said as he undid the bow at the front of his top that held the whole thing together. "And just think, if you'd have gone to Ibiza, you'd never have met me." I thought he'd been aiming for it to come out teasingly, but there was an earnest note to his words that pulled me up short.

Whatever this was, Colin and I meant something to each other. And not just in a professional way.

We were more than just student and teacher, more than just friends, but neither of us had attempted to figure out where that left us.

Not that we needed to. I'd never needed absolute rules and guidelines for life, always preferring to do things my own way.

"And my life would be fucking awful," I said, dropping my dress on the floor and stepping out of it. Colin's gaze was fixed on me, his fingers hanging in mid-air like they'd forgotten what they were supposed to be doing.

"I don't think it would be that bad."

I reached for my breastplate and tugged it over my head, suddenly struck by a new urgency to get out of drag as fast as fucking possible. "I do." Colin shook his head. "I'm serious. Meeting you at The Court made my damn year. The last six months would have been a complete bloody write-off if it wasn't for you."

He smiled softly. "I haven't done that much."

"You have," I said. "And I need you to believe that."

I was too much of a coward to tell him the truth and spill my bloody secrets. It would be like opening a festering wound that was finally starting to heal, and I couldn't bear the idea of Colin thinking less of me for my mistakes.

"Okay, but only if you accept how much you've changed my life," he said. "This... tonight... none of it would have been possible without your help."

"I didn't do much either—it was just a few pointers.

You'd already made the first big leap by putting yourself out there."

"I guess we'll have to agree to disagree on that," he said with a glowing smile as his hands finally remembered what they were meant to be doing and finished undoing his top. He slid it off over his head then removed the breastplate I'd leant him, leaving him completely shirtless.

God, he was beautiful.

"Fine, I'll give you that one." I winked and reached for my tights, starting to remove the layers of nylon and cotton since I was wearing two pairs of pants as well as two pairs of tights. I found it gave me the smooth, doll-like look I was going for but it wasn't half a pain in the ass to get out of, especially when I was sweaty and tired.

"Do you need a hand?" Colin asked. He'd stood up and easily slipped his trousers over his hips, leaving him in a tiny skin-tight pair of briefs and a pair of socks patterned with ice cream sundaes.

"No?" I tipped forward as I wrenched everything down at once, the waistbands of all four layers bunching in my hand and creating a firm band around my thighs that cut into my skin and threatened to send me crashing to the floor. "Okay, maybe yes."

Colin laughed and padded toward me, his warm fingers grazing my skin as he helped tug down my mess of tights and underwear, leaving me completely naked. Barring the half a ton of make-up I was still wearing, but that could wait a minute.

"There," Colin said quietly. "That's better."

"Thank you for rescuing me," I said with a smile. "Otherwise I'd have probably broken something."

"Don't do that. I don't really want to have to try and explain to your mum why you're naked and screaming on your bedroom floor."

I laughed and stepped out of my tights, throwing them into the washing basket in the corner. "She won't hear anything, trust me. Once she's out, she's out, and she needs like, three alarms to get up. She's slept through storms, fireworks, fire alarms, and a thrash metal concert. The only thing that ever woke her up when I was a kid was either me crying or the words, 'Mum, I feel sick.'"

"I think that'd wake up any parent," Colin said.

"Yeah, especially when you've got a kid who has a nasty habit of projectile vomiting everywhere," I said dryly. "But you didn't need to know that. God, I should just shut the fuck up."

"You're fine." Colin stepped closer and I felt the heat radiating from his body. "It's nice to know you're just as awkward as me."

"You're cute awkward, though. I've got the worst fucking case of foot in mouth syndrome you've ever seen."

"Definitely not." Colin pulled a face. "I've met far worse."

"Yeah?"

"Yeah, but let's not talk about that."

"No," I said, putting my hand on his waist to draw him closer. He was still fully made up too, but I could see him under the layers of make-up and enormous eyelashes. "Let's talk about how amazing you were tonight. You fucking slayed, baby. Everyone was talking about you, telling me how fucking fabulous you looked. You served. Violet couldn't even believe it was your first time out. I'm so, so proud of you."

"Thanks," Colin said shyly. "It felt so good. Even sitting in the dressing room with everyone or watching them on stage, it made me feel like I belonged. And I can't wait to do it again."

I smiled as my other hand gently cupped the side of his neck. "It's infectious. Once is never enough." My thumb stroked the edge of his jaw. "You should take your make-up off," I added. It wasn't what I wanted to say but the responsible part of my soul was harrumphing loudly and pointedly in my ear. "And if you want a shower, then—"

"Will you join me?" Colin asked.

My lips twitched into a smirk. "It's a bit small. We might have to squish together."

"I don't think that will be a problem."

"I didn't think it would," I said, pulling him flush against me and pressing my hips forward until my naked cock rubbed against his fabric-covered one. Colin's breath hitched and he moaned softly.

"And afterwards... I want..." He looked down at me with those beautiful doe eyes and my soul sang. "I want to bring you more pleasure than you ever thought possible."

"Fuck." I moaned as my hips jerked forward, grinding against him. "Will you fuck me, Colin? Please. It's been fucking forever since I had a good dick inside me."

Colin brought his mouth down to mine and brushed his lips teasingly across it. "If that's what you want. Then yes, I will fuck you."

I swallowed the groan on my tongue as Colin claimed my mouth in a deep kiss, his hands sliding into my hair. I had to stand on my toes and clutch onto him for balance, and for some reason that made my cock jerk. I didn't know when the fuck being vulnerable or, literally, off balance had become something that made me horny, but I was going to roll with it. That was how I'd discovered virtually every other thing I liked. Well, that and porn.

"Make-up," Colin said as he released me suddenly, making my head spin. "These lashes are killing me."

"Yeah," I said, still trying to catch my breath from being kissed like that. God, it was like he'd laid claim on my fucking soul. "They, er, they can be a dick if you're not used to them. I'm surprised you didn't peel them off already."

"I didn't want to lose them."

"Fair enough." I swallowed, not even sure of my bearings. I knew I was in my room, starkers, horny, and standing right in front of the man I desperately wanted to do absolutely filthy things to me. Beyond that, I had no damn clue. Did I have make-up remover in here? I must have, but I had no idea where. Colin had shut off all power to my brain when he'd kissed me.

He took my hand and steered me towards my make-up table where I realised I'd already left out wipes, micellar water, and some reusable make-up remover pads along with the various serums, creams, and moisturisers I used afterwards. I flopped down in the chair and practically tore my lashes off as I grabbed the wipes and pads and began to scrub the layers of make-up off my face.

The Court was not a place you painted prettily or daintily for. You painted for the back row. And that meant a lot of product.

It took me longer than I wanted to scrub myself into something vaguely resembling fresh-faced, and when I glanced over my shoulder, I realised Colin was sitting on the floor in front of the long mirror with a small pile of make-up wipes on the carpet next to him. He'd let his hair out, and it cascaded down around his shoulders in a shimmering wave.

The horny, needy part of me hated that we'd stopped to clean up before we'd started, but the rest of me was glad because if Colin and I were going to fuck, I wanted to see his actual face, not his painted-on one.

And I also didn't fancy trying to scrub foundation out of my pillowcases tomorrow, because even though they were dark green, that wouldn't hide anything.

Once I was done, I dumped the wipes into the little bin by the desk and grabbed a pair of boxers out of a nearby drawer just in case of emergencies between here and the bathroom. "How're you getting on?" I asked, crouching down behind Colin and kissing the top of his head. His hair smelt vaguely of sweat and something sugary, almost like maple syrup.

"I'm done. I'm not sure if I got it all, but it'll do for now." He turned and smiled. There were a few dark stains of make-up under his eyes but his face was back to being his again. "Do you still want to go and shower? I realised it might be awkward with your mum in the house."

"I definitely need a shower because I feel gross," I said, reaching for his hand and pulling him to his feet. "And like

I said, once Mum's asleep you'd be better off trying to wake the dead. But she will insist on you staying for breakfast tomorrow, sorry."

Colin had been over here enough that he'd met my mum a few times, and she was polite enough not to ask pointed questions about our relationship, but if she caught me trying to sneak him out without feeding him, I'd never hear the end of it.

"Breakfast sounds nice," he said as he leant in to kiss me. "And your mum is sweet. I like her a lot."

"Good." I squeezed his hand and led him towards the door and the darkened hallway beyond. The bathroom was sandwiched between the two bedrooms and painted a deep, warm green. The tiles around the bath with its overhead shower were black and white, and there was a small airing cupboard at the end nearest the door. I dug a couple of clean towels out of it while Colin slid out of his briefs, tied his hair back up, and looked in delight at the prints on the walls, which were various animals in baths, surrounded by heaps of bubbles and colourful tropical flowers. The room was the most recent of Mum's decorating projects and one idea I wanted to steal when I finally got a place I could paint.

I flicked the shower on and stripped off while I waited for it to warm up, the small room quickly filling with steam. When it was ready and not likely to freeze us to death, I held out my hand to Colin and grinned. "What do you say, sweetheart? Want to get wet?"

CHAPTER TWENTY

Sugar Pill

I LAUGHED as I took Anthony's hand and climbed into the bath, the hot spray of the shower catching my skin. "That was terrible," I said as he pushed me under the water and I ducked my head out of the way, trying to keep my hair dry. As much as I loved how long and thick it was, it was a pain in the butt to wash and dry, and I didn't want it dripping everywhere while we were in bed.

"Terrible, cheesy-as-fuck pick-up lines are my speciality," he said, wrapping his arms around me and shooting me a bright smile. He looked so happy and carefree—the most relaxed I'd seen him since we'd met. I hadn't realised quite how stressed and sad he was until I saw him shining like this, his personality bubbling like a bottle of shaken-up pop.

Not being on stage for a while seemed to have affected him badly, since for people like Anthony, performing wasn't simply a job—it was a way of life. Moving away from his friends and from the place he'd built his career must have been devastating, and I wondered if there was another reason besides the debt and the breakup with Steve that had forced him out of London.

Not that those weren't reason enough. Renting in London cost an arm and a leg in the first place, and that was without attempting to prove your income as a freelance creative and trying to convince people you'd never met that your debt wasn't an issue.

It was enough to make me heave just thinking about it.

But for tonight, at least, we could put all that behind us and enjoy a stress-free moment.

"What else is your speciality?" I asked, drawing him in for a kiss under the hot spray. His lips were deliciously soft and tasted vaguely of mint, and it made me want to kiss him for hours until the taste finally dissolved. "Apart from make-up, lip-syncing, dancing, singing, and being all-around fucking fabulous?"

Anthony laughed and looked up at me with heat and mischief dancing in his eyes. Everything about his expression screamed that he wanted me, and it was such a heady realisation it nearly brought me to my knees. I couldn't remember the last time someone had looked at me with such desire.

Was that what it was like to be wanted? Truly wanted?

It made me want to kiss and laugh and fuck and scream with joy, my insides twisting themselves over and over as fireworks exploded under my skin.

"Hmm, I'm pretty good with my mouth," he said slyly. "And my fingers... my dick too. And I've got a great ass."

I kissed him again, trying to stifle laughter—not at him, never at him—but I couldn't seem to stop myself from wanting to laugh. It was like all my happiness and excitement didn't know how else to escape. "Sounds like you have a lot of specialisms."

Anthony pressed his body against mine, his hard cock rubbing against my thigh. "I do. Want me to show you?"

"Please."

His kiss was teasing as he nipped my bottom lip and playfully slipped his tongue between my lips, stealing all my thoughts before sinking to his knees. He knelt under the spray and used one hand to push his sodden hair out of his face, reminding me of all those gorgeous blond surfer boys I'd seen on various shows over the years.

I'd never thought of it as a weakness of mine, but just looking at Anthony with slicked-back hair, water dripping down his chest and clinging to his face, was enough to send every drop of blood in my body rushing towards my dick.

He smirked up at me as he ran his hands up my thighs, fingers teasingly skirting across my groin and avoiding my achingly hard cock. For a horrible minute, I thought he was going to draw this out and make me beg, but then he wrapped his fingers around my shaft and stroked it slowly.

My breath hitched, a tiny groan escaping from my lips. My gaze was transfixed and I didn't dare blink in case I missed something.

Then Anthony leant forward and opened his mouth, flicking his tongue across the head of my cock. I gasped, hands balling into fists beside me. How had such a tiny touch threatened to undo me so quickly?

He winked at me and then wrapped his lips around the soft mushroom head, stroking the sensitive skin with his tongue as he slowly took me inside him. As he did he reached out with one hand and grabbed my fingers, guiding them towards his head.

"Tell me if it's too much," I said as I pushed my hand into his thick, wet hair. "I don't want to hurt you."

"You won't," he said, pulling back off my cock for a second but still stroking it with his hand. "I like having it pulled. And if it's too rough, I'll just tap your thigh."

"Okay." I let out a shaky breath as he resumed sucking my cock, taking me deeper into his mouth and swallowing around me. "T-That works."

Anthony chuckled, the sound reverberating through me and making me moan. He seemed to be revelling in this, licking, sucking, and pumping my cock in a way that felt like more than casual sex.

It felt like need and desire and something fun, almost playful. Joyous even.

Like adoration.

The decadent sounds of sex mixed with the heavy drumming of the water on the floor of the bath, making it impossible to think about anything else. All I could do was feel.

And it was fucking glorious.

"Shit, Anthony," I said with a gasp as heat began to build rapidly under my skin, the feeling of my oncoming orgasm speeding towards me. "Y-You have to stop. I'm gonna… shit, I'm gonna come!"

My fingers tightened in his hair as pleasure swept

through me, almost knocking me off my feet. I slammed my mouth shut and bit my lip to stop myself from shouting out his name, swallowing it down as my cum painted Anthony's tongue and ran down his throat.

He drank every drop of my release, groaning as he did like it was some sort of fine wine. It sent tremors of delight rolling across my skin, eking out my orgasm until there was nothing left and oversensitivity threatened to spoil the moment.

I tugged on Anthony's hair, pulling him off my cock and staring as he sat back under the flow of the water, lips pink and slick and a drop of my cum trickling out of the side of his mouth. If I could've taken a picture, I'd have been jerking off to it forever.

"Was that good?" he asked as he licked the last of my cum off his lips.

"Yeah," I said, still trying to catch my breath. "That was… wow. Thank you."

"You're welcome." He put his hand out for me to pull him up, wincing slightly as I helped him to his feet. "Fuck, when did I start getting too old to kneel in a bath?"

"Maybe it's because you spent all evening in seven-inch heels?" I asked with a soft smile as I drew him in for a kiss, both my hands cupping his jaw. I could taste myself on his tongue and it was intoxicating. "I'm sure your thighs don't appreciate that."

He chuckled, lips brushing against mine. "They should be used to it."

"Doesn't mean they can't hurt."

"I suppose, but don't use logic on me. I'm too horny and tired for that."

"I'm sorry." I kissed him again. "Let me take care of you."

"In a minute," he said, putting his hands around my waist and leaning back far enough to look at me. "Think you'll be up for another round? I still want you to fuck me. Please? Let me ride you."

I groaned, dragging him back in for another kiss. "How can I say no?" I was still young and lucky enough to have a fairly short refractory period, and the idea of giving Anthony whatever he wanted was enough to have refreshed desire humming through me. "But please, let me spoil you. I want to explore every inch of your body before I open you up with my tongue, because you have the most perfect ass I've ever seen and I need to taste it."

He moaned, hands frantically gripping my body. "Fuck! How can I say no to that? I can't remember the last time anyone wanted to eat my hole."

"Your ex wasn't a fan?"

He scoffed. "No. He only wanted to receive... giving was an alien concept to him."

"What a selfish bastard," I said with a hum as I brushed his hair back. The more I heard about Anthony's ex, the more I believed he was a raging twat. My voice dropped to a low whisper as I continued. "I'll have to make up for his mistakes. Or maybe I'll just remind you how much better off you are forgetting he ever existed."

Anthony groaned and cursed under his breath. He kissed me hard then reached past me to turn the shower off and yank the curtain back. "Fuck finishing the shower, we can come back in the morning. I'm not waiting any longer."

I laughed as he pulled me out of the bath and practically threw a towel at me. I just about managed to wrap it around my waist before he opened the door. The blast of cool air made me gasp, but luckily it was pleasant rather than shocking. I barely had time to register it anyway because Anthony was dragging me back to his room and slamming the door shut behind us.

The pair of us were breathless and laughing as our towels dropped to the floor, our hands reaching for each other because it already felt like too long since we'd kissed.

"Do you have lube? And condoms?" I asked, forcing the words out between kisses.

"Yeah… in the drawer…" He waved vaguely behind him and I assumed he meant the drawer of the bedside table. "There's a new box."

I kissed him again, revelling in the taste of his mouth. "Good." I walked him backwards, aiming for the new double bed, which took up nearly a third of the small room. He let out a small huff as his knees hit the edge of the mattress and I laughed as he toppled backwards onto the bed, dragging me down with him until we landed in a tangle of limbs, miraculously avoiding smacking our heads together.

Because the last thing either of us wanted was a bloody nose. It would be the least sexy thing ever.

I pushed my knee between Anthony's thighs as I stretched out over him, kissing him deeply and feeling the heat of his cock against mine, which was already starting to get hard again. I rolled my hips gently, grinding down against him in a teasing, exploratory motion I hoped would drive him wild. Anthony groaned and thrust up against me as he nipped my lip, his kisses turning frantic.

"Colin..." The way he groaned out my name had my body on edge and I couldn't stop myself from repeating the motion. I wanted to know every noise he could make, and then I wanted to hear them again and again until we were too exhausted to move.

I'd promised to spoil him, and I took that seriously.

"I've got you," I said quietly as I broke our kiss to trail my lips down his neck, finding all those little spots that made him moan when I touched them. I kissed across his chest, feeling the tiniest bit of soft stubble brushing against my mouth where his chest hair was starting to come back through after he'd shaved it. His nipples pebbled under my touch and he groaned softly when I sucked each of them between my lips.

I moved my mouth lower, pressing a stream of soft kisses down his abdomen, and as I reached his groin, he spread his legs wider so I could stretch out between his thighs. He was so beautiful like this—confident in his desires but desperately needy too. From what he'd said, it seemed like both of us had suffered from years of bad sex and self-centred partners who'd forgotten we had needs too. That ended now.

"You have such a nice dick," I said, wrapping my fingers around his shaft and pumping it slowly. I hadn't been able to stop thinking about it since the first time we'd gotten off together and I'd spent so many nights since fantasising about getting my hands on his dick again and dreaming what it would feel like on my tongue and in my ass. "Would you ever want to fuck me with it?"

"Yeah," Anthony said, pulling himself up slightly on his elbows so he could watch me. "I would. I've always preferred switching to being strict."

I hummed happily as I leant forward and slowly ran my tongue across the velvety head of his cock, savouring the taste of him. "Good, because I want all of you in every way we can think of."

"That sounds, fuck—" Whatever else he was going to say was cut off by a deep groan of delight as I wrapped my lips around him and started to suck. I kept my fingers around his shaft as I slowly worked him deeper into my mouth, savouring every moment as he filled me. It was everything I'd been dreaming about.

Anthony gasped as I began to bob my head, sliding his cock in and out of my mouth and groaning around him when he dripped precum onto my tongue. It was salty but somehow sweet, and I wondered if I could get addicted to the taste as I tightened my lips around him and sucked harder. I was so tempted to keep going and take him all the way because I wanted to know what it would feel like to have his cum coating my tongue… but I could always lick it up later.

I released his cock with a slick pop, jerking it slowly as I moved my mouth lower. If Anthony had been thinking about begging for more, anything he'd been going to say melted into moans as I ran my tongue over his balls and sucked them into my mouth one at a time. My saliva dripped down his taint as I licked it slowly, trailing my tongue down towards his waiting hole.

Wordlessly, he spread his legs wider, lifting his thighs off the bed and reaching his hands down to spread his cheeks, showing off his pucker for me. The furled skin was dark pink and dusted with dark blond hair, and my cock throbbed against the mattress, desperate to split him open and fill him up.

"Such a pretty hole," I said softly as I ran my thumb across it, loving the way Anthony moaned at my touch. It sounded like he was biting his lip, trying to stifle the noises he made. One day, I was going to make sure we went to a hotel or rented an Airbnb—somewhere we had some privacy with no roommates or parents so we could be as loud as we fucking wanted.

"Colin… please…" His voice was already wrecked and it made something inside me hum and twist, knowing I'd made him this way. So much of Anthony belonged to the world when he was Barbie, but right here, right now, he was mine and all this was just for me.

But I still wanted more.

I swept my tongue over his hole, savouring the sweet sounds dripping from Anthony's lips as the scent and taste of him flooded my senses. I flicked my tongue over his rim before licking and sucking the sensitive skin, pressing my tongue inside him as I started to work him open. I didn't know how long I stayed between his thighs, using my mouth to give him everything he'd been deprived of for so long.

The only measure of time I had was Anthony's moaning, which grew more and more desperate as I took him apart.

I finally relented and looked up when his thighs started to shake and he was practically humping my tongue, his broken voice begging for more.

"Can you reach the lube?" I was startled by the sound of my voice, which was rough and hoarse. The perfect reminder of what I'd been doing.

"I'm not sure," Anthony said, lowering his thighs and finally letting go of his ass, which he'd been gripping on to with white knuckles. He chuckled dryly. "I don't think I can move."

"I'll get it then." I kissed the inside of his trembling thigh and slowly slid into a sitting position. My dick had softened while I'd focused on Anthony, but it slowly began to chub up as I moved across the bed and dug in the drawer for the lube and a condom, ripping the plastic off the new box and pulling out a foil square.

When I turned back to face him, Anthony was watching me with wide, hungry eyes.

"Are you having fun?" I asked casually as I moved next to him, leaning down to kiss him before pouring lube onto my fingers and reaching down between his thighs.

"Understatement of the fucking century," he said with a chuckle. "I thought I was going to die."

"I'm glad you didn't. I don't know CPR."

He snorted, then groaned as I brushed slick fingers across his softened hole, barely giving him a moment to think before I pushed one inside him. Tight heat enveloped me as I pressed my finger deep, letting him adjust before I started working him open, adding a second as soon as he was ready for me.

I curled my fingers, searching for that spot inside him and smirking when he groaned. He turned his head to bury his face in the bed to muffle his moans as I teased his prostate, my other hand reaching over to slowly stroke his dripping cock.

"Colin," Anthony said, lifting his head slightly and looking up at me. "Fuck… I… fuck this… I need you to fuck me!"

I slid my fingers out of him and reached for the condom. "How—" But I didn't get a chance to finish my sentence because Anthony pounced, and all I could do was laugh as he pinned me to the bed and straddled my hips, grabbing the condom out of my hand and ripping the foil open. He quickly rolled it onto my cock and gripped me tightly as he slowly lowered himself onto me.

My hands flew to his hips, both of us groaning as my cock filled him. The tight heat of his ass and the weight of him on my lap was almost enough to make me come, and that was without looking up at his beautiful face with his rapt expression and the way his chest heaved.

"Shit…" He gasped, almost laughing. "I'd forgotten how fucking good it feels to take cock. Mmm, fuck, sugar… you feel so good inside me. So much fucking better than my dildo." I wasn't going to argue with him, even if I did think he was exaggerating. I was too enraptured by the look on his face and the way his body felt. "Shit, Col, you've gotten me so fucking worked up. I'm not gonna last long. Fuck…

the things you were doing with your tongue? Fucking heavenly."

"Yeah?"

"Fuck yeah." He grinned, resting his hands on my chest as he began to bounce on my cock, sending shock waves of pleasure rippling through me. "I'm never gonna be able to stop thinking about it."

I bit my lip and groaned at that thought, my dick aching at the idea of my tongue living in his memory forever. Anthony's cock bobbed in front of me as he rode me hard, milking every drop of pleasure from my body. I needed him to come soon because I wouldn't be able to last—everything was too hot, too tight, and too fucking perfect for this to turn into a three-hour-long fuckfest. I'd already wound both of us so tightly that we were ready to snap.

I just needed it to be him that broke first.

I wrapped my fingers around his cock, loving the way he groaned as I created a perfect tight tunnel for him to fuck as he bounced on my dick. Anthony cried out, his fingers digging into my chest as he used me for leverage, losing himself in pleasure.

"Colin," he said with a groan, his eyes wide as they met mine. "I'm gonna… fuck, I'm so close!"

"I'm there with you," I said as one hand gripped his hip. "I want to feel you… please… fucking come on me."

Cum splashed across my chest as his body stiffened, his ass tightening around me as he lost himself to his orgasm. I tried to watch every detail of his reaction, but it was impossible. Anthony was still riding my cock as his channel squeezed my shaft and one final grind down onto my lap was all it took to throw me over the edge, sending pleasure racing through every inch of my body as I filled the condom, stars bursting behind my eyes as I fought for breath.

I could barely do anything except feel, but underneath the ecstasy one thought crystallised in my mind.

I never wanted to let Anthony go.

CHAPTER TWENTY-ONE

Barbie Summers

"Morning," Mum said as Colin and I strolled into the kitchen late on Sunday morning, both of us cursing our new-found desire to fuck instead of sleep. She was making what was probably her third cup of tea because, knowing her, she'd been up since seven. Apparently, years of being woken up every weekend by a small but determined child had destroyed her ability to sleep in. "Sorry, Colin, I didn't know you were still here. I didn't hear either of you come back last night."

"Sorry," Colin said with an apologetic smile he didn't need. "I hope you don't mind. Anthony said I could stay so I didn't have to drive back."

I didn't know whether to hold his hand because, despite the fact we'd now had sex four times, we still hadn't gotten around to the whole "what the fuck are we doing" conversation. Which we needed to have but neither of us seemed willing to initiate. I couldn't blame us either, because who'd willingly choose talking about the whole mentoring-drag mother relationship thing over getting their dick sucked?

Mum grinned as she began refilling the kettle, glancing over at the pair of us with a casual scrutiny that I knew meant she was trying to figure out what was going on without asking questions. She'd always been good at giving me privacy and space to figure things out, but as I'd gotten older I'd realised she'd worked out a lot more than she'd ever let on. Usually before I'd realised things myself. "Oh, of course, you were going out in drag! How did it go? Do you have any pictures? I bet you looked amazing and I'm sure your make-up was much better than his first attempt."

"Hey! My first night out was fine!" I said with a tired huff. "It could have been a lot worse."

"It could. And we can forever be thankful you decided against shaving your eyebrows off and drawing them back on."

"Thank fuck for small mercies then." I yawned and stretched, trying to ignore the aching in my muscles. I wanted to pretend it was from my shoes but even my seven-inch Pleasers didn't make my butt ache in the way it was now. Maybe bottoming three times in one night hadn't been the best thing to do after not having been fucked in years, but it wasn't like I hadn't been fucking myself stupid on dildos in the meantime.

But next time, I did want to know what Colin looked like on my cock. I thought he'd look beautiful taking dick.

"I can't believe you considered shaving them off," Colin said with a teasing smile.

"Hey, I know a lot of artists who shave them! Like Maddi. And at least three girls on my season didn't have them either. For a lot of people, it's just easier."

Colin nodded and then peered at my face. "Okay, I can see that. But… I don't think no eyebrows would suit you."

"Absolutely not," Mum said. "Besides they'd have either grown back all patchy or not at all."

"Is this just because you plucked yours to death in the noughties and now have none?" I asked, knowing the answer was yes because Mum was the one who'd shown me how to shape, sculpt, and draw on the perfect eyebrows to begin with.

"Don't push it," Mum said with a laugh. "You're making me look bad." She glanced over at Colin, who was watching us with soft amusement. He'd said his relationship with his own mum was patchy, and I wondered if this was bringing up some weird feelings.

Mum and I had always been close, even when I'd lived in London and hadn't come back much, and over the last few years we'd moved into this comfortable friendship. And as much as I hadn't wanted to move home, I had to admit living with Mum was fun and comfortable in a way I'd never expected. She was the best roommate I'd ever had. "Sorry, sweetheart, just ignore him."

"Fucking charming," I said, leaning against Colin and sighing forlornly. "And after I told the whole world how lovely you were."

"Don't start, or I won't make you breakfast."

"Cereal doesn't count."

"Alright then, I'll just make eggy bread for Colin and me

then," she said as she pulled two mugs out of the cupboard and fished out some teabags.

"I take it back. All is forgiven," I said quickly, scooting over to give her a hug and kiss her cheek. "Oh, by the way, Colin doesn't have milk in his tea. He has lemon."

"I know, you told me last week," Mum said. "That's why there are lemons in the fridge." She turned to Colin. "I assumed you'd prefer that to just lemon juice. I got some almond milk too, so I'll use that for the eggy bread."

"Thank you," he said, sounding completely shocked by the gesture. That was Mum, though. If you told her something once, good or bad, she very rarely forgot it. It had been both a blessing and a curse growing up. "You didn't have to."

"It's not a problem, honey." She smiled at him and then looked between us. And I knew she'd figured everything out, even if we hadn't.

Two days later, I was still no closer to talking to Colin and instead I was finding every possible opportunity to distract myself. And today, the world was giving me a helping hand in the form of my initial wig and costume fitting for *Cinderella.*

I knocked on the door of one of the downstairs dressing room doors of The Court, waiting until I heard a very chirpy "Come in" before I opened it. While we weren't using The Court as a venue, Bitch had sweet-talked Phil into letting him use it for fittings since it was free during the afternoon and wasn't going to cost him anything.

"Hey," I said as I stuck my head around the door, doing a double take at the sheer number of wigs covering the surfaces of the dressing room. Or maybe my shock was due to the fact the room was tidy and I could actually see how big it was. "I'm Barbie Summers. I'm here for my fitting."

"Hi, come on in!" The speaker was a pretty, twinky man who looked barely older than twenty, with blond hair and an excited smile in shorts, a loose tank top, and some bright blue Nikes that were virtually the same colour as the summer sky outside. "I'm Orlando. It's wonderful to meet you finally. Eli—Bitch Fit—has been talking about you for weeks."

I smiled because at least I could trust Bitch to big me up. "Thanks. He said you two were friends."

"Yes! We've known each other for years," Orlando said cheerfully. "He's my best friend in the world. I've seen everything and I know where all the bodies are buried."

"What else are best friends for?"

"Exactly! Now come and grab a seat, and we can get started." Orlando patted the back of a tall chair in front of the make-up counter. I hadn't seen anything like it in any of the other dressing rooms and I idly wondered if Orlando had brought it in specially. "Before we do anything, though, I have to say that working with you is, like, an absolute dream. I loved you on *Drag Stars* and your wigs were spectacular. Like that one you wore for the Sweet Dreams runway... ugh, I gagged. My... one of my boyfriends thought I was actually going to pass out." He laughed breathlessly and then clapped his hands together. "I'm done, sorry. You must be so sick of people fawning all over you."

"You're fine. It's really sweet of you to say," I said, sliding into the chair and shooting him a bright, polished smile while my heart soared. "Honestly, sometimes it's nice to hear. I know that sounds really fucking egotistical but we film in a bubble and then social media is such a mixed bag. So thank you, I'm so glad you enjoyed it. Sweet Dreams was one of my favourites too."

"Oh God, don't get me started." Orlando scrunched up his face like he'd swallowed something very sour. "Da—Jude threatened to take my laptop away during last year's *Legends* season because I kept arguing with people on Reddit. I wasn't planning on it but some people are assholes and I'm stubborn."

I snorted, trying to stop myself from dissolving into a fit of laughter. "See, now I wanna know who you were defending, but I know if I ask I'll just want to go and find it and Maddi made me swear a virtual blood oath that I wouldn't go on Reddit again. Not after I was *this* close to making an account just to rip some cunts a new one."

Orlando made a cross over his heart. "Don't worry, I won't tell you. We'll talk about fun things instead, like pretty wigs."

"Sounds good to me," I said. As much as I wanted Orlando to spill the beans about his Reddit crusade, I knew no good would come of it and I didn't need to get sucked back into some shitty self-pitying cycle of destruction when I'd finally managed to start clawing my way out of the pit.

"I know you've had wigs styled for you before," he said,

grabbing a couple of blonde wigs from a shelf on the other side of the room. "Can I ask who did them?"

"A couple of different people. Layla Moon did quite a lot of them. She's based in North London."

"Oh, I know Layla! She's a sweetie."

"Yeah, I met her through a friend when I moved down there," I said as I thought back to the state of my wardrobe and wigs when I'd landed in London, naïvely thinking it would be easy to break into the drag scene there.

Luckily, a couple of artists had taken me under their wing and one of them had introduced me to Layla, who'd politely not laughed when I showed her my wig photos. I'd gotten better at styling my own wigs since then, mostly because I made sure to practice doing some basics to get by, but nothing beat a professionally styled wig done by someone who knew what they were doing. "And then I've got a couple by Taz Miller. He's up in Manchester."

"Oh my God, I love Taz! He's so gorgeous and his work is like... ridiculously cunty. I love it."

"Same, and his style. How does he look so fucking good in everything? I swear."

"I showed his picture to my Sir... Charles..." Orlando paused for a second like he was waiting for me to say something, but if he'd been worried I'd be weirded out over him having a Sir, and I assumed a Daddy based on the word he'd tried to cover up earlier, he needn't have worried. It wasn't like it was an unusual relationship dynamic for our community, although I supposed it might be more difficult in smaller towns and cities like Lincoln. "And even he thought Taz was stylish, and Sir is the sexiest man I know. Although I guess I'm biased. Daddy thinks so too."

I laughed. "I think when you're in love with someone, you're supposed to think they're sexy as fuck."

"True! Although that doesn't stop anyone else being sexy," Orlando said. "Everyone is sexy! I mean, look at you."

"Cheers." I winked at him. "You're pretty fucking cute too."

"I know." He grinned and grabbed a wig cap out of a nearby bag. "Although I'm being a bit naughty because I'm going to meet Sir after this and he's going to *die* when he sees these shorts. I can't wait. Luckily, he'll have finished work because he'd never let me in the office."

I snorted and resisted shaking my head as Orlando pulled the wig cap onto my head, effortlessly tucking my hair underneath it in a way I'd never managed. "Does he work nearby?"

"Yeah, he's about a five-minute walk away. He's a solicitor and a partner in his firm, so they've got a fancy office near the city centre. They've even got air conditioning!"

We both sighed mournfully because having air conditioning during British summers felt like winning the lottery.

Orlando began chatting again as he grabbed a blond wig and began to ease it onto my head, mentioning something about checking it for fit and that it would suit the undertones of my skin. But I was stuck on what he'd said about his partner.

Maddi had been encouraging me to talk to someone about the whole Candy Club thing and her gentle nudges were starting to sound less and less like suggestions and more like demands. I knew she only wanted the best for me, but reaching out to someone meant admitting the whole thing was real. Besides, it was hard to know from Google whether people were queer friendly and weren't just going to laugh me out of the office or totally misunderstand my problem.

But here I was being served up a queer, kinky solicitor on a plate. It was like the universe had decided I needed the most unsubtle shove it could give me.

"Orlando," I said softly, accidentally cutting him off. "Can I… I'm sorry, this is going to be weird but… can I ask you a question?"

"Of course," he said. In the mirror I could see a tiny worried frown on his face. "Everything okay?"

"Yeah… er, I can't tell you why, but you said your Sir is a solicitor, right?"

"Yes, he deals mostly with contract law and stuff like that, but if he doesn't know the answer, he'd know someone who does." He smiled gently and put his hand on my shoulder. "Do you want his email address?"

I stared, wondering how he'd known. Orlando grinned and patted my arm gently. "I'm a hairdresser; I'm good at reading people. Don't worry, I won't ask but I will tell him to keep an eye out for it. And not to be grumpy!"

"Thanks, I appreciate it."

"You're welcome!" He pulled a strand of hair over my shoulder. "I think we need to try a shade lighter. What sort of foundation do you usually use?"

"Oh, I brought it with me. Does that help?" I leant down

to rummage in my bag and pull out the smallest of my make-up bags, which was still bigger than most people's everyday ones. The perils of being a professional.

"Perfect. Can you put a little on? I'm just going to grab another wig."

Orlando bounced away as I sat back in my chair for a moment, realising some of the weight I'd been carrying around for a while suddenly felt lighter.

CHAPTER TWENTY-TWO

Sugar Pill

I'D SPENT the whole day working out what I was going to say to Anthony about our relationship and balancing the mentoring with a sexual, possibly even romantic connection. But all of my plans went out of the window as soon as he knocked on my front door.

He was wearing shorts and a white T-shirt with a loose collection of necklaces and his dark blond hair pushed back. He looked so casually sexy every rational thought left my body and was instantly replaced with a surge of lust that was nothing short of feral.

"Hey," Anthony said, barely getting the word out before I was slamming the front door shut and backing him against it so I could kiss him senseless. "Someone's pleased to see me."

"I missed you," I said in between desperate kisses,

sliding my hand under the edge of his T-shirt to the lightly tanned skin underneath. "Can't stop thinking about you."

He chuckled, fingers gripping the front of my shirt. "Take me upstairs then before we scar your roommates by fucking in the hall."

"They're not here."

"Don't care," he said firmly. "Upstairs, sugar. I'm not getting screamed at and thrown out of your house."

"That sounds like the voice of experience."

"Yeah, it is. And I've both shouted at someone to get the fuck out and been the one getting chucked out, so…"

I didn't wait for him to finish his thought. I just grabbed his hand and began towing him towards the stairs, not caring about anything except getting into my room as fast as possible.

The afternoon sun was streaming in through the window, which I'd opened in the vague hope of letting a breeze in. I danced over and pulled it shut but left the curtains open because there were no houses opposite us, and it was impossible to see into my room from the street. And I wanted to see Anthony in the gorgeous glow of the early evening sunshine.

He'd shut the door and started stripping off his clothes, throwing them onto the floor with wild abandon. I stopped for a moment, my fingers frozen on the hem of my shirt as I watched him. He really was the most beautiful man I'd ever seen, and there was something bewitching about the casualness of it. It was as if he didn't know how handsome he really was.

In drag, as Barbie, he knew he was stunning. It was

obvious from the confidence he exuded and the playfulness of his personality. But out of drag... it was as if he'd gotten lost somewhere along the way. And the more time we spent together, the more I wondered if something else had happened in London to make him so sad. Because now I'd seen Anthony at his brightest and most bubbly, it had become obvious that he was carrying around a monstrous weight on his shoulders.

The only problem was that I had no idea how to bring it up. How did I even start that conversation?

"You know, for someone who was desperate to get in my pants two minutes ago, you're doing an awful lot of fuck all," Anthony said with a wry smile as he stripped off his skintight boxers.

"I'm sorry, there was a very sexy man getting naked in my room and it short-circuited my brain."

Anthony closed the gap between us, his lips grazing against mine as he reached for the front of the loose linen shirt I was wearing. "Where is he? I'll fight him."

"He's you."

"Damn, not sure I want to punch myself in the face."

I laughed and pulled him in for a kiss, the fire of my desire rekindling into a raging inferno. Anthony gave up on the buttons on my shirt and tugged it over my head, dropping it onto the floor before reaching for the waistband of the loose trousers I'd pulled on after my post-work shower. Which hadn't got anything underneath...

"Damn," Anthony said as he pushed the colourful trousers over my hips. "Look at you walking around all ready and waiting for me." His fingers brushed over my cock and I groaned into his mouth. He pulled back slightly and put his other hand on my chest, walking me backwards to the bed. I hit the edge of the mattress with a soft thump and shuffled backwards until I was spread out in the middle of the bed, the fabric deliciously cool against my overheated skin.

Anthony climbed on the bed and crawled towards me, straddling my lap and smirking as he held out his hand, lifting his fingers to my mouth. "Suck them for me, baby."

I was happy to oblige, sucking two between my lips and wrapping my tongue around them. My eyes never left his and I could see heat burning inside them, waiting to be unleashed.

I wanted it to consume me.

Anthony moaned as he watched me, then slowly pulled his fingers out and reached down to wrap them around both our cocks. I gasped as he created a tight, wet, hot tunnel around our shafts, squeezing them together just enough to create the perfect amount of friction as he slowly began to pump his hand.

"How does that feel?" he asked coyly, like he couldn't see the expression on my face or hear the moans sliding from my throat or feel how hard I was in his hand. "Is it good? Not too much?"

"No," I said with a broken moan. "It's... shit, it's perfect."

"Good." He leant down and kissed me softly, his necklaces brushing against my chest. He kept jerking us off as he kissed me, sliding his tongue into my mouth and making me melt. It was like he fucking owned me, and fuck, I almost wanted that to be real.

He nipped my lip and then sat back, smirking as I followed him, chasing another kiss. He just put his hand on my chest to push me back down. "Just relax. And watch."

I groaned because I couldn't have stopped watching him if my life depended on it.

He let go of our dicks for just a second, lifting his hand to his mouth to spit in his palm before he gripped us again. This time he rolled his hips, fucking his cock into the tight tunnel he'd made and rubbing it along my shaft. The friction was perfect and I felt myself starting to lose control.

"Mmm, fuck, Col," Anthony said with a groan as he thrust against me. "You feel so good. Been thinking about this all day."

"Me too," I said. My brain was still stuck on the way he called me Col. Nobody else had ever called me that before. "Kept trying to make notes but all I could think about was you bending me over the desk."

"Fuck, baby. In your lab?"

"N-No." My face burned but it was too late to keep the rest to myself. "In my office. The one I share with some of the other PhD students. I was the only one in today… and the door locks… but…"

"Shit." Anthony moaned and thrust harder into his fist, sending a bolt of pleasure racing up my spine. "That would be so fucking hot. I'll—fu-fuck—I'll have to come and see you one day. Make those dreams come true."

I groaned as the fantasy unfolded in my imagination. I'd

probably never be brave enough to try it, but the idea was hot enough to make my cock drip precum into Anthony's hand and my balls tighten. My orgasm was right there but...

Then Anthony gripped us even tighter and twisted his hand as he fucked against me, crying out with pleasure as he chased his own orgasm. And that was all I needed.

I cried out, my fingers digging into his thighs as I sprayed cum into his fist, making his grip wet and slick as he kept thrusting. Filthy sounds filled the room, mixing with my own heaving breath as my head spun, the room suddenly feeling far too warm. Every move Anthony made prolonged my orgasm, sending wave after wave of pleasure through me and stretching me to the point of oversensitivity.

"Anthony," I said, my voice wrecked as a whimper filled my mouth. "I..."

"Colin..." He cried out, his head falling back as he thrust into his fist once more and came. Cum leaked out of his fist, dripping onto my skin and painting me with our pleasure. Sweat was dripping down his chest, the golden afternoon sun highlighting the soft lines of his muscles and making him look like he'd been sculpted.

He released us both slowly, flexing his fingers as more cum splattered across my stomach. On a whim I reached out and ran my finger through it, curious to see what we tasted like.

I'd never been the biggest fan of cum, and it turned out I still wasn't, but there was something heady about knowing it was both of ours.

Anthony grinned as he leant down to kiss me, tasting

our release on my lips. "Mmm, that was fun," he said with a happy hum. He rolled off me and flopped onto the bed, gazing up at the ceiling with a relaxed smile that lit up his whole expression.

I wished I could see that smile more often.

And maybe one day, I would.

We lay there for a while, basking in the afterglow. I knew we needed to talk, but I didn't want to spoil the moment by bringing reality into it.

In the end, it wasn't me who started it.

"You know," Anthony said, turning his head to look at me with that same soft smile. "We should probably talk about this"—he waved his hand lazily in the air—"at some point. This whole getting off together thing. And drag." He gave a half laugh and sighed. "Fuck, why did I even bring it up? It sounds so fucking serious."

"That's probably because it is," I said as I rolled onto my side to look at him. I was still covered in cum but clean-up could come later. If we started now, it would feel like avoidance.

"Yeah." He groaned and ran his hands through his hair. "Also doesn't help that we've been avoiding this conversation for weeks but we've kept fucking around. Although…"

I bit my lip, debating whether to take the risk and put myself out there. But if I didn't, I risked losing something that had started to mean more than I'd ever imagined. "It doesn't feel like fucking around?"

"Yeah," Anthony said, twisting onto his side and gazing at me, a little smile curling the corner of his lip. "Look, I know we've done this arse-backwards, and I know we shouldn't get involved with each other, especially not if you're my drag daughter, because there's every chance this could get messy as fuck and I'll accidentally screw you over and—"

"It's okay." I put my hand out and interlaced our fingers together on the bed, hoping to calm some of the fear I'd heard rising in his voice. "You're not going to screw me over."

"I might. I won't mean to, but there's a good chance I will."

I wanted to know why he thought that. He seemed so convinced and I wondered if it was purely down to his ex or whether there was something else too. The nagging feeling that I was missing something—a key piece of the puzzle that was Anthony—was growing stronger. And while I wanted to come straight out and ask, I didn't want to pry. It wasn't like we'd known each other that long, and if he was keeping secrets, it was likely for a good reason.

"I don't think you will," I said softly. "Especially because you're aware of it. We've both come out of shitty relationships and neither of us wants to be in that situation again, and we're both very mindful of not screwing the other person over. And I know there's a power dynamic here with you being my mentor and everything, but"—I smiled at him and squeezed his hand—"I like you, Anthony. I think you're the most interesting and beautiful person I've ever met, and I don't want to stop doing whatever this is. And if you think I like you simply because you're Barbie or because you're helping me, then you're wrong. I mean, Barbie is amazing, but Anthony is even better."

"You say the sweetest things," he said, shuffling closer and leaning in to brush our noses together, kissing me softly. "Are you sure about this? I don't want you to feel, I don't know, forced."

"I'm sure. Are you? I don't want to feel like I'm taking advantage."

"You're not. You're like the least fucking demanding baby queen I've ever met. Sometimes I think you're allergic to asking for help."

"But I've asked you for lots of things."

"Sort of," he said with a grin. "But most of it is just me being like, do this, do that, have you done this."

I chuckled and pressed my forehead against his, my hair falling down around us. "Do you want me to be more demanding? Do I have to throw some kind of diva tantrum?"

"Fuck no, only I'm famous enough to do that. And even then I'll still look like a cunt." He kissed me again and we lay there for a moment, our chests rising and falling in sync. "How do we make this work then? Are we dating out of drag and in drag we're just friends? Mother and daughter? Hmm, not sure I like that. It makes me feel old. I'm too young and pretty to have a daughter as beautiful as Sugar. It might turn me into a jealous bitch."

A little bubble of happiness burst in my chest, filling me with warmth. "Dating?"

"Well, yeah, I thought that was what you wanted? I mean—"

I cut him off with a kiss. "Yes! Yes, it's what I want."

"Good." He let out a little sigh and kissed me. "You scared me for a second there."

"No, it's just... it's nice to hear you say it."

"It does sound pretty fucking good," he said.

"So dating out of drag, in drag we're friends and you're my mentor. And we'll remember to talk about how we're feeling. Then if anything's not working, we can change it."

"That sounds very mature and sensible." Anthony grinned. "Does that make me mature by default then? Maddi will be so proud of me. Well... maybe not."

"Why not?" I asked, suddenly curious.

"Eh, she has this golden rule about people not fucking their drag daughters. She thinks it gets too messy." He shrugged. "Don't worry, we're going to prove her wrong. Plus Maddi breaks her own rules all the time, and mine too."

"What rules are those?" I hoped asking would distract me from the fact that Anthony's best friend thought this was a bad idea.

"Like my rules around make-up, especially eye make-up. Never, ever share eyeliner or mascara unless you want to risk an eye infection. You don't want to know the gross shit I've seen." He shuddered and then snorted. "And Maddi's got a million golden rules, like never ask when someone last washed their tights when she literally messaged me on Friday telling me to wash mine."

"Okay, I'll remember those," I said. "What else?"

Anthony grinned. "Okay, do you remember that episode

of *Drag Stars* season four? Where Maddi was doing the pantomime acting challenge dressed as a cow?"

"Yes…" I said as I tried not to laugh, wondering where on earth this was going. I knew we needed to get up but I was too busy enjoying this moment, lying together on the bed nose to nose, sharing secrets and figuring out where we went together.

It was everything I'd wanted this conversation to be.

"Right, well, after that…" Anthony said, gesturing with one hand as he prepared to launch into what I assumed was going to be quite a long story. I smiled as I watched him, unable to tear my eyes away.

I knew this wasn't going to be easy, and there were going to be bumps along the way, but if we were prepared, hopefully we'd come out the other side unscathed.

CHAPTER TWENTY-THREE

Barbie Summers

"Good afternoon, can I speak to Anthony Kennedy, please?" The voice on the other end of the phone was deep, warm, and rich, catching me totally off guard and leaving me sat stunned in the middle of my room with a small screwdriver in one hand and a half-assembled IKEA unit at my feet. I'd been trying to use my afternoon to build some of the furniture that had finally arrived but that plan looked like it was about to fly straight out the window.

"Er, speaking," I said, trying to sound vaguely like I hadn't been swearing and cursing flatpack furniture thirty seconds earlier.

"Hi, my name is Charles Hunter from Hunter and Greenwood. You sent me an email last week about a potential legal issue you were having with a former employer. Apologies for the delay in getting back to you, but I wondered if you had a few minutes to talk me through the details."

Oh shit. It was Orlando's Sir.

After Orlando had encouragingly pressed a little card with Charles's email address written across the back in purple into my hand, I'd gone home and fired off a quick email before I'd thought everything through. I hadn't expected him to get back to me, and I definitely hadn't been expecting a call out of the blue.

I wasn't even sure how I felt about talking about it. Only it was a bit late to turn him down without looking like a complete tit, especially after Orlando had gone out of his way to make sure I had his email.

"Yeah, sure," I said, putting the screwdriver down and arranging myself into a slightly more comfortable sitting position. "Thanks for calling me. I didn't expect to hear anything. That's not on you—sorry, I just thought you'd be too busy."

"Don't apologise," Charles said smoothly. "Orlando mentioned you might need a bit of help, although he didn't say what about, and your email was a little vague too. Which means I do have to ask if you're comfortable talking about this over the phone. Would an in-person meeting suit you better? That way you could bring along someone to support you."

"It's fine." It wasn't like I had anyone to bring with me. Maddi was in London and neither Colin nor my mum knew the full extent of what had happened, and I didn't feel comfortable burdening them with that knowledge. "We can talk about it now. It might take longer than a few minutes, though."

"That's absolutely fine. Just take your time. I might not be able to get you all the answers now, but if not, I can go away and do some research and come back to you."

"Cool. Cool, thanks. Er, not to be rude, but how much is this going to cost me? I'm a little short on funds at the moment," I said, hoping I didn't sound like a defensive dick. Legal advice cost a lot of fucking money, especially from someone like Charles—because yes, I had spent a large amount of time Googling him and his firm instead of doing admin shit. I'd only stopped when I'd found myself down a LinkedIn rabbit hole and realised I'd gone too far.

"Don't worry about the cost. This call is complimentary and any other help you receive will be pro bono."

"Seriously?"

"Of course," he said. From here it sounded like he was smiling. "There's not always a lot of accessible support out there for queer artists, and I like to help out my community where I can. Besides, you were our favourite on *Drag Stars* and Orlando would never forgive me if I didn't help you—although that won't be on the public record. Otherwise, it just sounds like obnoxious favouritism."

I snorted because even just from meeting Orlando once, I could well believe he was the sort of sweet, bratty man who had both of his partners wrapped around his little finger. "Thanks—for the favouritism and the help."

"You're welcome. Now, how can I help?"

"It's a bit of a long story, but it kind of starts when I went on *Drag Stars*," I said, picking the screwdriver back up and twisting it in my hand as I tried to organise my thoughts and memories. I had a rough timeline of events in my head, but it was getting it all out in the right order that was the problem.

I started by telling him about how much it had cost me once I'd been accepted, about the fact that in the UK, *Drag Stars* offered no prize money because of broadcasting rules for the BBC, and about some of the paperwork and conditions of participation—the things I could tell him, anyway, since I'd signed a lengthy NDA.

I told him about winning and being approached by Andi and the contract and tour package with Candy Club that she'd presented me with and about selling out the tour despite some date changes. He listened carefully and only stopped me now and then to clarify a detail or a date or ask me if I had any of the original paperwork from Andi. I was pleased he let me waffle away because, now I'd started, it was difficult to hold back.

It felt like all the pain was rushing out of me, having now broken through the barriers I'd been forcing it down with. I tried to keep my voice neutral and stick to facts, but it was hard when I felt myself reliving every emotion like it was the first time.

And when I finally got to the part about reaching out to Andi and then Caesar Hurst about getting paid and being rebuffed over and over until they straight up started ignoring me, I felt like I was about to cry. And when I mentioned the day I called from a different number, because they'd blocked mine, to find out the phone line had been disconnected and the email bounced back, I finally broke down sobbing.

Maybe it was because it was the first time I'd told someone who wasn't Maddi, or maybe it was because Charles was someone who might be able to help. From his questions and the way he'd spoken to me before we'd even started, I didn't think he was about to turn around and tell me I was an irresponsible loser, even if that was how I felt.

And maybe some of it was the terrible pain of true acceptance.

I had been duped, played, and taken advantage of by those who were meant to have my best interests at heart. They'd manipulated me and used my trust in them to get exactly what they'd wanted, and then when I'd stopped being useful, they'd dumped me and run. Leaving me anxious, depressed, and waiting for money that was never going to come no matter how much I kept fucking wishing.

It hurt more than anything else I'd ever experienced.

"I'm sorry," I said eventually, wiping my eyes and looking around for something to blow my nose on. I sounded like a right bloody mess and I was grateful nobody else could see me because I doubted hot mess even covered it. "Fuck, you must think I'm a proper idiot."

"No, I don't," Charles said, his voice warm and kind. "I'm sorry for asking you so many questions but thank you for telling me everything."

"It's fine." I pulled up the hem of my T-shirt and wiped my face while Charles hummed.

"Do you know if any of the other artists they've worked with have had a similar problem?"

"No. I've not actually asked any of them. I don't know if I want to know the answer, to be honest. Because if I'm the only one, then I'll feel worse and if I'm not…" I trailed off and Charles hummed again. I wondered if he'd be able to make some enquiries and find out. I wasn't really sure how the law worked or if that was a thing he could do. I didn't know if anyone would tell him even if he did ask.

"That's understandable," he said. "I'm just going to run over a few details to make sure I've got the right information, and then I'm going to ask you to send me a list of things through, if that's okay? Then I'm going to do some digging and see what we can come up with. But there is one thing I have to warn you about first."

"What's that?"

"I can't guarantee anything will come of this. One of our team here who specialises in employment law and I will do everything we can, but unfortunately we may be up against the limits of the British legal system." There was a hard undertone to his voice that suggested he wasn't impressed by that, and it made a tiny note of optimism flutter in my chest. Because even if there was a good chance they'd get nowhere, at least they were going to try. And that was more than I'd ever expected.

Apparently, my expectations were so low they were virtually six foot under the fucking floor.

"If they have disconnected every method of communication associated with them and if we can't find them—if their registered business address is just a room in an office building under a fake name, for example—then we won't be able to take any legal action against them. Unfortunately, it's pretty easy for people in these situations to take the money and run and never be seen again. Sometimes they'll pop up under a different name and try their luck again, but if that doesn't happen, there may not be anything we can do. I'm very sorry, but I wanted you to be aware of that now in case the worst does happen," he said. He sounded sorry too.

But despite the potentially dire prospect, I didn't feel as bad as I'd thought. I'd never expected someone who wasn't Maddi or me to actually care about this shitshow of a situation, and now someone did it felt like I was being heard for the first time.

Charles might only have been being professional, but I doubted many other high-powered solicitors would've sat and let me ramble on at them. Or cry.

Fuck, I was such a fucking mess.

I needed to get my shit together.

"Okay," I said as I nodded my head, surprised by how fine I felt about everything. "I wouldn't be surprised if they've totally disappeared but I guess one way or another I'll have an answer."

"You're being surprisingly reasonable about this."

"I'm kinda surprised myself," I said with a wry chuckle. "I think it's because I've mentally written the money off. Like yeah, I'd love to get any part of it, but I think part of me already knew it was very unlikely to happen. It's probably why it took so long for me to even ask for help with this, even though my friend Maddi has been nagging me for months."

I didn't know why I was telling him any of this, but I

got the feeling this was a judgement-free zone. Besides, it wasn't like Charles could tell anyone, which gave me a strange sense of safety. And if I was that willing to dump my woes on an unsuspecting solicitor, then I probably also needed to find a therapist.

"With things like this, it helps to have that perspective, I think. Always be hopeful but don't put all your eggs in one basket, just in case. But it sounds like you have at least one supportive friend, and that helps."

"Thank you. I really do appreciate all of this."

"You're welcome," he said. "Are you ready to check a few details? It's mostly just names and contact details, etc. Anything more complicated and I'll get you to send it over in an email."

"Sounds great."

The details weren't as hard the second time around. In fact, thinking about the whole situation felt easier than it ever had before. It was as if knowing I had someone in my corner who knew what they were doing had lifted some more of the weight from my shoulders, taking it away so I didn't have to carry it anymore.

The stress and scars it had given me were still there, they always would be, but maybe now it would be easier to move on and focus on my life and my career again.

It was time to put myself back out there and embrace my work, letting Barbie shine in the way she was meant to.

CHAPTER TWENTY-FOUR

Sugar Pill

"Do you want to try it again?" Connor called from his position at the front of the studio. "Make sure you really use those hips, and when you're coming up off the floor remember to push your butt back and use the momentum so you're not putting too much weight through your shoulders."

"Okay, I can do that," I said, putting my hands on my knees and trying to catch my breath as sweat trickled down my back, sticking my loose T-shirt to me like glue. Despite having the door propped open and two industrial fans going, the dance studio was baking. There was an oppressive humidity to the air that seemed to lodge itself in my lungs, and every part of me was hot, sore, and sticky.

I knew performing in full drag under stage lights was going to be just as bad if not worse, but at that moment I couldn't imagine anything more hellish than doing my routine again.

But I wasn't going to get better without practice.

"Good, grab a drink and take your position. I'll get the music. Do you want me to film it so you can watch it again later?"

"That would be great, thanks." I tottered over to the nearest wall where my phone was sat on the floor beside my nearly empty water bottle. My feet ached and although I'd put precautionary plasters on my toes and the back of my ankles, I had a horrible feeling something was bleeding.

My ruby slippers might have been the most comfortable heels I currently owned, but that didn't mean they weren't going to punish me for dancing in them for an hour straight. Comfort had its limits.

I bent down to pick up my phone and bottle, draining the last drops of water and resisting the urge to flop on the floor starfish style. Because I knew if I sat down now, I wouldn't be able to get up again. Instead I flopped against the wall and tried to leach as much coolness from the bricks as possible.

That was the one benefit to the studio being in an old building—in the summer, at least, the walls stayed pretty cold.

"Are you doing okay, babe?" Connor asked as he walked over to collect my phone, his footsteps so light I barely registered him being there until he spoke.

"Yeah... I think so. Just a bit dead," I said, huffing out a laugh that morphed into a sad groan as I shifted my position and felt the deep burn in my thighs. Why had I thought getting Connor to help me choreograph and learn a heels routine I could perform in drag was a good idea? I knew I was going to need a routine for shows if I ever managed to land a gig, and having little performance snippets to post online—even just from the studio—would help show people what I could do, but couldn't I have picked something simpler?

I almost laughed at that thought, holding it back because I knew it would make my abs ache. The routine was fairly simple but Connor had designed it to look impressive to anyone watching, especially if they didn't know much about dance. Still, that didn't mean I couldn't have picked a simpler talent.

Although after watching Barbie lip-sync live, I knew I'd have to practice for years to even come close to her.

There was just something about the way she could hold a crowd with a single look and the way she *felt* the music as if they were her songs, not to mention her creativity when it came to routines.

Barbie Summers was the motherfucking queen of lip-syncs and nobody else would ever hold a candle to her.

Which meant I had to learn to dance.

"You've got this," Connor said with a beaming smile. "Seriously, you're super fucking talented—on and off the pole—and I know everyone is going to love you! Ooh! Also! I looked at the supplier we use for our poles and I can order you a freestanding performance one for about twenty percent less than the one you showed me, so let me know if you want me to order you one. I can get it shipped here and we can have a play around with it and see how you find it before you start using it in shows."

"That would be amazing, thank you." If I could fold pole into my drag routines, even in some small, simple way, I'd feel instantly a thousand percent more comfortable on stage. My outfits would need to change, but I'd already started bookmarking some gorgeous two-piece pole sets and talking to some of the women in my class about their favourite suppliers.

I just needed some fabulous shoes, a performance pole, and a routine.

And a gig too, but at least if I had the rest down, I'd be prepared.

"Perfect! Now, let's run it again. And remember, *hips*!"

I sighed as Connor sauntered down to the other end of the studio with my phone in hand. Then I rubbed my thighs and heaved myself off the wall as I told myself that it was only once more. Or maybe twice. Either way, I just had to get through it.

As Anthony had said, being a drag artist always came with a small dose of suffering.

I took my position in the middle of the empty studio and wondered if I could convince him to give me a massage later.

And if it ended up with his dick deep in my ass, then I definitely wasn't going to complain.

"Holy shit, sugar, you look awful!" Anthony said as soon as I opened my front door later that evening. I'd not long gotten back from the studio and from the horrified look on his face, I looked about as good as I felt. "Did Connor fucking torture you or something?"

"Not torture, I mean I voluntarily signed up for this when I asked for his help," I said, ushering him inside and slowly closing the door. "But I think the things he did to me might be considered cruelty to drag queens. I should have learnt to lip-sync."

My thighs were still burning, as were my calves, my abs, my feet, and basically every other part of my body. Except for maybe my ears. And my nose. Getting out of bed in the morning was going to be horrible. I'd probably have to come downstairs on my bum like a toddler, only very slowly so I didn't jostle my muscles too much.

"You'll probably need to learn to do that too," Anthony said with an apologetic grimace. "That or sing."

"Hmm, I'll definitely go for lip-syncing."

"We can practice." He closed the gap between us and gently brushed a loose strand of hair out of my face. "I'm proud of you, though."

"Thanks."

He leant in and kissed me softly. "Want to go upstairs? I'm in no way a qualified massage therapist, but I'll definitely give you a rubdown. I can't guarantee you'll feel any better in the morning, but it'll be fun in the meantime."

I giggled. "Sure, that sounds good. I don't have any massage oil, though."

Anthony shrugged and kissed me again. "We'll manage without. I think I've got some cocoa butter in my bag. That'd probably work."

He slid his hand into mine and slowly led me towards the stairs. I tried to hide a wince as my calves twinged. And how was there pain in the balls of my feet? I'd only been wearing heels for a couple of hours. How did people wear heels regularly without dying?

"Come on, sweetheart," Anthony said with a wry chuckle. "Let's get you upstairs."

Climbing the stairs wasn't as bad as I'd imagined but maybe I was just excited about the possibility of snuggling up with Anthony.

And maybe getting naked too.

I hadn't thought about getting dinner, but my plan was just to order something whenever we got hungry. There was an amazing curry house just down the road that did the best lamb biryani and the softest chapattis, plus their samosas were enormous and crispy and so freaking heavenly I could live on them. I'd debated learning to make my own, but then I realised I could just order them whenever I wanted.

Anthony shut the door and put his bag down, kicking off his shoes before turning to me. I was just wearing the tiny gym shorts and giant old T-shirt I'd pulled on when I'd gotten out of the shower, with my hair still tied up in a messy bun.

The T-shirt had once belonged to my older brother and was for some ice hockey team in Canada. I'd never been the biggest sports fan, but the shirt was big and comfy and reminded me of him. He'd moved to Toronto for work nearly five years ago and I'd barely seen him since because flights were so expensive and he was so busy with work and his family. We spoke regularly, though.

Maybe I'd try and save up and go next summer.

"You look so cute like this," Anthony said as he slowly reached for the hem of my T-shirt. "Can I take this off?"

"Please."

He smiled as he lifted it over my head, tossing it onto the pillows so it was out of the way. "Do you want to leave your shorts on for now?"

"That depends."

"On?"

"If I take them off, do I get a butt massage as well?"

He snorted and shook his head fondly. "You're trouble. If you're in pain, we probably shouldn't fuck."

"Maybe," I said, tugging down my shorts and watching with pleasure as Anthony's eyes flashed when he realised I wasn't wearing any underwear. "But orgasms do release a fuck ton of dopamine, which makes you feel amazing—I mean it's literally referred to as the feel-good chemical. It basically encourages you to keep seeking pleasure, or whatever is making you feel good in that moment. Anyway… if I'm full of dopamine, I might not notice how much my thighs hurt. At least for a while."

Anthony raised an eyebrow. "I'm not sure it works like that. But you're the one doing a PhD in jizz, so…"

I laughed. "I don't think mathematically modelling sperm has anything to do with orgasms, unfortunately. Well, I mean we need orgasms for sperm, but I don't deal with that part. I just work with the samples we get delivered to the lab, but—"

He cut me off with a soft kiss and I sighed happily into his mouth. "Still doing a PhD in jizz, babe, no matter how you frame it." He rubbed his nose against me affectionately, and I realised he was standing on tiptoes. "We'll have to find a way to work it into your drag routine."

"Oh lord no, then I'd actually have to try to be funny," I said. "I don't think I've ever been intentionally funny in my life."

"Comedy is hard as balls. Any performer who does stand-up comedy and is good at it is like, God-tier talented."

"I'll just stick to pole dancing. Oh! Connor said he could order me a freestanding performance pole at a discount from the supplier they use for the studio."

"Fuck yeah!" Anthony kissed me again, harder this time. "And I'm sure there's a dick joke in there about free-standing performance poles but I'm too fucking tired to make it."

I frowned and tilted my head back to look at him. "Long day?"

"Yeah... just... tiring." He shrugged but not before another emotion flashed across his face. Pain maybe? Or sorrow? But I didn't understand why. Was Anthony hiding something from me? "I built all that furniture and finally managed to get my room sorted. I'm not sure I like where everything ended up but I can move it around when I get bored."

"That's wonderful, though," I said. "I'm proud of you! Does it look good?"

"Yeah, I think so. Makes the room look a hell of a lot

tidier. It still looks cramped, but at least I can see the floor." He put his hand on my chest and gently pushed me towards the bed. "You'll see it when you come over on Saturday. Now, lie down and make yourself comfortable. I promised you a massage, and as bad as it might be, I'm going to give you one."

I climbed onto the bed and stretched out on my stomach, hugging a couple of pillows as Anthony went to dig out his cocoa butter. His IKEA furniture escapades and the sheer amount of tidying he'd have needed to do explained the tiredness and why his day had probably felt like it'd lasted a million years.

But it didn't explain the other emotions I was sure I'd seen.

Maybe I'd been imagining them.

All the same, the nagging feeling in my stomach that there was something else going on wasn't going away.

In fact, it was only getting stronger.

CHAPTER TWENTY-FIVE

Barbie Summers

I MIGHT NOT BE a massage therapist, but there was no way on earth I was going to pass up the opportunity to touch Colin's beautiful body and make him feel good.

I'd managed to find the small tub of cocoa butter hiding at the bottom of my bag, left over from the winter when it was the only thing that helped my dry skin, as well as a small bottle of lube and a couple of condoms. They were more recent additions just in case Colin and I ever found ourselves in need.

Colin had floated the idea around of fucking in his office, and even if he didn't want to make his fantasy a reality, I'd wanted to be prepared in case the opportunity arose.

After all, preparation was a drag queen's best friend.

I walked over to the bed, goodies in hand, and let my eyes roam over Colin's stretched-out body. There were a few bruises forming on his pale skin, and although it looked like he'd put plasters on his ankles, his shoes had obviously rubbed one of them.

His hard work and dedication were inspiring, but he needed to remember to take breaks too so his mind, and body, could heal. Doing everything he could to put himself out there and craft amazing routines was one thing, but if he was too emotionally and physically exhausted to respond to calls or perform, it would all be for nothing.

And while I'd never take my own advice on this subject, I was treating this much more as a "do as I say, not as I do" situation.

I climbed onto the bed and over Colin's sumptuously long legs so I could kneel beside him, putting the lube and condoms down and opening the tub of cocoa butter. Colin had turned his head to watch me and he smirked as he saw the lube.

"I thought you said we shouldn't fuck if I'm in pain," he said slyly as I scooped up some of the thick, creamy butter and began to warm it between my fingers as the distinctive rich, sweet smell filled the room.

"Yeah, well, I'm easily persuaded," I said. "And I wouldn't want to disappoint you."

He hummed happily and then sighed, relaxing further into the bed. "Good, because I've been dreaming about you fucking me all day. It was the only thing keeping me going while Connor was torturing me."

"Yeah?" I put my hands on his calf, gently beginning to rub the hard muscles. Even to my untrained hands I could tell they were tight and I watched Colin's face carefully for any signs of pain.

A couple of artists I knew who did a lot of dance often went to see sports massage therapists to help prevent injury, and I was going to suggest Colin did the same, if he didn't already.

"Yeah," he said, pulling his lip between his teeth. "Connor's an incredible teacher and choreographer, but he doesn't half make you work hard. I think I'm going to be hearing him say 'again' in my sleep."

I chuckled as I moved my hands to his other calf. "And thinking about me fucking you when you should be concentrating makes it better?"

"I can do both."

"Without getting distracted?"

"Sometimes." He grinned and then let out a soft sound of satisfaction as I slid my hands further up his leg to the bottom of his thigh, sweeping my thumbs in broad, firm circles across the stiff muscles. "Mmm, that feels good."

"Is it helping?"

"I think so."

"Good." I moved my hands a little further up and Colin spread his legs wider to allow me to dip my fingers between his thighs. I smirked to myself as I rubbed his thigh slowly, gliding my hands up to graze the bottom of his ass before sweeping them down again.

Colin groaned softly as I did it again, trying to push back into my touch. "No, sweetheart," I said, moving my hand back down. "Lie still."

"It's hard when you're teasing me," he said, a grumpy pout forming on his pretty mouth.

"Am I teasing you? I thought I was just giving you a massage."

"You know you are," he said, spreading his legs a little further and giving me a glimpse of his taint and his balls pressed against the mattress. It would be so easy to spread his legs even further, open up his hole, and slide into him like this.

"Is this what you were thinking about?" I asked as I moved my hands to his other thigh and starting to rub it slowly, sweeping my hands up and down the firm muscles. The cocoa butter I'd slathered on my fingers had run out, but I didn't want to take my hands off him to get more.

"Yes."

"Is that all you're going to tell me? Don't I get details?"

Colin groaned as I let my fingers brush against his ass again, and I watched his eyes fall closed. He'd pushed his hips up again, but I wasn't going to tell him no. I just kept rubbing his thighs, trying to ignore how fucking tempting his pert little ass looked.

"I... I imagined you giving me a massage," he said softly. "Just like this."

I hummed. "That's one part of your dream that's already come true then. What else?"

"You... mmm, you started playing with my ass, rubbing it slowly and then using your fingers to tease me..."

"Like this?" I asked, slowly moving my hands up to his bottom, rubbing one hand over each cheek. Colin groaned as I squeezed his ass, gently pulling his cheeks apart to look at his hole, which was dusted with soft red hair.

"Yes. M-More..."

I dipped two fingers between his cheeks, slowly running them over the sensitive skin and circling his pucker. Colin gasped, gripping the sheets in his hands as he tried not to push back into my touch.

"What next?" I asked as I gently teased the furled skin of his entrance, my cock throbbing as I imagined sinking into it. I hadn't stripped off and I was now regretting that decision, even if getting naked would take me less than thirty seconds.

"You... fuck, I imagined you licking me... then fingering me... shit! Thought about you sinking your fingers into me, opening me up for your cock while you told me how good I looked..." He groaned again, pushing desperately back into my touch. "P-Please, Anthony. Give me more."

I pulled my hand back, very willing to give him whatever he wanted. "Spread your legs for me," I said, moving back so he could spread them without hitting me. "Fuck, Col, you have such beautiful legs. And a gorgeous ass—so pert and pretty for me. I can't wait to be inside you."

I lifted myself up and quickly stripped off, throwing my clothes off the edge of the bed before stepping over his leg and kneeling between his knees. "Mmm, so gorgeous, Colin," I said as I reached for the lube and quickly squirted some on my fingers. "Talk to me, baby. Tell me what else you were thinking."

"I... I was thinking about you fucking me," he said, gasping out the words as I slowly ran my slick fingers across his hole, using the tip of one to tease his rim. I wasn't quite pushing inside, and when he tried to press his hips back, I put one hand on the base of his spine to hold him in place. "Thought about you sliding deep inside me, until I've taken every inch. Then... ungh... you fucked me slowly... pinning me down so I could only take what you give me."

"Like this?" I asked, using my other hand to stroke my cock as I finally pushed one finger into Colin's ass, loving the way he moaned and gasped. "Want me to fuck you on your stomach? Fuck you slow and deep until you can't take it and beg for more? Your cock would just rub on the bed and it would feel good, but we both know it wouldn't be enough."

"Fuck," he said and groaned as I began to pump my finger in and out of him. "Would you make me wait? Would you let me touch myself?"

"I would," I said, leaning down over him to trail kisses across his shoulders and down his spine. "I love making you come, Colin. Even if I wanted to tease you, I'd never be able to. I'd give in the moment you begged." I gently pressed another finger into him, loving how tight he felt around me. "I'll always give you whatever you want. All you have to do is ask."

Emotion swelled in my chest as I kissed his heated skin, listening to the sweet sounds he made as I worked him open. The way I felt about Colin was unparalleled. There was nothing in the world that could match it.

He'd given me a purpose again, a reason to get out of bed and put one foot in front of the other. He was the one keeping me on my feet when it felt like I was going to fall, and he was the person whose smile had the power to change everything.

Our friendship meant the world to me, but what we had now was something even greater.

I'd told myself that love was a curse which brought nothing but pain, but now I was realising that what I'd thought was love in the past had never even come close. Because if what I felt for Colin really was love, then it was nothing like I'd ever experienced before.

I meant what I'd said: I would give him everything he wanted. All he had to do was ask.

"Anthony, please," Colin said as he twisted his head to look back at me, desperation written openly across his face. "I need you."

"Can I fuck you like this?" I asked, pressing one last kiss to his spine before reaching for a condom.

"Yes! God, yes, please."

I ripped the condom packet open and rolled it onto my cock, adding more lube before I moved to hover over him, planting one hand beside his head as I used the other to line my cock up with his waiting hole. Colin had lifted his ass slightly, and it was so easy for me to slowly sink inside him, filling him and stretching him with my cock.

He groaned sweetly and the sound sent a little shiver of pleasure across my skin.

"Is this good?" I asked, putting my other hand beside his head so I was totally blanketing him with my body. Heat radiated off him, and even though I was above him, it felt like I was totally at his mercy.

I was Colin's to command.

"Mmm, yes," he said with a happy sigh of pleasure. "Feels so good. I love how your cock feels inside me."

"Yeah? Are you ready for me to fuck you?"

"God yes." He groaned and slowly rolled his ass, taking me even deeper so my balls brushed against him. "Give it to me, please. Make me come."

I moaned as I pulled back then pushed back in, fucking him slow and deep, giving him everything he'd dreamed about and more. Desire burned through my muscles, demanding more, but I held it in check.

Colin's soft moans and gasps crowded my senses, threatening to overwhelm me, and I thrust a little harder and faster, desperate to see what happened. Colin cried out, mixing my name with desperate pleas for more. And I wasn't going to say no.

He pushed back against me as I fucked him harder, pounding deep into him with every thrust. I moved slightly to put my knees at a better angle, and Colin groaned as my cock ground against his prostate.

"There?" I asked, smirking delightedly to myself as I pressed deep into him. "Is that good?"

"F-Fuck, yes. Don't stop! Right there, Anthony. Please!"

"I'm not going to stop, Col," I said, picking up the pace again and hammering my cock into that perfectly sweet spot that made him sing for me. "I want you to come. Can you do that for me? Touch yourself, sweetheart. Hump the fucking bed. Whatever you need. Just come on my cock for me, baby. I need to feel you come."

Colin slid his hand underneath him and the slapping sound of skin on skin sent another shiver of pleasure shooting through me. I groaned as blissful need bubbled under my skin. I was so close, my orgasm already right there. "Come for me, Colin. Please, baby, I fucking need it. Won't come without you."

"Yes, I'm so close…" He groaned louder, his desperation clear. "Fucking give it to me. Fuck me!"

My arms burned from supporting me as I fucked him harder, but I wasn't going to stop. Not until we both came.

Colin cried out suddenly, my name bursting from his lips as his body tensed, his ass squeezing around my cock as he moaned. "Oh god, oh shit… fuck," he babbled. "Don't stop… so good."

"Is this what you wanted?" I asked, thrusting into him again and again.

"Yes, oh fuck yes!" He twisted his head, his mouth finding mine in a messy kiss. "Come for me, Anthony. Need to feel it."

I groaned, my body obeying him as my orgasm rocked through me, sending wave after wave of pleasure rolling through my muscles as I filled the condom with my load, burying my cock deep inside him as I panted out every breath.

"Fuck," Colin said with a satisfied hum as he kissed me again. "That was… mmm…"

"Good." My mouth met his and we exchanged what felt like a hundred soft kisses before I felt him wince at the angle of his neck. I pulled out slowly and quickly disposed of the condom in a tissue from his bedside table before I flopped back onto the bed next to him.

Colin was smiling at me, and it made my chest ache.

That smile.

That perfect, beautiful smile.

I wanted to see it every single day.

"Can I have a massage like that after every training session?" Colin asked, a devious twinkle dancing in his eyes.

I chuckled and leant over to kiss him again. "Works for me."

CHAPTER TWENTY-SIX

Sugar Pill

"I'm so glad they're making another season of this," Anthony said as the opening credits for the final episode of *Llewelyn* rolled across my laptop screen. "I don't think I could cope without more naked Henry Lu in my life."

I hummed in agreement as I used the last chunk of chapatti to wipe my bowl clean. Getting curry had been the best decision after Anthony's deliciously sexy massage, and now I was full and comfortable, and there were enough leftovers for me to have some for lunch tomorrow, which was always one of the best parts about getting takeaway.

"Agreed," I said as I put my bowl on top of Anthony's empty one on the floor. I'd take them down to the kitchen later. "And Jude Kane. The two of them just have this chemistry. It's…" I tried to search around for the right word when Anthony chimed in.

"Hot as balls."

I laughed and flopped down beside him, pushing back into him so he could spoon me. "I was trying to find a better way to say that."

"There isn't one." He kissed the side of my neck. "They're hot as fuck together."

"I think Henry actually posted a picture of him, his boyfriend, and Jude and his fiancé, Austin Carter—"

"The porn star?"

"Yeah," I said, reaching for my phone to try and find the photo. "They've been together for a couple of years now?"

"How the fuck did I miss that?" Anthony asked. "I spend half my fucking life online."

"I think they try and keep it fairly low-key. They don't constantly post about their relationship and I *think* Jude has a very strict policy about talking about it in interviews." I scrolled through Instagram, sure I'd only seen it earlier that afternoon. "I'm pretty sure I saw something about it last year."

"That would make sense. I'd get pretty pissed if all I was ever asked about was who I was shagging."

"Yeah, it must get…" I trailed off as my eye caught another post on my feed. It was an image of pure text, the starkness of the black text on the white background drawing my attention. I frowned as I read, my stomach sinking and starting to churn.

It was from the drag artist Astronomica, who'd won season four of *Drag Stars*—the same season Maddi had been on—talking about her experiences with the tour company

Candy Club and how, nearly three years later, they still owed her nearly six thousand pounds in earnings.

And that the owner, Caesar Hurst, and her agent, Andi Smith, had refused to answer her calls and emails, blocked her, and disappeared without a trace.

She didn't even know if those were their real names.

"Hey," I said slowly, rolling over in Anthony's arms to face him. I had an awful feeling in my chest that Barbie had also gone on tour with the same company, and I was suddenly hoping that Astronomica's story was a horrific one-off. "Do you know Astronomica?"

"Yeah." He raised an eyebrow, a concerned look furrowing his brow. "What's wrong? Is she all right?"

"No…" I turned my phone towards him so he could read it. "Have you seen this? It's about Candy Club. Apparently, they still owe her about six grand. You… did you…"

Anthony's face went white as all the colour drained out of it, his eyes widening and filling with panic as he sat bolt upright. He snatched my phone out of my hands and began to read, curling over like he wanted to climb straight through the screen. "No… no… this can't… it… fuck, no… it can't be happening to her too…"

"Anthony," I said softly, quickly closing my laptop and putting it on the floor. Panic was clawing at my chest but I fought it back, trying my best to remain calm because if both of us lost control of our emotions, everything was going to hell in a matter of minutes. "What's going on?"

He looked up at me with wild eyes, like he'd almost forgotten I was there. He was still holding my phone tightly in his grip, his whole hand shaking as he glanced frantically between me and the screen. My heart sank.

The gnawing feeling that had been building in my chest, the missing piece of the puzzle behind Anthony's sudden move that I'd never been able to figure out, his casual avoidance of certain topics, the way he looked so sad when he didn't think anyone else was watching... they all suddenly made sense.

"Anthony," I said again as I gently reached out to pry my phone from his grip. "Please... tell me what's going on."

"I... She... No... this can't be happening," he said. "I thought... I thought it was just me."

"Did they... are you waiting for money too?"

"What?" He didn't seem to have heard me. I put my hand on his leg, trying not to startle him. I'd never seen him like this. It was like he was a wounded, frightened tiger in a cage, ready to lash out at any moment. My heart broke because how had I not known? How had I not seen something was wrong?

Then again, how could I? It seemed like Anthony had kept this secret so bottled up it had eaten away at him, stripping away tiny pieces until he was barely existing.

I wondered if he'd told anyone at all.

"Are you affected by this too?" I asked, carefully taking his hand with both of mine, squeezing it just tightly enough that it would give him an anchor point to reality. "Did Candy Club steal from you as well?"

He turned his head away like he couldn't bring himself

to meet my gaze as his whole body slumped. "Yeah," he said quietly, his voice a broken whisper. "Yeah, they did."

"Fuck, I'm so sorry." I squeezed his hand tighter, wondering what the hell I could say. I didn't want to offer advice because now was not the time to try and fix it, and everything else I thought of felt like a meaningless platitude. And as much as I wanted to ask what the fuck had happened, I couldn't bring myself to ask Anthony to open that wound any further and pour his trauma out for me simply because I was curious.

"It's fine," he said. "It's my fault anyway."

I frowned, his words pulling me up short. "What?"

"I should have gotten a proper contract. Or gotten someone to read it. I should have been smarter. None of this would have happened if I'd used my fucking head." He sounded so broken, and at that moment I could have burnt down the entire fucking world.

My fear and sadness turned to anger, boiling up into something that threatened to engulf me and making me tremble with rage.

How fucking dare these people take advantage of my beloved Barbie Summers.

How fucking dare they exploit my beautiful Anthony, who was so kind and generous he'd give his fucking soul to someone if they asked.

"No." The word came out sharper than I'd intended as fire and fury simmered under my skin. "This is not your fault. They took advantage of you. How the hell could that be your fault?"

"I... I should have pushed more. Should have got everything in writing. Should have—"

"Do you think that would have stopped them?"

Anthony shrugged. He still wasn't looking at me.

How could I make him see?

How could I show him this wasn't his fault?

I let out a slow breath, trying to release some of the anger threatening to consume me.

"It wouldn't," I said, tugging his hand and hoping it would somehow pull him towards me. "The people who did this... they don't care. I don't think you could have done anything to change that. This isn't on you, I promise. You were just..."

"Gullible? Naïve? Stupid?"

"No." I pulled his hand harder and when he wouldn't budge, I slid across the bed until I was practically on top of him. I reached out and gently drew his face towards me. He resisted at first, but I held firm and eventually he gave. There were no tears in his eyes. Instead they just looked... empty. Hollow. Like someone had reached in and scooped out his soul.

It crushed me.

"No," I said again, trying to hold back tears. "No, my darling. No. Never."

"Then what am I?" he asked quietly. He took my hand with shaking fingers. "What am I, Col? I'm a failure. I'm supposed to have everything. I won. It's not meant to go like this. My life was supposed to be different. I gave them *everything*. And they... they used me."

"You're not a failure, I promise. This isn't your fault."

"It feels like it."

"It's not," I said, my voice shaking because I was so desperate to make him see. "And I'll keep telling you that every single day until you believe me."

"You'll be sick of me by then." He let out a sad little sound. "I would be."

"Never."

"You don't know that."

"Maybe I don't," I said, my voice still trembling. I wasn't good at this; I didn't know how to make him believe me. All I could do was tell him the truth and hope it was enough, even though it felt like far too little. "But I do know that you are the most amazing man I've ever met. You're funny, and kind, and so fucking generous—I mean, you barely knew me and you still offered to help me with drag."

"That was selfish. You were cute."

"Even if that was your reasoning, you didn't have to do half of the things you've done for me. You've given me wigs, clothes, taught me how to do my make-up. You even gave me your name. You are the most unselfish person I've ever met," I said. He sighed but didn't argue and I let out a soft breath. A tiny fraction of relief.

"The first time I met you, you went out of your way to talk to me. I was a nobody, I still am, and you're Barbie fucking Summers. You didn't have to do anything. But you did because you, Anthony, have the most beautiful, generous soul and I wish you could see it."

"I... you... you were so pretty," Anthony said quietly. "And you looked so lost. Besides, if I didn't talk to you, I'd have just looked like a dickhead and I promised myself I'd never become one of those stuck-up cunts who thought they were better than everyone else, even if I was queen of the fucking world."

I leant in and kissed his forehead, almost climbing into his lap. "See? When you say things like that, I *know* the only way I'm leaving your life is if you make me. Because whatever we have, whatever this is, it's the best thing that's ever happened to me."

He sighed and for the first time since the start of our conversation, he seemed to relax. "I'm not letting you go anywhere," he said. "But I'm still not convinced you're going to want to stay."

"Maybe one day you will be. Maybe not tomorrow, but one day."

Anthony looked up at me with those heartbroken eyes and I wished with all my heart that I had a way to make it better. To magically erase all the pain and strife. But life didn't work like that. I couldn't take back everything that had happened to Anthony—I could only be here and create a supportive space for him to heal.

"Thank you," he said. "I'm sorry I didn't tell you."

"You didn't have to." I thought for a second then decided it wasn't worth telling him I'd had my suspicions. It wasn't going to help. "Does anyone know?"

"Yeah, Maddi does. She was the one who tried to help me hunt them down, and she's also been nagging me to find a solicitor for months."

"That's a good idea. Are you thinking about it?"

"I actually spoke to one this afternoon," he said sheepishly. "You remember I mentioned Orlando—the cute guy who's doing the wigs for *Cinderella*? One of his partners is a solicitor. I emailed him and he called me this afternoon."

"How did that go?" I asked, trying to keep my voice neutral and not wanting to get my hopes up. Anthony still hadn't told me the ins and outs of the situation, but from his reaction and the little he'd said, I assumed it was a similar situation to Astronomica's.

"Okay. He was really helpful, but he did warn me there's a pretty good chance he won't be able to do anything. Apparently, it's pretty easy for someone to fuck off with your money."

"Bollocks!"

"Yup." He sighed again. "Apparently, if they don't have active contact numbers and their email and business address are dead ends, then you're kinda fucked because if you can't find them, you can't take any action. Oh, and there's probably a really good chance that Caesar Hurst isn't his actual fucking name either, which makes things worse." He let go of my hand to scrub his face. "God, I wish I'd never fucking heard of Candy Club."

"Do you mind… what happened? You don't have to tell me if you don't want. I'm gonna assume it's like what happened to Astronomica?"

"Yeah, something like that." He bit his lip then reached out to pull me into his lap, putting his arms around my waist and holding me close. "Is this okay?"

"Yeah," I said, kissing the top of his head. "We can lie down if that's better?"

"Here's fine." He paused for a second, then took a deep breath like he was steeling himself to talk about something deeply unpleasant. I hadn't wanted him to open these wounds for me, but maybe it would be for the best. It wouldn't halve the problem but maybe I could share some of the burden.

At the very least I'd know exactly who to plot vengeance against when I couldn't sleep.

CHAPTER TWENTY-SEVEN

Barbie Summers

I'D THOUGHT I'd started to feel better about this whole bloody mess after talking it over with Charles but seeing Astronomica's post had brought everything crashing down in a tidal wave of pain.

For months I'd begged the universe to let me be the only one because I didn't want anyone else to feel the way I did while simultaneously shamelessly wishing I wasn't because at least then I'd feel like less of a fool. I'd gone back and forth between the two emotions so often I hadn't been sure which option I preferred.

Now I knew it was the first.

I wished I was the only one.

But I wasn't. And no amount of longing could change that.

"It all began when my season started to air," I said slowly. I knew the order I needed to say things in and that made it easier. After this afternoon, repeating it felt like going through the motions. It was funny—despite all the shock and pain, it somehow felt more distant than ever, like it had happened in another life, to another person.

I told Colin all about being approached by Andi, who'd promised me the world, and that I'd been too starstruck and overwhelmed to consider saying no. Especially because of who else she represented. I told him about meeting Caesar Hurst and going on tour with Candy Club, performing my heart out up and down the country.

And then I told him about them fobbing me off when I asked about the late payments. Them telling me to be patient, their endless excuses about banking problems and promises it was coming soon as they wrung out every drop of my goodwill by casually reminding me what they'd done by giving me a platform. Making me feel like I owed them despite the fact I was the one wearing the fucking crown.

My mouth dried out as I talked about the phone calls that hadn't been returned, the countless voicemails, texts, and emails that had gone unanswered. The social media messages that had gone unread until they'd blocked me.

And the final nail in the coffin of the disconnected phone lines, when I knew for good that I'd been fucking had.

Throughout it, Colin sat quietly in my lap but I could feel his body tensing, tightening like a coiled spring, and when I finally looked into his eyes, they were burning with a fury I'd never seen before. Anger radiated off him, his eyes dark with rage and the loose strands of his auburn hair standing on end like they were full of electricity.

I'd expected him to think I was the world's biggest twat for being duped, or maybe even be angry that he'd trusted me to help him build a career in drag when I clearly couldn't even take care of my own.

Instead, he seemed ready to burn the fucking world down for me.

I wasn't sure if I was scared, grateful, or turned on.

It was probably a bit of all three.

"So yeah…" I said. "That's all of it, really. I keep telling myself I should have done something… gotten a better contract… chased more… I don't know. I feel like I should have done more."

"You couldn't have," Colin said, fixing me with a look that was so full of certainty it bowled me over. I'd heard those words from Maddi a thousand times, but they sounded so different coming out of Colin's mouth. I didn't know why. They were the same fucking words.

Maybe it was because there was something about Colin —his passion, his sweetness, his determination to make me believe I wasn't at fault even if it took him a thousand years.

His attitude was so fucking different from Steve's, who'd shrugged the whole thing off, telling me it was definitely my fault and how the fuck could I let them do that to me? Because to him, without the money, I was as useful as a chocolate teapot.

Fucking wanker.

"What're you thinking?" Colin asked as he put his hand on my chest, right over my heart.

"Not much, just realising my dickhead of an ex-boyfriend might be part of the reason I blamed myself so much. Because he told me over and over and fucking over how useless I was for not following through. Mostly because he hated the fact he couldn't use me for my money anymore. Funny how suddenly being poor gets rid of leeches."

Colin growled under his breath and I tried to ignore the way my stomach twisted. A sound that angry had no place coming out of the mouth of someone so sweet, but fucking hell it was hot.

I wondered how difficult it would be to convince Colin to fuck me as a distraction. It'd stop me thinking about all this shit for a bit at least.

He raised an eyebrow at me, a smile pulling at the corner of his mouth. "I can feel you getting hard."

"Yeah, well, this whole sexy protective growling is doing it for me," I said.

He chuckled softly and kissed me. "I might look nice, but I'm the sort of person you don't want to piss off."

"I kinda like the idea of you being my knight in shining armour." I'd never had a partner willing to protect me. I was big and stubborn enough to stick up for myself most of the time, but knowing Colin wanted to be right beside me instead of leaving me to fight alone was such a novel idea it was doing funny things to my insides.

"If you need me, I'll be there. All you have to do is ask."

"I've never been much good at asking," I said. "I've always expected myself to be perfect."

"That's something else we have in common."

"Right fucking pair we make." I smiled wryly. "I thought you'd hate me, y'know? If I told you everything."

Confusion scrawled itself across his face. "What? Why?"

"Because I'm a loser. I mean, sure, I won *Drag Stars* but I fucked up everything else. I'm not exactly mentor material. Why the fuck would you want me as your drag mother if I can't even take care of my own damn career?" I tried to play the whole thing off as jovial, but even I could hear the fear underneath my words. "I failed, Col."

"You didn't fail," he said. "None of this is failing. You can't blame yourself for something that wasn't your fault."

I laughed. "Are you sure about that? Because I've been doing that for the last... nine months? Something like that. Fuck, that's a long time."

"Yeah, it is, but look at you. You're still putting one foot in front of the other. You're carrying on."

"I don't really have a choice," I said. "I can't stop."

"Why?" He tilted his head to one side, a few more long strands of hair falling out of his loose bun. I reached out and gently tugged the bobble free, letting his hair cascade around his shoulders. One day, he should do drag without a wig because his natural hair was so stunning he'd leave everyone breathless.

"Because... then I really would be a failure."

"No, you wouldn't." He sounded so certain, and it shocked me. All this time I'd convinced myself that I *had* to keep going because if I stopped, I'd be letting the bastards win. "I wouldn't blame you if you never wanted to get into drag again. You don't have to keep doing something simply because you think you should. It's called the... sunk cost fallacy. Like, where you think you have to keep doing something because of the amount of time, energy, or money you've sunk into it."

I thought for a second, turning the idea over in my brain. Colin was the first person to ever suggest a way out and tell me it was okay to walk away. But hearing it made me more certain than ever that I didn't want to do that.

"I'm not going to stop," I said. "Not because I can't but because I don't want to. I love being Barbie. She's everything to me. Yeah, she and I have had some shit times, and sometimes I wish we'd never won, but I wouldn't give being Barbie up for the fucking world. When I'm in drag, everything is different. I might still be a hot mess, but Barbie isn't. Barbie's a fucking queen, and all these bitches can try and bring her down, but she won't fall. She's the strength I wish I had."

"You have that strength too. Maybe it's harder out of drag, but I'm sure Barbie won't mind if you borrow some of it now and then. When you need it." He brushed his hand through my hair and leant in to kiss the top of my head. "And when you can't have that, you'll have me. I'm not above kicking a few shins and stomping on some feet. Have you seen the heels on my Pleasers?"

"Fuck, sugar, you'll do some fucking damage with them."

"Exactly. I'm not going to let the world fuck with either of us."

My heart ached and the corners of my eyes prickled. "What would I do without you?" I asked quietly, sliding my hand up his spine and pulling him in for a hug as I breathed in the sweet scent of strawberry and mint that I'd forever associate with this beautiful man.

"I'm sure you'd be fine."

"I doubt that. You're the only thing that's been keeping me going." I tilted my head back to look up at him. There was a soft blush spreading across his cheeks and up the side of his face, and his doe eyes were wide with shock. "I'm fucking serious, Colin. I'd be lost without you."

Emotion swelled in my chest, burning hotter and brighter than any star. It'd been so long since I'd felt like this about someone, and I wondered if it really was love or something else... safety, relief, support, acceptance. And trust.

I couldn't remember the last time I'd felt any of those either.

Perhaps that was what love was. Or part of it anyway.

"I promised you I'm not going anywhere," he said. "And whatever happens, I'm going to be there with you."

I smiled but there was a new twisting feeling in my chest. "Do you think... do I need to say something too?" I'd reach out to Astronomica privately to let her know she wasn't alone, but the thought of talking about my experiences publicly was making me feel ill.

As an artist with a platform, I knew I should be using it to speak out about shit like this, especially since there were so many other artists who might also be caught up in it. There were new queens too, who could easily fall victim to a similar scam, especially if they desperately wanted the platform companies like Candy Club promised.

But this was my life and going public would mean

exposing myself to the world. Everyone would put me under a microscope, picking and pulling at my story until they found a flaw or a mistake. I could already see the endless scroll of comments blaming me and spewing abuse. And blocking them wouldn't stop those words from doing an endless loop in my brain.

"That's up to you," Colin said. "You don't have to say anything if you don't want to. And you can always offer support without talking about your experiences."

"Maybe." I sighed. There was a headache forming in my temples, the sort that made my skull throb and my sinuses ache. It was like my brain was telling me I'd done enough thinking for the day and now I needed to shut down so it could process.

Hopefully, I wouldn't wake up in a cold sweat at three in the morning trying to escape endless rounds of nightmares that insisted on parading my pain in front of me in crystal clear detail.

"You can think about it tomorrow." Colin kissed my forehead softly. "Do you want to get some sleep? You look exhausted."

"Yeah, sleep sounds good."

Colin nodded and slid off my lap onto the bed beside me, pulling me down into his arms with a surprising amount of strength. He pressed tiny kisses down my face, from my forehead to my lips, as he held me close. "Sleep," he said. "I'll be here when you wake up. I promise."

CHAPTER TWENTY-EIGHT

Barbie Summers

"Good morning, Sleeping Beauty." The soft voice prodded at my brain and I was vaguely aware of a hand on my calf. It didn't sound like Colin, but I was sure I'd gone to sleep in his bed, so who the fuck else would it be unless I'd been kidnapped by aliens in the middle of the night?

If I had, I hoped it was the sexy kind. I didn't fancy dealing with the earth-conquering ones.

"Come on, Babs, I haven't got all bloody day."

"Maddi?" I screwed up my eyes and opened them, not convinced my senses weren't lying to me. The room was full of light streaming in from the window beside the bed, illuminating the figure of my best friend sitting on the edge of the mattress. Her hair was scraped up into a messy bun and she wasn't wearing any make-up, which was a rarity unless she was in a rush. She was wearing a black dress with little puff sleeves that seemed to be patterned with either tiny flowers or skulls, it was hard to tell from this distance, and sipping a large iced coffee. "What the fuck are you doing here?"

"I thought you might need a friend," she said, patting my leg gently. "I saw Astra's post last night."

I sat up slowly and pushed my hair out of my face. "You did?"

"Kinda hard to miss it. I tried to call you a couple of times but you didn't respond, so I figured you'd probably already seen it." She smiled grimly. "Anyhoo, I remembered you were coming to see your man, so I reached out to him instead—he's a sweetie, isn't he? I can see why you fucked him. Then I got up at five this morning to beat London traffic and here I am."

"Mads... I..." I couldn't believe it. And yet I could because this was Maddi and like Colin, she'd fucking throw hands to defend me without asking questions.

"I know, I'm amazing."

"That you fucking are," I said with a grin. I looked around, suddenly noticing Colin's conspicuous absence. "Where's Colin?"

"He's just—" Maddi's words were cut off by the bedroom door opening and Colin's willowy frame ducking through. He was wearing the same tiny pair of shorts he'd had on yesterday afternoon but instead of his T-shirt, he'd grabbed mine off the floor. He looked really fucking good in it.

In one hand he was holding a plate stacked high with slices of toast and in the other he'd managed to grasp two mugs.

"Hey," he said brightly. "You're awake. How're you feeling?"

"Bloody knackered," I said, throwing back the duvet and trying to scramble up before poor Colin dropped one or both of the mugs. I didn't get very far because Maddi went to rescue him before I'd managed to put my feet on the floor. She took the plate and handed it to me while Colin slid the mugs onto the bedside table.

One was full of tea with lemon and the other was a perfectly made cup of coffee.

"Eat something," Maddi said, stealing a slice of toast and perching on the edge of the bed. "You've had a shock."

"That was last night, Mads. I'm not sure eating something now will help with that," I said. I wasn't going to turn down the toast, though, because it wasn't every day I had a sexy man bringing me breakfast in bed. And if Maddi wasn't here, I'd show Colin how much I appreciated it.

"Get that look off your face," Maddi said with a knowing smirk. "I'm not buggering off so you can blow your boyfriend."

Colin made an embarrassed squeak and I snorted. "I wasn't going to blow him."

Maddi rolled her eyes. "Dickhead."

"Yeah, and? Have you seen him?" I gestured at Colin, who was watching the pair of us shyly. I'd told each of them so much about the other, but this was the first time they'd ever been in the same place.

And it was all because they wanted to support me.

I really was the world's luckiest bastard, even if I felt like shit.

I patted the bed next to me and scooched across slightly so there was room for Colin to sit. He slid into the spot and I leant across to kiss him because it was the least I could do to say thank you. "Good morning, gorgeous," I said. "How're you doing?"

"I'm okay," he said as I offered him the plate. "Sore. My feet feel like I've been walking on knives. And my thighs. And my butt. And my hips." He sighed sadly and rested his head on my shoulder. "And I'm supposed to be going to pole tonight too."

"I'm gonna get you some gel inserts for your shoes," I said as I grabbed another piece of toast and offered the plate to Maddi, who was watching us with a wry smile. It was very similar to the look my mum wore when she knew something I didn't. "Mads, where did you get yours?"

"Just from Amazon. I can find the link for you."

"Cheers," I said. "Poor Colin's working on dancing in heels and it's—"

"Painful as hell," Colin said as he nibbled his toast.

Maddi clucked sympathetically. "It's gonna be, sweetie. It'll get easier with practise. Try wearing your heels around the house when you can. It'll help your muscles get used it." She sipped her coffee and swirled the large cup around, making the ice rattle. "Do you remember your first pair of heels, babe? Mine were these cheap, shitty Mary Janes I got off eBay."

"Shit, I think I got mine in Primark or something. They only cost me like, a tenner, but they didn't fit properly and rubbed the back of my feet fucking raw." I shuddered. I remembered peeling them off in the kitchen and

Mum finding me. She'd helped me clean my bloody ankles up and then made me promise I'd buy better shoes.

I'd promised but she obviously hadn't believed me because a week later the most gorgeous pair of pink platforms had arrived in my size from a brand that specialised in shoes for drag artists. She'd left them on my bed with a note that just said *love Mum xxx*.

Those shoes had been worn to death over the years but I still had them, packed neatly in a box with the battered note tucked in alongside them.

"That sounds horrific," Colin said. "Why didn't you take them off?"

I chuckled. "I didn't notice. I was drunk off my tits."

"We should go out sometime," Maddi said. "You'll have to come down to London for the weekend—both of you. It's been *forever* since I went out and I'm fucking gagging for a good night out. Plus everyone misses your mug, and I promised them I'd drag you down as proof of life."

"I've been posting on socials," I said, picking up the last piece of toast. "Not my fault if they haven't noticed."

Maddi rolled her eyes and prodded me with a long, pointed nail. "You know what they're like. Also, you need to take me out round here. I promised Bitch Fit I'd drop in at some point. What are your plans for tonight?"

I bit back a laugh because of course Maddi had packed an overnight bag. It was so her.

And knowing her, it probably had about six different outfits neatly folded inside it so she could be prepared for anything and everything that might be thrown at her—from a coffee shop date to a night at a kink club. Nobody could say Maddi didn't have range.

"I don't know! I don't even know what day it is," I said before taking a huge chunk out of the toast.

"Friday," Colin said. "We didn't have any plans tonight —well, I'm supposed to be at pole, but we're going to The Court tomorrow. Barbie's part of the line-up, and I'm just going along to support. And it gives me a chance to practice being in drag."

"That settles it," Maddi said. "I'll stay until Sunday morning then and come with you tomorrow. Do I need to get a ticket? I'll just message Bitch. And don't worry, I'm not going to insist on crashing with you. I'll ask my favourite trash goblin if I can stay with her, and if not I'll get a hotel. But we are definitely going out tonight, even if it's just for dinner and one drink since I'll probably have to drive. We also need to talk about this whole Candy Club shit."

Ah yes, the whole reason Maddi had driven a hundred and twenty miles at the crack of dawn.

I put the last half of my slice of toast on the plate and slid it onto the floor, suddenly not hungry. The events of last night had been buzzing around in my skull since I'd woken up, but I'd successfully managed not to give them any attention until now.

Colin slid his hand into mine and squeezed, his silence saying more than any words could have.

"I know you don't want to," Maddi continued. "You're probably fucking sick of this whole situation."

"Understatement of the fucking year," I said dryly.

"But I think you should say something. Publicly." I stared at her, mouth open as I processed. It was one thing for me to suggest it to Colin, but Maddi saying it was another thing entirely. "I know it'll hurt to be open like that, but we both know your voice matters. You've got a platform, and when you say something, people listen. And if you speak out, then anyone else who's been affected is more likely to join you."

"Yeah, I know," I said. Maddi had a point. She'd said everything I'd been thinking. But that still didn't mean it wasn't a fucking terrifying proposition.

"Nobody's going to think badly of you," Colin said, squeezing my hand tightly. "Yes, there will probably be a few trolls but unfortunately there are assholes everywhere. But if you don't mind giving me your phone, I can delete them."

"We'll just turn off the fucking comments," Maddi said.

"No," I said with a shake of my head. "If they have something to say, they can say it. They'll just look like pricks."

If I was going to do this, I was going to do it with my head held high. This whole experience had haunted me for far too long and it was time for me to start taking control of the story instead of being a victim of it.

It was going to hurt.

But if I could help one person feel less alone, then it would be worth it.

"It's your choice," Colin said. "This is your story. Only you can decide what you share. And whatever you decide, I'll be here. Just like I promised."

I turned to look at him, a new tightness in my chest. I didn't deserve this man. I doubted I ever would. But that didn't mean I wasn't going to keep him in my life for as long as he'd have me, because without him, my life wouldn't feel complete. And I'd forever feel like a piece of me was missing.

"I'm gonna do it," I said. "But you two will have to help me write it, or it'll just be a series of never-ending swear words and death threats."

Maddi laughed and patted my thigh. "Don't worry. Between the three of us, I'm sure we can manage something."

CHAPTER TWENTY-NINE

Barbie Summers This is one of the hardest things I've ever had to write but I refuse to stand by silently any longer. Like my fabulous sister Astronomica, I have also been taken advantage of by Candy Club and am now owed a significant amount of money.

For months I have tried to contact Caesar Hurst, the owner of Candy Club, and my former agent, Andi Smith, who I believe is also part of this organisation. Both of them have ignored my calls, messages, and emails, and have now gone as far as blocking me so I cannot contact them.

To date, Candy Club owe me close to ten thousand pounds from tour, merch, and meet and greet earnings.

They took advantage of me and used me and there is a good chance I'll never get a penny from them.

This situation has meant I've had to leave my home and jobs in London to move back in with my family because I am unable to support myself, despite all my hard work and your support.

These last nine months have caused me a huge amount of pain and distress and I'm still struggling.

To all my fellow drag artists, if you are affected by this, please know it's not your fault.

And to all my fans, thank you for your continued support. I'm picking myself up slowly and doing my best to find a new normal. I am also taking legal advice.

All my love,
Barbie Summers x

CHAPTER THIRTY

Sugar Pill

"Right, honey bunnies, you two owe me at least one drink," Maddi said as we left Papaya, full of noodles and satay. After we'd written and posted Barbie's statement, we'd spent the rest of the day chilling out together before venturing into town to play a couple of rounds of mini-golf, where Anthony had casually handed Maddi and me our asses. Twice.

It was easy to see how close Maddi and Anthony were, but at no point did I feel left out. The two of them included me in all their conversations, making me part of their in-jokes and sharing their secrets.

Maddi was sharp and funny, and I was more than a little in awe of her. She'd already invited the two of us down to stay with her at some point over the summer, although she had dropped a couple of hints that she was going to be away for some of it. Anthony had raised an eyebrow and smirked, and when Maddi had nipped to the toilet, he'd quietly wondered if she was going away to film the first season of *Drag Stars Legends: UK*. There'd been rumours it was in the works and queens weren't allowed to talk about where they were going or what they were doing when they went off to film.

I hoped she was because she'd absolutely smash it and Anthony and I could shamelessly root for her.

"Colin, as our Nottingham resident, where's good to drink?" Maddi asked, looping her arm through mine. "As a student you must have some recommendations."

I laughed and shook my head. "That would mean I'd left my house this year to do more than work or go to pole." I thought for a second then dug in my pocket for my phone. "I know a couple of people to ask, though."

I pulled up the twins on WhatsApp and fired off a message to both of them.

> **Colin**
> Hey, random question. Where's good for a drink in the middle of Notts? Anthony's friend Maddi is visiting and we promised her one drink.

> **Ianto**
> Do you want something casual or are you planning to go out out?

> **Rhys**
> How's Anthony doing btw? I saw Barbie's post. That's fucking bollocks!

> **Colin**
> He's okay. That's kinda why Maddi is here, she wanted to check in.

> **Ianto**
> Try Cherry Bimbo. It's a bit hidden away but it's not far from the city centre. Here.

I clicked on the map link he'd dropped into the message and studied it. It wasn't far from where we were and was already open, which was good because it was only half eight.

"I've got one," I said, holding up my phone. "Ianto recommended it."

"Score, let's go," Anthony said. He was on my other side and looking slightly better than he had this morning. Distracting him had definitely been the best plan today because otherwise he'd have spent the whole day scrolling through social media. It was nice of Rhys to check in, though, and I was sure if Anthony actually checked his phone—which was currently in Maddi's spiked handbag for safekeeping—there'd be a slew of supportive messages.

It didn't take us long to get to Cherry Bimbo, which was down a small alley between two buildings I'd walked past hundreds of times. Outside the alley there were two impressive-looking bouncers who checked our IDs and waved us towards a door with a pair of pink neon cherries above it.

Once inside, we went down a flight of stairs into a large room with bright lights and booths along one wall, a few tables, and a large bar opposite the door with a huge progress pride flag hung behind it alongside enormous shelves of bottles. Off to one side was a dance floor, which was virtually empty at the moment but I could see a small DJ booth in the corner.

I assumed at some point they'd turn the music up and the lights down, but I didn't think we'd be out that late.

"Right, you two grab a booth," Maddi said, gently steering me towards an empty one at the far end of the room. "I'll get drinks."

"Don't you want to look at the menu?" Anthony asked with a laugh.

"Honey, I fucking know you. And Colin…" She gazed at me for a second. "Strawberry daiquiri?"

"Yes, please," I said, not attempting to hide my surprise as I slid into the curved booth that had a dark wooden table in the middle of it. "How did you know?"

Maddi winked. "I bartended for six years. I know what everyone wants, even if they don't."

"It's her hidden talent," Anthony said as he slid in beside me, casually resting his hand on my thigh. It was such a simple gesture but it left me breathless, my head spinning. The last twenty-four hours had been a rollercoaster ride of intensity, and even though he seemed to be handling everything okay, I was worried he was putting a brave face on for Maddi and me.

"How're you doing?" I asked, putting my hand on top of his and interlacing our fingers together, feeling the silver rings he was wearing bumping against my bare skin.

"I'm all right." He smiled but it was small and didn't

quite reach his eyes. "I appreciate you and Maddi keeping me company. I can't wallow then."

"Yeah, I don't think doom scrolling would be good for you right now."

"Did you look at the post?"

"No," I said with a shake of my head. "I was tempted but I was worried I'd start a fight with anyone being a dick, so I decided it was best not to even look. I'm still too angry. Not at you, obviously, but at this whole situation."

Anthony's smile widened slightly, his eyes twinkling with amusement. "You know, it's kinda hot that you're ready to start a fight for me."

"It's not me at all," I said quickly. "But—"

"It's hot, sugar. Take the compliment." He leant in and brushed his lips against mine, his hand coming up to cup my jaw and draw me in for a deeper kiss. I melted into his touch, silently begging for more. "One drink. Then I need to take you home."

"Okay," I said. "Yeah, let's do that."

"Oi, oi, less of that, please," Maddi said as she appeared before us carefully carrying three glasses. "You can fuck later when I'm not here."

"Did you decide where you're staying yet?" Anthony asked, taking his drink. It was in a tall glass with a round base that reminded me of a pineapple, especially with the pattern cut into the glass. It smelt very strongly of rum and sugar.

"I booked a Premier Inn," Maddi said as she sat down and took her own drink, which looked like a mango slushie with sugar around the rim. "I can't be asked to drive up to

Lincoln tonight. Besides, I think I'm gonna want more than one of these."

"Oh no, Mads," Anthony said. "We're not going out out. We're just having one."

"Why not? You deserve to have some fun after all this shit. Come on. You don't have to say yes now. Just have a drink and see if you fancy another."

"You're fucking trouble."

"What's new?" Maddi said with a smirk. I sipped my drink, a beautiful strawberry daiquiri with sugar and half a strawberry on the rim, without saying a word. I'd never been much of a party person because I'd never felt safe with the people around me, but a night out with Maddi sounded fun.

"God, this is gonna be like that night in Soho when…" Anthony trailed off as his gaze wandered over to the door. Mine followed. "Mads, did you tell—"

"Tell who?"

"No," I said quietly. "This might be on me…"

Standing by the door and looking around with purpose were the twins, Evan, and Connor. Connor spotted me and waved and the four of them suddenly descended upon us. They were all dressed casually and Connor's make-up was rather simpler than I'd expect for a night out. It was like they'd all gotten ready in a hurry.

"We heard you were coming for some drinks," Connor said brightly. "And we thought we'd join you."

"Thought you might want some company," Evan said with a wry smile as he looked over at Anthony. "You doing okay, babe?"

"I've been better," Anthony said, sipping his drink with a grin.

"Yeah, thought you might say that." He glanced at Rhys. "Can you get us some drinks, please? Oh, and we'll need another booth too. Connor, can you grab that one?"

"Another booth?" I asked, my head suddenly spinning. What had I done?

"Yeah, the others are on their way," Evan said casually. "Might take them a while, but they'll be here."

"Who's they?" Maddi asked, smiling sweetly at Evan. "I'm Maddi, by the way."

"I know." He nodded and there was a small flush to his cheeks, giving me the suspicion that Evan was trying really hard to keep his cool. "I'm Eva. That's my boyfriend, Rhys, his twin brother, Ianto, and their friend, Connor."

"Who also teaches me pole," I said. "Sorry, I should have introduced you all."

"Don't worry about it," Anthony said, shock written across his face. "I'm… can I… what are you doing here?"

Evan grinned and shrugged. "Like I said, we thought you might want some company. We saw your post, and we wanted to make sure you're okay. Bitch, Bubblegum, Peaches, Legs, and Ink are coming down too—might take them a while because some of them are at The Court tonight. Moxxie's DJ-ing, so they're not, but the murder twins might. Depends if Bubblegum can get hold of them."

Anthony stared and I felt laughter bubbling up inside me. "How did you…"

"Rhys told me you were coming out," Evan said. "We wanted to check in anyway, but nobody's got your address. Otherwise, Bitch would've probably been at your front door at, like, nine. She's got a habit of doing that."

"At least she brings snacks," Rhys said, handing Evan a drink and leaning down to give me a hug. "You all right, darling? This your man, then?"

"Oh yes, sorry," I said. This whole situation had thrown me completely off guard and now I didn't know my head from my toes. When I'd asked Rhys for recommendations, I hadn't expected him and Evan to throw out the Bat-Signal. But maybe it was just what Anthony needed. "Anthony, this is Rhys. Rhys, this is Anthony, also known as the brilliant Barbie Summers."

"So you're the one who sat in the front row of Eva's show after stalking him on Instagram?" Anthony asked with a grin as he sipped his drink, which I noticed was nearly half-empty already.

Rhys groaned. "Jesus Christ, I'm never going to live that down, am I?"

"Not while I'm around," Evan said, kissing his cheek. "Luckily, I thought it was endearing."

"Now this is a story I have to hear," Maddi said. "Grab a seat!"

We spread ourselves across the two booths and I grabbed some more drinks for Anthony, Maddi, and me to keep us going before the bar got too busy.

I wasn't keeping track of time, but at some point, probably after the third round, Bubblegum Galaxy, Legs Luthor, and Incubussy appeared in full drag, having driven straight from Lincoln.

"Hey, babes," Bubblegum said, throwing her arms around Anthony and squeezing him. "How're you doing?"

"Better now I've got a few drinks in me," Anthony said with a laugh. "What are you doing here? Aren't you fucking knackered?"

"Don't be silly, we're here for you! You're one of us now, honey. You're family! And that means we're here for you, no matter what." She released him and beamed. "Especially when shit like this happens. God, what a fucking nightmare, right? You must be stressed out of your mind. Is there anything we can do to help?"

"Do you need a lawyer?" Ink asked from beside Bubblegum, his rhinestoned leather jacket twinkling under the lights.

"I think... isn't Orlando's Sir a lawyer?" Legs asked. All her looks were themed around comics, cartoons, and anime, and tonight's look was inspired by Storm from X-Men, complete with the most incredible white mohawk.

"Ohhhh, yes! You met Orlando, right?" Bubblegum asked excitedly. "He's doing the wigs for the panto."

"Yeah, we met," Anthony said. "And he mentioned his partners. I've actually spoken to his Sir too. He doesn't have much hope, just because of the way things work, but he's gonna try."

"Fuck, that's bollocks, isn't it?" Ink sighed. "Sounds like we need more drinks."

Bubblegum nodded and clapped her hands together. "I'm going to get two. I need to catch up. If we're going to drink to forget with you, we're going to do it properly."

Legs shook her head and hooked her arm through

Bubblegum's, dragging her towards the bar. "We should get shots too. That'll help!"

I laughed and slurped up the last of the cherry and mint cocktail I'd been drinking. My head was starting to feel more than a little fuzzy and a warm lightness was floating through my muscles. I hadn't planned for any of this to happen, but here we were. And it looked like Maddi was about to get her wish for a night out.

"Is this okay?" I asked Anthony, who was perched at the edge of the booth, watching everyone around him. "We can go if you want."

"No, I want to stay," he said, leaning back against me. "I still can't believe they'd come out for me. I thought they'd think I was a loser."

"They don't think that," I said, kissing the side of his face. "They're just worried about you."

"But I'm not worth worrying about."

"Yes, you are! You're amazing, Anthony." All my emotions were suddenly fighting to get out of me. I knew I was drunk and saying anything more was a bad idea, but I'd had too many drinks and my filter was gone. I'd always been a lightweight. "You're the most amazing man in the whole fucking world. And I love you! So there! You are worth it."

Anthony turned his head to stare at me. "You... what?"

"I. Love. You." I grinned and leant in to kiss him. "And yes, I know I'm drunk but that doesn't change anything. I love you and you're fabulous and you're never, ever going to get rid of me."

He chuckled and then burst out laughing, the sound

drawing everyone's attention as he pulled me in for a kiss that drew more than a few cheers. "I love you too, Colin."

I kissed him again, my heart and stomach fizzing with joy. My whole body felt ready to float away and I didn't think I'd ever want to come down to earth. I giggled and kissed him once more. "Now we have two reasons to have more drinks."

CHAPTER THIRTY-ONE

Barbie Summers

I WAS NEVER DRINKING with Maddi ever again.

The next time she even *suggested* going out for "just one" I was turning around and running in the opposite direction as fast as fucking possible.

As long as it wasn't today.

Today was for doing absolutely fuck all as quietly as possible.

"I think I might be dead," Colin said with a groan, burying his head into my neck and putting his arm across my chest.

"If you're dead, then I am too." My voice sounded like I'd rubbed sandpaper all over my vocal cords and my mouth tasted like cheap tequila and grease. It felt like something had died on my tongue. I desperately wanted a glass of water, but that would mean getting out of bed and I wasn't convinced I knew how to do that. God, why couldn't I magic some adorable houseboy into existence to bring me water, paracetamol, and a toothbrush while soothingly explaining what the fuck had happened last night.

Although I wasn't sure I wanted to remember all of it given the acrid smell of cold kebab and chips coming from somewhere in the room.

"When did we get the takeaway?" I asked, turning my head slowly and breathing in the familiar scent of Colin's shampoo.

"I'm not sure," he said, his voice still muffled from where his head was buried in my neck. "I think we got it on our way home? No... wait... we ordered it in the Uber so it'd be here when we got back. It sounded like a good plan at the time."

"A lot of things sounded like a good plan last night."

Colin hummed. "Yeah. What time did we get in?"

"No fucking clue. Two? Three?"

Colin groaned. "No wonder I feel awful."

I tried to nod but it made my head spin, so I just lay there for a few minutes listening to Colin breathe. I thought he'd gone back to sleep until he said, "Do you remember any of it?"

"Yeah, quite a lot actually," I said, pressing a kiss to the top of his head. "I remember everyone coming out, all the hugs... Bitch and Peaches turning up at eleven and buying everyone shots."

"Ugh, yes... they tasted awful. I preferred the ones Legs got us."

"I remember Bubblegum death dropping on the dance

floor and nearly breaking her ankle and then trying to dance on a table."

Colin chuckled. "She was so mad when they told her to stop."

"I remember catching Maddi and Ink making out in the booth while everyone else was dancing," I said, smiling to myself as the memory resurfaced. "And I remember promising both of them I wouldn't tell, but I'm pretty sure they went back to Maddi's hotel room."

"I know nothing," Colin said. He turned his head so he could look up at me, his red hair fanning out like a halo. His face looked a little pasty and green. I didn't think either of us had thrown up last night but there was still time. "But I do remember Rhys taking his shirt off... I'm not sure why."

"I think it was so people could tell him and Ianto apart? I'm not sure." Trying to piece everything together was making a nasty headache form around my temples. But there was one memory that stood out in perfect clarity with a spotlight shining on it. "I remember you telling me you love me."

Colin smiled, something that looked like relief flashing across his eyes. "You do?"

"Yeah, did you think I'd forgotten?"

"I wasn't sure," he said. "We were a little drunk. Well, I was at least."

"I remember all of it," I said, moving just enough so I could lean down and kiss him, gross morning breath be damned. "Every single word."

He pressed his lips gently to mine. "I probably shouldn't

have told you while I was drunk."

"Why not?"

"I don't know... it makes me sound insincere."

"That's bollocks." I rolled the pair of us so we were lying side by side and I could see all of Colin's beautiful face. "Doesn't matter to me when or where you said it, just that you did. And that you mean it."

"I do," he said. "I love you, Anthony. I know we haven't been together long and maybe it's too soon but—"

"Who says? If we feel it, then why the fuck does it matter? Some people get married after only knowing each other for, like, two weeks." I shrugged. "Fuck anyone else, it's none of their business. You love me, and I love you. That's all that matters."

I nudged his nose with mine and rested our foreheads together. "I don't want anyone else's opinion, Col. I've already got enough of that. I just want you."

"I want you too," he said. "I want *this*. Us."

"Good." I kissed his nose and tried to ignore the way my head was spinning.

He sighed quietly and put his hand on my chest. "I really don't want to move, but it feels like something died in my mouth and my head is killing me."

"Same. Do you want to use the bathroom and I'll take the leftovers downstairs and find us some water? I think I need to plug my phone in too."

"Did you get it back from Maddi then?"

"I think so." I frowned at the vague memory of Maddi pressing it into my hands and telling me not to look at it until tomorrow. She might have even turned it off. "It's probably in my jeans."

"Cool." Colin nodded and then stopped quickly with a sad moan. "Ouch. Ugh, I'm going to message the twins too, make sure they got back okay. I think Bubblegum was going to crash with Eva too, as were Bitch and Peaches. I think Rhys said something about them having his house and him staying at Evan's? Oh... because they live next door to each other. Oh fuck, we'll have to see some of them later. We're supposed to be at The Court."

"Fuck! Well, that can be a problem for this afternoon, not whatever time it is now," I said as I mentally prepared myself to sit up. My stomach was already churning at the idea. "Okay... I'm going to get up now."

"If we survive our ordeal, do you want to finish *Llewelyn*?"

"Fuck yeah. Henry Lu's abs can be my reward."

Getting up and around was fucking torture and by the time I got back to Colin's bed with two glasses of water and a tub of Pringles I'd nabbed out of the cupboard, I thought I was going to be sick.

Colin didn't look any better, so we climbed back into bed and slowly sipped our drinks while we scrolled through our phones. It was only eleven, so we still had plenty of time before we had to head to mine to get into drag.

As I'd hoped, my phone had been in the pocket of my jeans and when I turned it on, I was bombarded with notifications. There were a few messages from The Court kings and queens from yesterday afternoon, all checking in, and quite a lot from artists I'd worked with in the past as well as queens from my season, all touching base.

Like everyone from The Court, they were all horrified by what had happened and my heart sank when more than a couple of them told me they were in the same situation. It was fucked up beyond belief and I wished a series of small curses on anyone associated with Candy Club—like they'd always have a small stone in their shoes they couldn't get rid of or the lift they were hoping to catch always left just as they arrived—while I replied to as many messages as I could before dizziness and nausea made it impossible.

I made a mental note to come back to the rest of them later because I didn't want to leave anyone hanging. They needed to know I was on their side and they weren't alone.

That it wasn't their fault and they shouldn't take responsibility for the failures of others.

I told all of them the same things Colin had told me, typing the words out over and over instead of just copying and pasting them because I wanted them to feel genuine every time. And the more I typed them, the more I started to believe they might be true.

Even if my brain was reluctant to accept it, my heart knew Colin was right.

None of this was my fault, and I couldn't blame myself for what had happened. I'd given these people everything, and they were the ones who'd chosen to take advantage of my kindness, my generosity, and my dedication.

And if I could make one more person believe that about themself, then I'd feel like I'd achieved something.

I didn't even touch the hundreds of Instagram notifications. They'd keep until my head didn't feel like it was going to split in fucking two every time I blinked.

"How're you feeling?" Colin asked as he slid his phone onto the bedside table and rolled into my side, throwing his arm lightly across my chest. "Less like death?"

"Just about," I said. "Once upon a fucking time, I could've done that, gotten up, and gone straight to doing bridal make-up at eight. God, I'm so fucking old."

Colin snorted. "You're twenty-six!"

"God, what'll happen when I hit thirty? I'll fucking keel over after one drink." I sighed and locked my phone, tucking it under my pillow to retrieve later. "How's everyone else getting on?"

I'd messaged Maddi and not heard anything back, so I assumed she was busy getting to know Ink. Or she was lying in a hot bath with an iced coffee, an eye mask, and a true crime podcast, which was Maddi's method for returning to the land of the living.

"Bubblegum is fine and Legs said they've felt worse, but apparently Evan, Peaches, and the twins are suffering—I think Legs and Bubblegum are going to try and make everyone breakfast. Poor Evan's got a night shift later too, so I think his plan is to sleep for most of the day and hope that shakes his hangover," Colin said with a pitying smile. "And Connor said he's just about made it to the sofa with his cat, and he's trying to convince his husband, Patrick, to make him some cake since he's a pastry chef."

"Cake sounds like the worst thing right now," I said, putting my hand on my stomach, which was twisting at the thought.

"Agreed. I don't think I want anything."

"We should probably eat something later before we go out."

"Yeah, being hungry while in drag sounds horrible. But so does being tired and hungover, so…" He yawned and snuggled deeper into my side. "Oh… I had an email too, from Phil at The Court. Because quite a few of his artists are away for the summer or getting involved in Bitch's panto, he's looking for some potential new artists for smaller slots—like hosting drag bingo and karaoke and doing some short performances in their summer variety shows. He wondered if I'd be interested. There's more details in his email, and he said we could talk about it tonight, but"—he yawned again—"I thought it might be fun. I'm not very funny, but I think I could host. Especially if I was with someone else."

"Shit, seriously?" I tried to sit up but thought better of it. Instead I pulled Colin further into my arms and began pressing kisses all over his face. "That's fucking amazing, sugar. I'm so fucking proud of you."

"Yeah?"

"Fuck yeah. You're going to fucking smash it." I kissed him deeply, ignoring the protests from my body.

"Thanks," he said. "This is all because of you, Anthony. You've changed my life. All my dreams get to come true because of you."

"I didn't do anything, Col. I just gave you a push." I kissed him. "I love you so much."

"I love you too." He kissed me again and we melted into the bed. I wanted to keep kissing him, showing him exactly how I felt, but my hangover was sinking its claws into my skin and if I kept going, things weren't going to end well.

"Nap first," I said, pulling away to kiss the top of his head before taking a deep breath to settle my stomach. "Nap first, then fucking, then drag."

"Yeah… nap first." Colin yawned again before shooting me a sleepy smile. "We've got all night."

"And all tomorrow too."

And the next day.

And the day after that.

And, if I had my way, every day for the rest of our lives.

CHAPTER THIRTY-TWO

Sugar Pill

"Are you ready, sweetheart?" Barbie asked, taking both of my hands in hers and giving them a quick squeeze. "Do you need anything?"

Her gaze was full of encouragement and it settled a few of the nerves fluttering around in my stomach like anxious butterflies. The time for my debut performance as Sugar Pill was virtually upon me and I wasn't sure if I felt more worried or excited. This was everything I'd been working towards for the past ten weeks, and I was desperate to make a good impression.

"No." I shook my head and wiggled my toes, making sure my feet didn't fall asleep in my ruby slippers. While they weren't designed as pole shoes, they were easier to dance in and I hadn't wanted to risk falling flat on my ass in front of everyone. Not during my first time out, anyway. "No, I think I'm okay."

"Good girl." Barbie winked and released my hands, stepping back to give me a once-over with a careful eye. "You look gorgeous. I love that set on you."

"Yeah? It's not too much?" I glanced down at the brand-new pole set I was wearing, with bright red garter shorts with pretty buckles and straps around my thighs and a glittering halter top with extra straps that wrapped around my chest below the cups. It was fun and sexy, especially when paired with my ruby slippers and my trusty black knee pads. I'd debated performing without them but quickly changed my mind when I realised The Court's stage would shred my knees in a second.

Over the top I had a little cropped shirt that I'd tied around my chest, and my wig was artfully styled into a stiff, high ponytail that wouldn't get in my way.

Barbie had also helped me set it with wig glue so there was no way it was going to drop off when I turned upside down.

She'd also put a ton of setting spray on my face so my make-up wouldn't move either.

"Nope, it's perfect," she said. "Next time, I might even add more glitter."

"Definitely more glitter," Bubblegum said from behind her. "There's *always* room for more glitter."

"Just because you want to look like a craft store vomited on you doesn't mean Sugar does," Eva said calmly, shooting Bubblegum a pointed look.

"I don't know," said Moxxie, who was also lingering, their customary cowboy hat perched jauntily on their coiffed hair. "I think I'm with Sparkles on this one. More is definitely better when it comes to rhinestones and glitter."

"See! I told you."

I giggled, their bickering providing the perfect distraction to my nerves. On stage, the opening act for the second of The Court's summer variety shows was coming to a close and I was eternally grateful that Violet had put the incredible Legs Luthor on first to wow everyone with her latest routine, which involved lasers, smoke, and a giant D20. Apparently, she'd gotten heavily into Dungeons and Dragons over the last few months and had built an entire drag show around it.

It was truly stunning and I hoped the audience was so blown away they wouldn't notice if I made any mistakes.

Although compared to Legs, I definitely would look like an amateur. Hopefully, everyone would be kind.

To my left, a member of The Court's small stage crew was preparing to drag my new performance pole into place and my stomach fluttered again. I'd practised this routine more times than I could count, until my muscles burned, my skin turned purple from bruising, and my ankles developed calluses. I could do this. I just had to prove it.

Legs's routine ended with a flash of light, and everyone cheered as she bounced off stage waving an EVA sword and beaming. "That was fun," she said before fixing her gaze on me. "Are you ready, baby girl?"

"I think so," I said, letting out a deep breath as the crew began to move, taking my pole onto the stage and making sure it was placed on the X we'd taped onto the floor during the technical rehearsal that afternoon. I poured a tiny bit of liquid chalk onto my hands and rubbed it between my palms, putting the bottle down next to my water. "Yeah... I'm ready."

"You've got this," Barbie said, flashing me a proud smile. I really wished I could kiss her, but we'd agreed to keep our relationship professional while in drag and crossing that boundary would just make things messy. "Deep breath."

I nodded, the voices of everyone around me fading into the background as I inhaled slowly and released it, thinking through my routine in my head. I watched Violet glide onto the stage, today dressed in primrose yellow. She was speaking to the crowd and I heard my name as she began to introduce me, but I wasn't really listening to the words.

I stepped to the edge of the wings, waiting for my cue and trying not to look at the crowd. I knew it was going to be busy even in the middle of August, because the variety nights always sold out, but if I could pretend they weren't there, that I was just in the studio with Connor doing my thing, then I'd be fine.

"Please give your everything for the newest member of our drag family here at The Court, the adorably sweet and gorgeously talented Sugar Pill Summers!" Violet's words echoed in my ears and from somewhere in the audience I heard cheering. That would be Connor, the twins, and the rest of our pole class, who'd all been determined to come out and support me.

Another deep breath.
Another exhale.

Drawing my left foot up to rest on my toes, I was ready to step forward. My head dipped down.

Then the opening beats of Hozier's 'Too Sweet' kicked in, the smooth, swinging combination of the bass guitar and the drums sending a pulse through my body. I strolled onto the stage, swinging my hips as the crowd applauded. The little burst of support made me smile and as I reached for the pole with chalked-up hands, a sense of unmitigated joy filled me.

The routine Connor and I had devised was another one that looked impressive but was technically simple, at least for someone of my skill set. It would allow me to show off, adding flair and showmanship to every spin, drop, and trick. There was a nice mix of pole and floor work too, with the final section taking me right to the front of the stage so I could engage with the audience.

The first cheer came as I spun myself around the pole, kicking my legs out impressively and then catching the pole between my legs. I climbed up, which was harder to do in shoes than barefoot, and gripped the pole tightly in my hands as I tipped myself backwards, opening my legs into a spilt for just enough time for everyone to applaud before I hooked my knee around the pole and let myself hang for a second.

The music thrummed through me, the beat keeping me in check as I pulled myself up and into another simple but impressive hang before I slowly spun down to the floor.

I rolled my hips and drew my legs up to clap them on the floor behind me. It was harder to do without the huge platform of the Pleasers and my ruby slippers didn't make a satisfying crack when snapped together, but it still looked impressive. And doing it in different shoes would give me something to work up to.

My heart raced as I pulled myself up onto my knees, adding a little bit of burlesque and teasingly removing the tied crop top over my halter neck, dropping it to the floor and flipping my wig. Someone whistled and I laughed with delight as I crawled towards the front of the stage.

I could see the faces of the audience in front of me. Unsurprisingly, my gorgeous pole family were sat right in front of the stage, smack bang in the middle where I wouldn't miss them.

I shot them a wink as I danced, letting the music move through me. I'd never felt more confident or sexy and I revelled in the feeling.

Barbie had always said that drag gave her strength and confidence, allowing her to be the person she'd always wanted to be. And being on stage under the spotlights with everyone watching me, I understood exactly what she'd meant.

Sugar Pill was the confident, fun, sexy, and wild part of myself that I'd never explored. She was the party girl, the dancer, the carefree spirit who embraced life as a whole. She didn't have worries and responsibilities like funding applications to fill out, endless research papers to read, bills to pay, or shitty ex-boyfriends to avoid. She was the dreams and desires I'd never allowed myself to explore, and freedom from the parts of my life I couldn't escape.

I loved my PhD, but academia was hard and thankless, and the real world came with a million strings, every one demanding my attention. But when I was Sugar Pill, I could forget about all of it, even if it was just for an hour.

I'd still be exhausted and sore afterwards, but it was a different kind of exhaustion, one that filled me up with happiness and left me refreshed and restored.

If that had been all Sugar Pill had given me, it would be enough joy to fill a thousand lifetimes.

But somehow I'd found more—a loving community that supported me, a new group of friends who'd be there for the good, the bad, and the ugly parts of life, no questions asked, a mentor who inspired me to push myself and go beyond what I'd thought possible, and a boyfriend who I adored more than anything.

Without Barbie Summers, without Anthony, I'd still be nervously lurking in the audience, too afraid to put myself out there. Sure, I'd have made a start thanks to my push from Rhys and Bubblegum, but I doubted I'd have made it this far.

I definitely wouldn't have found love along the way.

And the most wonderful part was that it was only just beginning.

My routine drew to a close and as I dropped into my final pose, I felt my heart thundering and my lungs fighting for air. If I didn't know any better, I'd have thought I'd forgotten to breathe for the last four minutes.

The music faded away and for a split second I wondered if I'd done enough. Then a wave of applause hit me, jolting me to life like I'd been shocked. I grinned as I climbed to my feet and bounced off stage, riding the high of what I'd achieved straight into the waiting arms of Barbie.

"You did it! You fucking did it, sugar!" Barbie's embrace was crushing as she planted an enthusiastic kiss onto my cheek. "You were incredible. I'm so fucking proud of you."

"Yeah?" I asked with a gasping, shaking breath as Barbie released me and the full force of what I'd done hit me, threatening to take my legs out from under me in shock. "Was it okay?"

"You smashed it," Barbie said, grabbing my hand and leading me further into the wings. "Absolutely smashed it."

"It was incredible," Bubblegum said, appearing next to Barbie with my water bottle in hand. "I wouldn't have known it was your first time."

"Definitely not," said Moxxie as they pulled a slightly squashed vegan marshmallow Rice Krispie bar out of their jacket pocket. "Here, eat this."

"She's not going into shock, Moxxie," Bubblegum said.

Moxxie shrugged. "Still good for her to eat something."

"Stop fussing, you two," Eva said, tapping both Bubblegum and Moxxie on top of their heads with a large folded fan. "And give our baby some breathing room. She doesn't need you two hovering over her like a pair of enthusiastic but uninformed farmyard fowl."

"I'm okay," I said, putting my hand on my chest and feeling my heart racing.

"Let's go somewhere quiet," Barbie said as she took my water bottle from Bubblegum and began to steer me towards backstage and the dressing room we were sharing downstairs. "You need to decompress."

I let her lead me to our room and guide me into the little chair in the corner, which I flopped into ungracefully. There were still stars bursting behind my eyes as Barbie knelt down before me. "You did amazing, baby," she said. "Seriously. I'm the proudest person in the world right now."

"I didn't disgrace you then?" I asked with a grin as exhaustion started to flood my muscles. I'd been told to expect it, but I hadn't realised it would hit so quickly.

"Fuck no, you were awesome. You did the Summers name proud."

"Thank you."

Barbie patted my knee and smiled softly before handing me my water. "Drink that, eat your Rice Krispie treat, and maybe take your shoes off. Then we'll go back out and watch the others."

I nodded, watching as she looked in the mirror to touch up her lipstick. One day, I wanted the two of us to do a routine together. Something truly legendary.

But I had a lot of work to do first.

"Are you ready?" I asked as I ripped open the wrapper of the squashed marshmallow bar. Barbie was closing the show with another medley—longer and grander this time. She'd become a staple on The Court's roster over the summer and everyone loved having her around.

Barbie turned and winked at me, making my heart skip and stomach flutter. "Sugar, I was born ready."

CHAPTER THIRTY-THREE

Barbie Summers

I WAS SO FUCKING proud of Sugar Pill that I wanted to grab a damn megaphone and walk around Lincoln announcing it to the world. Unfortunately, I didn't have a megaphone to hand, so I had to settle for posting hundreds of photos and little snippets of video on Instagram instead, sharing my pride and joy with nearly half a million people around the world.

My platform had grown rapidly over the last few weeks because calling out the behaviour of shitty tour operators and going viral for my opinions had done wonders for my visibility. It definitely wasn't what I'd expected to happen, but neither was being interviewed by various news channels and podcasts or getting an email about a potential spread in *Cosmopolitan*.

I'd still not gotten any of my money and nor was I likely to since Caesar Hurst and his entire organisation had disappeared into thin air, leaving absolutely no trace of themselves, but calling him out on various international media platforms made me feel a little bit better about it.

If I couldn't get paid, then getting even was an acceptable replacement.

Although the ten grand really would have been useful, I couldn't lie about that.

"I still can't believe I did it," Colin said as we pulled up outside my house. There was a light on downstairs which Mum had left on for us before she went to bed, and seeing it made me smile to myself.

Mum's reaction to finding out all the details about my situation had been a mixture of stunned silence and icy calm rage, which had ended up with both of us arguing about whether or not I should pay rent since apparently my debts were more important. I'd worn her down to just covering my half of the bills, which she'd begrudgingly accepted. I hadn't originally intended on staying with her for long, but since Colin had signed up to extend his lease for another year before we'd even met, I'd decided to stay put until next May when Colin and I could find a place of our own.

At least it gave me another nine or ten months to save for my half of the deposit.

"You did, and if you want proof, it's all over Instagram," I said teasingly, reaching out to put my hand on his thigh. Since we'd had a proper dressing room, he'd gotten changed before we left and pulled on a loose tank top he'd stolen from me and a pair of shorts. His wig along with his shoes and pole set were in his bag on the back seat and the only reminder of tonight was the face of make-up he was still wearing. I was still in full drag because we'd left not long after I'd finished, and I'd wanted to get home where I could change in comfort.

And leave my shit all over the floor without worrying I'd lose something.

"I saw I had a bunch of notifications," Colin said. "But I haven't looked yet. I'm too nervous and I don't want to ruin this moment by seeing a comment from some asshole."

"Don't look then," I said. "Leave it until tomorrow." I smirked and leant across to kiss him. "And if you need a distraction, I'd be happy to provide one."

"Hmm, I might have to take you up on that," Colin said with a soft, happy hum.

"Good, then let's go inside."

I stole one more kiss before I climbed out of the car, grabbing my bag with my shoes out of the back before we headed into the house. I was itching to get undressed and show Colin how proud I was of him for everything he'd achieved tonight. And stop him from going down a social media black hole.

I needed him to see how fabulous he was, how talented and beautiful and goddamn incredible. How he could steal my breath with one look and make my heart race with a simple smile.

Colin had only been in my life since May, and already I knew that even if I searched every inch of the earth, I'd never find anyone else like him. He was everything to me. It didn't need to be any more complicated than that.

Once we were inside, we headed upstairs and I bit back

a smile when I heard Mum's snoring echoing down the landing. I could probably set fireworks off in her bedroom and she wouldn't notice.

I closed the door to my bedroom softly, dropping my bag on the floor and kicking off the old trainers I'd driven home in. Colin had put his shoes beside the bed and was sitting on the end of it, watching me carefully.

"Do you want to take your make-up off before I distract you?" I asked as I gently peeled my wig off and put it back on its stand. It was a new one, courtesy of Orlando, and I didn't want to damage it. He'd been very gracious to squeeze me and Maddi in for a couple of last-minute pieces, and I had a few more slots booked with him as well because his work was exceptional. "You can shower too if you want."

"Make-up yes, but I'll skip the shower," he said, leaning back to show off his long legs. "There's no point if I'm just going to get messy again."

I grinned and reached behind me to undo my dress, sliding it over my shoulders and stepping out of it before I started to remove my padding and tights. Performing in drag in the middle of summer was never glamorous, and I felt swampy and gross. "I'm going to shower," I said. "I feel fucking disgusting. Why the fuck did I decide to wear two pairs of tights?"

Colin laughed and stood up, walking gracefully over to me and helping me tug them down. I could've sworn my skin was actually sticky. "Because Barbie has standards, even when Anthony doesn't."

"Damn right. Ugh, I can literally feel sweat rolling down my back. Where the fuck did it come from?"

"Under your breastplate?"

"Probably." I shuddered with disgust then reached for the tall fan by the bed, flicking it on full blast. The air in my room was stifling, reminding me how much I hated the rank humidity of British summers. "Fuck it, I'm definitely showering. Otherwise I'd feel like shit for suggesting you go anywhere near my dick."

Colin chuckled again, leaning in to kiss me. "You know I'm equally sweaty."

"Not true, you spent all evening parading around in tiny shorts and a bra."

"I was wearing tights too!"

"You had an exposed midriff. That counts as air conditioning."

Colin snorted and shook his head. "Yes, Mum."

"Don't be cheeky," I said, drawing him in for another kiss. "I taught you everything."

"Mostly," he said as he pulled back. His confidence had definitely grown over the summer and he'd blossomed into someone more secure in his teasing. Although he still got flustered sometimes with the cutest blush on his cheeks and it made me want to pounce on him, pin him down, and kiss all over his body until he squirmed and groaned.

"I'm going to take my make-up off now," he continued. "You should do the same. And then I guess I'll join you in the shower, as long as you promise to distract me."

I smirked. "Sugar, I wouldn't dream of doing anything else."

We removed our make-up quickly and quietly, not wanting to get sidetracked, and when we were done we headed for the shower to cool off and clean up. I turned the temperature down low and climbed in, offering Colin my hand. The cool water was a blissful relief after hours in drag and under sweltering stage lights, and Colin and I traded soft kisses under the spray as we washed off, trying not to laugh at the sound of Mum's occasional snores through the wall.

Afterwards we went back into my room where the fan had just about managed to lower the temperature to an acceptable level. I pulled Colin in for a kiss and slowly walked him backwards towards the bed, pushing him gently onto the mattress. He went down easily, smirking at me as he stretched out in the middle of the bed, loose hair fanning out around him and legs spread.

"Beautiful," I said as I grabbed the lube off the bedside table and tossed it onto the bed within easy reach. We'd stopped using condoms in July after we'd both hauled ourselves to the sexual health clinic in town for testing. One slightly embarrassing encounter with an older nurse later— she'd recognised me from *Drag Stars*, which her grandson had introduced her to—and I'd been free to go. At least Colin had gotten a good giggle out of it.

I climbed onto the bed, sliding between Colin's thighs and bringing my mouth down to kiss him senseless. Colin groaned and rolled his hips, rubbing his hardening cock against mine. I trailed my lips down his neck, kissing and sucking all the soft, sensitive spots I'd mapped out over the last few months while I slowly ground my hips down.

"More," Colin said with a gasp as I teased his nipples with my thumb. "I need more."

"I thought I was distracting you," I said. "Doesn't that mean I'm in charge?"

Colin grinned, desire flickering wildly in his eyes. "No." He pounced, rolling me over and pinning my hands above my head. He was straddling my hips and my cock pressed perfectly against the cleft of his ass. "You're mine."

I grinned. "That was never in doubt. I love you, Col."

"I love you too." He leant down and kissed me, his hair falling down around us and pooling on the sheets. It was one of my favourite parts of him and Colin was always happy to lie on the sofa, or in bed, with his head in my lap while I played with it.

Colin groaned into my mouth as I slowly rolled my hips again, rubbing my cock along his ass. "I want to ride you."

"Mmm, fuck, baby, that sounds so good."

"Want to watch me open myself up for you?"

"Always," I said as Colin released my hands, grabbed the lube, and pivoted in my lap to sit on top of my thighs with a grace and elegance I'd never seen anyone else possess. He brushed his hair over one shoulder as he tilted forward to give me the perfect view of his hole. I hummed with delight as I watched him sink two slick fingers into his ass, the moan he made going straight to my dick. I reached for my cock and began to stroke myself with a loose fist as Colin slowly started to ride his fingers.

His sweet moans made my dick jump in my hand and a shiver run down my spine.

"Anthony," Colin said with a groan as he turned to look

at me over his shoulder, his face a picture of desperation. "I... ohhh... fuck..."

"Do you need my cock, Col?" I asked, leaning forward to gently grip his hip. "Need me to fill you up?"

"Y-Yes! But..." He pulled his fingers out of himself and spun around again, hands landing on either side of my head. "I want to see your face. I love watching you come."

I tilted my head up and kissed him, slowly working my hand out from under his thigh where he'd accidentally landed on it. "Ride me then, baby. Use my cock and make yourself come."

Colin moaned as I kissed him deeply, my tongue sliding into his mouth. "I love you," he whispered as he sat up, reaching behind himself to grasp my cock, holding me in place so he could easily lower himself onto me. His eyes fluttered shut, another moan filling the room as my cock breached him and he slid slowly down my shaft, taking every inch until his ass rested against me.

He paused for a second and then began to roll his hips, resting his hands on my chest as he rode me. He looked so stunning like this, full of my cock and owning his pleasure. Taking what he wanted and giving me what I needed. Our days of bad sex with pitiful partners were long behind us, consigned to the past and a box of memories we never had to examine.

Once or twice he leant down to beg for a kiss and I was happy to oblige.

"A-Anthony," he said with a groan, nails gently digging into my chest as he rode me harder. "I'm... I'm getting close."

"Yeah?" I gripped his hips, just holding on for the ride. Pleasure hummed through me, my senses revelling in the feel of his ass around my shaft, the weight of his body on my lap, the soft moans and gasps bubbling from his lips, the heat of his skin under my fingers, the way his cock bounced as he moved, and the delight and bliss etched into his expression as he got closer and closer to his release. My own orgasm was there, waiting, but I held back because I needed to watch Colin come first.

"Fuck, it's so good," he said, slamming down onto my cock. "I... I can't... oh, fuck..." He groaned breathlessly as he sank down onto me again, his body tensing suddenly under my hands as his cock jumped and pulsed, shooting ropes of sticky cum across my stomach. Colin tipped forward suddenly and I almost had to catch him as he buried his face in my neck, breathing in deeply.

"Was that good, baby?" I asked as I trailed my fingers up and down his spine, slowly rocking my cock into him to prolong his pleasure.

"So good." His voice was muffled where his face was still pressed into my neck. "Fill me up? Please?"

I gripped him tightly in my arms and rolled us sideways until he was underneath me, smiling softly up at me with his hair fanned out around him like a burning halo. My cock was still inside him and I kissed him as I fucked him slow and deep, not stopping until my orgasm overwhelmed me, flooding my body with pleasure and making me gasp out Colin's name as I pumped my cum deep inside him.

We kept kissing, even after I'd pulled out and could feel my load trickling out of him and onto my thigh. We'd both need another shower, but I didn't want to move just yet. I wanted to stay here, in this moment, with the man who'd changed my life.

"I'm so proud of you," I said, brushing a strand of hair out of his face and nudging his nose softly with mine. "You did amazingly today."

"Thank you. So did you. Every time you perform… it blows me away. You're incredible, Anthony. I hope you know that." He kissed me again. "I love you so much."

"I love you too."

He sighed and smiled at me. "We should clean up before I fall asleep."

"In a minute," I said. "I want one more kiss."

"Only one?"

"Maybe more." I grinned. "Definitely more."

Colin put his arms around my neck and kissed me again.

Six months ago, in the depths of my hopelessness and misery, I'd never have been able to imagine anything like this. My life might not have turned out the way I'd planned, but I'd found the ultimate treasure amongst all the shit—Colin, the man I wanted to build my life with, who'd rescued me and kept me going when everything had threatened to overwhelm me. Who'd given me joy and love and hope and encouraged me to embrace the bad along with the good. Who'd seen the best in me, even when I couldn't.

I'd never admit that everything happened for a reason, because it still sounded like bollocks to me.

But maybe *some* things happened for a reason, and if all

the shit I'd waded through was the price I'd had to pay for finding the love of my life, then maybe it had been worth it.

I grinned as I kissed Colin softly.

Of course it had been worth it.

I had Colin.

And, in the end, that was all that mattered.

EPILOGUE
TEN MONTHS LATER

Sugar Pill

"I'M PRETTY sure making me move all this stuff during Pride month is illegal," Maddi said as she grabbed another box off the stack in the back of the van and began heading towards the front door of the little terraced house Anthony and I were now renting. We'd finally been able to collect the keys at nine o'clock that morning and had wasted no time in rallying our army of volunteers to start moving everything.

"You offered to help," Anthony yelled from the back of the van where he was shuffling more boxes forward and wedging them in next to one of the IKEA units we'd hurriedly disassembled when we'd realised it wouldn't go through his bedroom door in one piece. "I said we could hire people and you said, and I quote, 'Fuck that, I can help.'"

"I was wrong," Maddi said, pausing at the door. "You

should have gotten a bunch of sexy, strong men to do it instead."

"Can I get that in writing?"

"Fuck you, dickhead!"

I laughed as Maddi disappeared inside and I reached into the van to grab another box, which had Wigs scrawled across the side of it in bright red pen. "Did you not tell her that a couple of the rugby guys are on their way?"

Anthony grinned. "I might have forgotten to mention that. When do you think they'll be here?"

"Soon, I'd have thought. Rory messaged me that they were leaving about an hour ago." Part of the reason we'd ended up deciding to do the move ourselves had been because Bubblegum, who'd told me he was happy for me to call him Rory outside of drag, had kindly offered up his boyfriend, West, who was a strapping six foot three and could probably pick me up without batting an eyelash, and his friends, Mason and Jonny, as tribute. The fact that Mason was dating Legs, also known as Ryan, was another bonus because he was fully aware of the sheer amount of stuff that came along with being a drag queen.

Although I thought the number of wigs and outfits Barbie owned would put most other artists to shame.

And that was without even considering the amount of make-up.

"They had training first thing, right?" Anthony asked. "Do you think they'll turn up in their tiny shorts?"

"I'm sure they don't want you ogling them while they kindly move all our stuff," I said with a snort. "Besides, I bet Rory is the possessive kind. He'd probably drag West off to fuck somewhere if he catches you staring, and then we'll never get anything moved."

"And nobody is fucking in our house before us," Anthony said. He walked into the back of the van where half the heavier pieces of furniture were stacked. We didn't have a lot, just things like Anthony's bed and the bits and bobs from his bedroom, but I was pleasantly surprised we'd managed to get it all out of the house in the first place.

Perhaps it was because at that point, we'd been excited about the move rather than exhausted by it.

We'd spent the past couple of months trying to find somewhere to rent, which had proved more challenging than expected. Not only was everything we looked at being let as soon as it came onto the market, but quite a few letting agencies hadn't been a fan of the fact that Anthony was self-employed and I was a student. It didn't matter that I got a paid stipend—which wasn't much but would cover my rent and bills—or that Anthony had plenty of evidence of funds thanks to a couple of lucrative brand partnerships, the drag pantomime, a sold-out spring tour—organised by his amazing new agent, Delilah—regular slots at The Court and two other drag clubs, and proof of plenty of upcoming gigs. Some of them had still considered us a liability.

In the end, Anthony's mum had promised to act as guarantor for us, which had satisfied an agency enough to let us apply for the little house we could now call home.

It was on the outskirts of Nottingham, with easy access to the main road so we could make the journey up to Lincoln, and a nearby bus stop so I could get to the QMC and the main university campus. We also weren't too far from Rhys and Evan, who we already saw fairly regularly, and Evan, Anthony, and I would often all drive to The Court together to save on fuel.

I carried the box into the house and up into the tiny second bedroom we'd decided to turn into a drag studio and walk-in wardrobe, putting it on top of the stack we'd already started to build. I wasn't looking forward to unpacking everything but my plan was to do it all as quickly as possible so I didn't have to think about it again.

Then I was going to lie on the sofa and do absolutely fuck all while indulging in the brand-new season of *Llewelyn*.

I still couldn't believe we'd met Henry Lu. Bitch's youngest brother, Lewis, was married to Henry's brother, Jason, and Lewis had brought both the Lu brothers and Henry's partner, Alex, to the club last December. Henry had been very happy to pose for photos because apparently he'd been desperate to meet Barbie, who'd nearly died of shock.

I wasn't sure if I should feel guilty lusting over Henry's naked ass knowing how charming he was in person, but that was a thought for another day—when I wasn't exhausted from moving and wishing I could just snap my fingers and unpack everything, Mary Poppins style.

When I got back downstairs there was another car outside, and the three rugby boys accompanied by Rory and Ryan were standing on the pavement chatting to Maddi and Anthony.

"Babes!" Rory called, waving to me. "Over here."

"Hey," I said. "You made it. Thanks for coming."

"No worries," Ryan said, sipping from a large iced coffee. "Happy to help."

"And by that you mean volunteering us to do it for you?" Mason asked, putting his arm around Ryan's shoulder and grinning.

"Obviously. Now put those rugby muscles to good use and get this all unloaded," Ryan said, making a shooing motion with his free hand. "And don't forget to bend with your knees."

"Is this why you got me to wear shorts?" Mason asked with a laugh as he walked over to the truck. "So you can look at my ass?"

"Absolutely, babe." Ryan winked. "They could be sluttier, though."

"Wait, should I have worn shorts too?" Jonny asked, looking between himself, Mason, and West. "I feel kind of left out now."

"It's okay. The grey joggers are a perfect substitute. Besides, what would your man say if he couldn't see you wearing slutty shorts?"

"He'd just ask where his were," Jonny said. "We both know he loves showing off." He picked up half the bed frame out of the back of the van like it was a paperweight and began carrying it towards the house, chatting to West as he went.

Jonny finding a boyfriend had apparently come as a bit of a surprise to Rory and Mason, but the common consensus was that nobody was ever going to be better for Jonny than Devon.

"I suppose we should help too," Rory said with a sigh. "What's the lightest thing you've got?"

"Moira?" Anthony nudged one of our foam wig heads towards him with his foot. He was still stood in the back of the van, and I was enjoying the view. He'd always been confident, but he'd grown so much more self-assured over the past ten months. There was an easy happiness to him and a sparkling love for life that I adored.

Despite the bumps in the road, including finding out for certain that Caesar Hurst had disappeared along with all the money, our relationship had gone from strength to strength. We'd started to build a life together, and this house was the next part of that. We'd found friendship, community, and joy—something I'd never imagined having when I moved here eighteen months ago.

I'd told myself then it didn't matter if I had friends, and now I had more than I'd ever had in my life. I had love too, another thing I'd never thought would become reality. And I had a PhD I loved and a blossoming drag career.

My life was truly unrecognisable and I cherished every single second of it.

Even if those seconds involved lugging boxes and bags up and down stairs.

"I can deal with Moira," Rory said, not batting an eyelash at the fact we'd named our wig head. He picked her up and looking at Ryan said, "Come on, bitch, you can take something too."

"Fine," Ryan said before reaching for the other wig head. "Who's this?"

"Priscilla," I said with a smile as I watched Ryan scoop her up.

"Come along Madam," Ryan said, tucking her under his arm. "Your new abode awaits."

I chuckled softly as I watched the pair of them disappear into the house, giving Anthony and me a tiny moment alone. "How're you doing, sugar?" he asked, leaning down from the back of the van to kiss me softly.

"Okay. Tired, but I'm pretty sure that's par for the course. God, I hate moving."

"Same." He smiled. "We'll get curry later and veg out. Watch some *Llewelyn*. Then I can blow you on the sofa." He winked. "As long as you're not too tired."

"I'm sure I'll manage," I said, kissing him quickly. "I'll return the favour too."

"That's because you're awesome and I love you."

"I love you too." I grinned. "I can't believe we finally have our own little house."

"Me neither. It'll be so nice not to have to worry about roommates. We can actually sit on our sofa and watch whatever we want without someone huffing at us."

I winced because my previous housemates hadn't been keen on Anthony popping over regularly, which I understood but they could have just talked to me about it instead of rolling their eyes and grumbling from a distance.

"It's going to be great," I said. "I can't wait."

"No need to wait. We've already got the keys," Anthony said with another kiss. "It's ours, baby, and one day we're going to buy something instead, where we can do whatever the fuck we want—like paint it bright green."

I laughed. "Anything but beige."

"We could probably paint here if you want. We'd just have to change it afterwards."

"We can think about it," I said. "With the amount of stuff we've got, in some rooms it won't matter what colour the walls are."

He snorted. "Are you saying I have too many wigs?"

"No, I'm saying *we* have too many wigs. And you have too much make-up." I grinned and kissed him one final time before picking up another box. "I love you."

"Love you too, Col."

I walked towards the house, box in hand, and I could see the future before me.

It looked beautiful.

And I'd have Anthony right beside me for every moment of it.

A SURPRISE VISIT
BONUS SHORT

Sugar Pill

I SIGHED and rubbed my eyes, the spreadsheet of data in front of me starting to blur into one giant mess of numbers. That usually meant it was time to call it a day, but I'd gotten so behind in my work recently with all the excitement of starting drag that I needed to pull a few long days to catch up while the university labs were quiet over the summer.

If not, I knew I'd drown in stress, so it was better to spend a couple of days, or weeks, suffering now rather than spending the rest of the year chasing my tail.

Even so, I wished I was spending the evening with Anthony in the sunshine instead of being cooped up in the tiny postgraduate office I shared with three other PhD candidates. None of them had been in today or would be for the rest of the week since all of them were away visiting family or on holiday.

The quiet meant it was easier to get work done, but the

department was so empty this time of year it felt like I was working in a ghost town and it was starting to get to me a little.

Anthony had asked why I didn't just work from home, but I knew if I was in my room I'd get distracted by something—probably make-up or playing with a wig—and then I'd be even further behind.

My stomach rumbled and I realised I hadn't taken a break for a while. Now felt like as good a time as any to stretch my legs, stick a ready meal in the kitchen microwave, and make myself another cup of tea.

Just as I was standing up, there was a knock on the door. "Come in," I said, assuming it was one of the department's lovely cleaning staff come to ask if I was planning on staying much longer so they didn't accidentally lock me in or turn off all the lights, leaving me wandering around in the dark.

But to my delighted surprise, it was someone else entirely.

"Knock knock," Anthony said as he stuck his head around the door, his blond hair pushed back off his face. "Surprise!"

"Oh my God," I said. "What are you doing here?!"

"I knew you were planning on pulling another late night and I assumed you'd probably forgotten to feed yourself. And I thought you also might need me to force you to take a break, since it's nearly half-seven and you've been here for about twelve hours." He grinned and raised an eyebrow, waiting for me to tell him that he was wrong.

But he wasn't.

"I mean, I was thinking I should take a break. And I am getting kinda hungry."

"Good," he said, stepping through the door and closing it behind him. He looked around the tiny office, with the four desks crammed in, the overflowing bookshelves, the white board on one wall which was covered with formulas scribbled in colourful pen, and the tiny window which overlooked the roof of another part of the building.

The window didn't let much light in, especially over the winter, and was more decorative than anything. We usually kept the blinds closed, because the endless concrete vista and pigeons sitting on the tiny window ledge wasn't exactly inspiring.

"It's not the most glamourous place in the world," I said as I watched Anthony, who was wearing a loose linen shirt and the most perfect pair of shorts, with a bag slung over one shoulder. "But it's better than nothing."

"And it's quiet," he said with a hungry smirk. "And the door locks."

"Yeah but… oh…" I trailed off as a memory flashed into the front of my mind and I felt my face turning scarlet. I'd told Anthony about my fantasies of him bending me over my desk and fucking me senseless… was he here to make those dreams into reality? "Are you…?"

"Am I what, sugar?" he asked as he closed the gap between us and put his bag on the floor by my desk. "You have to actually say it."

"Are you just here to make me eat dinner or do you have an ulterior motive?"

"What would that be?"

I swallowed, the heat in his eyes melting me to my core. I didn't even know if this counted as teasing, but he'd already frazzled me to the point I could barely get my words out. "To fulfil my fantasies of you fucking me in my office," I said quietly.

"Do you want me to fulfil them?" he asked, putting his hand on my waist and pulling me against him. "If you don't want to, that's absolutely fine. We can just have some dinner and then go back to yours. I'm never going to force you to do something you're not comfortable with."

"I... I..." My heart raced, the idea both thrilling and slightly terrifying. But it was also an evening at the end of August. Nobody else was here, the door locked, and the blinds were shut: if there was ever going to be a time to try this out, now was it. "Yes. I want you to fuck me."

I grabbed the front of his shirt and pulled him onto his tiptoes and into a filthy kiss. Anthony groaned, grabbing my shirt and nipping my lip, his tongue sliding into my mouth and making my knees weak.

He pushed me backwards until my knees bumped against the edge of my desk and I gasped as I sat down on the edge of it.

"Let me just—" I broke out of his grasp to reach behind me and slam my laptop shut.

"Pass it here," Anthony said and when I handed it to it, he turned to the side and dumped it on the edge of one of the other desks out of the way. There were still a few bits of paper and knick knacks littering the top of my desk but nothing that was going to stop us from fucking on it.

Anthony kissed me again and I groaned, my hands

desperately working at the buttons on his shirt as he reached for the waistband of the loose trousers I was wearing. I lifted my hips so he could pull them down, swiftly dumping them on the floor along with my underwear.

He trailed his mouth down my neck and sucked marks into the soft pale skin. My neck tilted back, giving him more access as his hand wrapped around my cock, stroking it slowly. I spread my thighs and leant back, desperate for more.

This wasn't going to be slow and sweet, this was going to be fast and desperate, and it was everything I'd been dreaming about.

I moaned sadly as Anthony pulled away, ducking down to retrieve something from his bag: a small bottle of lube. He grinned as he poured some onto his fingers, his shirt half-open and rumpled, lips kiss-swollen and slick.

"I've got you," he said softly as he stepped between my thighs and dipped his hand between them. I leant back further and pushed my bottom forwards, gasping with delight as Anthony slowly pressed two slick fingers into my waiting hole.

"Fuck," I said with a happy groan, my eyes fluttering shut and a smile crossing my lips. "I needed this."

"Yeah? Needed to be filled up?"

"Mmm, yes. So much better than spreadsheets."

Anthony snorted and kissed my neck. "Sex: better than spreadsheets."

I tried to laugh but it just morphed into another groan as he curled his fingers and rubbed them over my prostate, making my cock jump as need surged through me. "More,"

I said, my voice coming out soft and needy. "Please, Anthony. Fuck me!"

"You want it like this?" he said, mouthing at my jaw and sending a shiver down my spine. "Or do you want to bend over the desk?"

"Like this. Want to keep kissing you."

He kissed me deeply, his tongue sliding into my mouth and claiming me, one hand cupping my jaw as he slowly pulled his fingers out of my ass and undid the button on his shorts. I heard him pulling them down but I was too busy kissing him to watch what he was doing.

He moved closer to me and I shuffled my butt as far forward as I dared. It was a little awkward but we made it work, and it was easier than working with the height difference of me standing and bending over.

Another moan punched its way out of my chest as Anthony pushed his cock inside me, filling me with one smooth thrust. It felt so good and I could feel all then tension in my body starting to melt away.

I didn't care how fucking cliché it sounded, his dick was the best stress relief in the world.

Anthony groaned and gripped my hip tightly as he began to fuck me fast and hard, pistoning his hips and pounding me with his cock. I wanted every inch inside me so I spread myself out on the desk, knocking things out of the way, not caring about the mess. I could pick everything up later.

Right now, I just needed to get fucked.

He let go of my jaw and grabbed my thigh, pulling my leg around his waist as he thrust deeper inside me. The rough material of his shorts brushed my legs, because he'd barely shoved them down far enough to get his dick out, and something about that made the whole encounter feel so much dirtier.

I loved the feeling of being spread out on my office desk, half-naked, and begging for his dick, while Anthony was still dressed, with his shirt partially unbuttoned and his shorts around his thighs, his hair pushed back off his head.

I reached down and grasped my cock, jerking myself fast as Anthony fucked me, filthy moans and cries of pleasure dripping from his lips. Thank God there was nobody else around because we weren't exactly trying to be quiet.

But I wouldn't have cared if anyone did hear, because I was getting my favourite fantasy fulfilled and it was everything I'd ever wanted.

"I'm… fuck, I'm getting close," I said with a broken gasp, my orgasm rushing towards me, burning up every nerve it touched. "A-Anthony, I'm gonna come!"

"That's it, sugar. Come on my fucking cock for me. Fuck, look so fucking pretty like this… gonna, fuck, gonna fill you up."

His hands tightened on my body as he thrust harder and as he growled out his release, my name on his tongue, my own orgasm hit me with unbridled intensity, cum splattering across my stomach and Anthony's shirt.

Bliss made my muscles soft, happiness enveloping me like a blanket. I sat up and cupped his jaw, kissing him over and over until my lips were sore.

"Thank you," I said, resting my forehead against his. "That was perfect."

"Good," he said as he took my hands in his and squeezed. "Would you like some dinner now? I bought some picky bits, figured we could have an office picnic. I've got some wipes to clean up with too."

"That sounds amazing. You're the best boyfriend ever."

"I try," he said, kissing me again. Then he glanced down at himself and noticed the cum soaking into his shirt… "Shit, I should've bought a change of clothes. Guess I'm going home shirtless tonight."

"Oh no, what a shame," I said with a fond laugh. "I might have a spare in my backpack. But I won't say no to you being shirtless, and we can walk back to mine from here later."

"Sounds good." He kissed me and then stepped back. "Okay wipes and then food. Because you've been working too hard."

"And I'm very grateful to you for the distraction."

"Well who else is going to make sure you take breaks?" He smirked at me. "And if you're going to keep working these long hours, it's my duty to distract you."

I hummed happily, a beaming smile on my lips. "I'll happily take every distraction on offer."

"Good to know," he said, shooting me a wink as he bent down to rummage in his bag.

I got the feeling this wouldn't be the last time I got a surprise visit… and I already couldn't wait for the next one.

IT'S GIVING CONVENTION FANTASY
BONUS SHORT

Barbie Summers

"W℮ℋ℮ℛ℮ ᴅᴏ you want me to put these T-shirts?" Colin asked, hefting an enormous cardboard box in his arms. His long hair was pulled up into a loose bun, little strands frizzing out of it like a halo, and a bead of sweat clung to his temple.

"Just shove them under that table for now," I said, looking up at from my place on the floor where I was attempting to put together some flamingo lawn decorations that Amazon had promised were easy to assemble. Easy my ass.

We were currently in the middle of set-up for the official *Drag Stars* convention at the London ExCeL centre, and I was starting to curse myself for signing up and paying the extortionate booth fee.

Although that was mostly because I was tired, hot, hungry, and frustrated.

I knew everything was going to look fucking amazing when it was done. I just needed to get it done first.

"How many more boxes are there?" I asked as Colin slid the box under the undressed table and I shoved a cheap bamboo cane into another flamingo.

"I think that's it," Colin said with a smile as he stood. "Or it will be once Rhys and Evan bring the last two in from Rory's van. They've got another box of hoodies and the art prints."

"Perfect," I said, triumphantly lifting up the finished flamingo. "Then we just need to put everything out. And finish decorating... and we have three hours... fuck me. Why the hell didn't I pay someone to do this?"

Colin chuckled softly and walked over to me, leaning down to plant a kiss on the top of my head before plucking the flamingo out of my hands. "Because the booth decorating company quoted you nearly three grand and you said, 'fuck that, I'll do it myself'."

"Yeah well, I should've just started selling pictures of my feet or something," I said with a laugh as I pulled another flamingo out of the nearby box and started putting it together. They'd already been bright pink when we'd ordered them but mum had helped me add a layer of spray-painted pink glitter across the top of them for added kitschy goodness.

Colin laughed again. "It'll all be fine, I promise. We can get it done." He looked at me fondly, a small frown appearing between his eyebrows. Then he walked over to his backpack, which he'd dumped in the corner when we'd arrived, and rummaged inside it to pull out a tub of home-made, dairy-free flapjacks. They were something he'd started making recently and were to fucking die for. I could've eaten an entire tub in one sitting.

"Have one of these," he said, holding out the tub. "You're getting cranky because you haven't eaten lately."

"Thanks," I said as I took one of the enormous flapjacks and stuffed it into my mouth, letting the dense oaty, syrupy goodness melt on my tongue. "I love you."

"I love you too," he said. "And I promise, it's all going to be okay."

I nodded as I chewed, looking around the booth and taking a minute to imagine what it would look like when it was all finished. I'd had a clear vision in my head as soon as I'd been invited to attend; a pink and teal sixties inspired kitsch-motel fantasy, complete with flamingos, palm trees, and a neon sign.

I'd spent months planning everything in my head, finding all the perfect pieces in my budget and doing a bit of DIY where necessary, and now I just had to put it all together.

"Right," I said as I finished the last of my flapjack, casting a longing glance at the tub in case Colin fancied passing me another piece. "Let's do this."

As soon as I'd said that, Rhys and Evan appeared around the corner of the booth carrying the last boxes of my brand-new merch, designed by the fabulous Legs Luthor, and right behind them was Rory, hefting a small tool kit. God bless drag queens with a wide skill set.

Between the five of us, it didn't actually take as long to set everything up as I'd feared and while we'd still needed all three hours, the booth actually looked polished and presentable by the time security came around to politely tell us to shove off.

"Okay, the show opens at nine tomorrow," I said as we walked out of the hall and into the half-empty central walkway. "So we need to get here for eight at the latest I think. Just so we can get coffee, get the merch all set out, test the card machine, and all that shit."

I glanced around at the small group, who despite being sweaty and exhausted, all seemed excited. It stunned me for a second, because when I'd done the show a year ago, my experience had been a much lonelier and more stressful one. Yeah, I'd had friends from London with me, but at least a couple of them had radiated jealousy at not getting to exhibit themselves and I felt like I'd had to make myself smaller to please them.

But this time, all my friends seemed nothing but happy for me. And I was so grateful for all their help, love, and support.

"And I just want to say thanks," I said as we kept walking. "I really appreciate you all giving up your weekends and dragging your asses down to London for me. You're the best bitches I could ask for."

"Duh, why wouldn't we come?" Rory asked, grinning at me. "It's fucking drag con. Of course we were gonna be here."

"That and you weren't going to allow any of us to play with electrics unsupervised," Evan said with a wry smile.

"That too."

"It's going to be amazing," Colin said as he slid his hand

into mine and squeezed gently. "You're going to blow everyone away."

"I hope so." I had two looks prepared for each of the two days the event was on; one for the booth, and one for the daily runway that took place in the middle of the con. And as a former winner, I really needed to turn it out.

I glanced up at Colin, soaking in all the details of his beautiful face as my heart fluttered. We'd only been together for just over six months, but he'd changed my life in ways I couldn't even put into words. "I'm really glad you're here, Col. I couldn't do this without you."

"Of course you could," he said. "But you don't have to because we're a team and I love you." He grinned teasingly, swinging our hands as we walked. "Plus you're my boyfriend and my drag mother, I'm pretty sure it'd be a crime if I didn't show up."

"You won't be so happy when my alarm goes off at five tomorrow."

"I'll live." He leant down and kissed me. "For you, it's worth it."

I wasn't sure the five o'clock wake up call was worth it when my alarm started screaming at me, but I dutifully hauled my ass out of bed and into the shower so I could begin my transformation from hot mess into queen of the fucking universe.

I'd wanted to give myself plenty of time so I didn't have to rush and, for once in my life, the plan actually worked. It felt surreal to be walking down the empty halls of the

ExCeL with Colin beside me, our trainers squeaking on the floor—because I wasn't putting my heels on until we were in the booth—and the digital advertising boards above us highlighting the event.

Despite the fact I'd been on tour multiple times, it still felt surreal to see the *Drag Stars* name on the boards and know I was part of it. My platform was still growing and sometimes I forgot just how big it was getting, because I still felt like little old me, a stubborn brat from the East Midlands with a talent for make-up and lip-syncing.

The fact that people were spending their hard-earned money and using their free time to come and see me still had the ability to stun me into silence.

It was times like that, seeing the fans excitement, that reminded me just how far I'd come and why I did this: I loved performing and bringing people joy.

When we got to the small entrance door to the hall, I stopped dead in my tracks and stared at the sight in front of me. Hundreds of people with VIP tickets, which allowed early entry, had already started to queue and the line ran all the way down past the huge door to the exhibition hall to the very front of the ExCeL centre.

It had been the same last year, but the sight still took my breath away.

"What the—" Colin said with a breathless laugh of disbelief. "Are people…"

"Yeah, sugar, they're all waiting to get it," I said, squeezing his hand tighter. "It's a bit overwhelming, isn't it?"

"Just a bit." His wide eyes followed the line. "Do you

want to go inside? I can get both of us a coffee and meet you in there. You're pretty noticeable right now and I don't want you getting mobbed."

"Thanks," I said and turned to duck past security and through the door. "I'll see you in a minute."

At the booth, I found Rhys, Evan, and Rory all waiting for me, decked out in Barbie Summers T-Shirts. They already had coffee and were hard at work laying out all the merch on the table in front of the booth, making sure everything had visible pricing, and that all the stock was in easy reach.

Virtually every artist had a minimum merch spend from attendees for a meet and greet and I'd tried to price mine fairly reasonably at twenty-five pounds, which was the cost of a T-shirt or a signed print. I hadn't split it into pricing categories either, where people had to pay more for a photo, because even if I didn't make as much out of the weekend, I hated the idea of some people not getting to see me because they couldn't make their budget stretch.

"Morning," Evan said, looking up from folding hoodies with the new teal and white Queen of Hot Messes slogan plastered across the front of it. "What time do you call this?"

"Too early," I said with a laugh as I put my stuff down. "Not all of us are used to five in the morning wake up calls."

"It's nearly quarter past eight," Rhys said and I winced, realising it'd taken me slightly longer to walk across from the hotel than I'd anticipated. Still, at least I was here before the doors opened.

"Well not all of us are used to being awake at quarter past eight either," I said as I walked into the booth the check on everything. In the new light of day, with fresher eyes, it looked even more incredible than I could ever have imagined.

There was a giant neon flamingo and a motel sign with my name in teal neon, both of which Rory had hooked up, the glittery lawn flamingos and fake palm trees, all in front of a backdrop that I'd had designed and printed to give kitsch sixties Americana vibes.

There was even a little blow-up paddling pool filled with pink and teal balls to create a mini ball pit, and several sun loungers with my name painted across them. Which were not only stunning but would give me somewhere to sit down if the chance arose.

I had a sneaking suspicion that wouldn't happen until the show closed. In which case I'd need somewhere close by to collapse in a heap.

I really hoped someone had remembered to pack snacks.

Colin arrived a few minutes later, bringing me a coffee and a large cinnamon bun, because he was the best boyfriend ever, and I hid in the booth to consume both before putting my shoes on—rhinestoned teal cowboy boots with a chunky heal to match my sparkling pink and teal outfit. It was very sixties kitsch meets cowgirl. Like Dolly Parton meets Barbie on steroids.

If that was even possible.

I'd wanted to finish helping with set-up but other people kept popping in to see me, and before I knew it the doors were opening and the chaos had begun.

.

I'd expected it to be busy, but I hadn't expected it to be so busy that I lost all track of time and space. It was a whirlwind of people wanting hugs and photos and to chat, all with their new Barbie Summers merch clutched in their hands.

Some of them had even bought me presents, including some gorgeous friendship bracelets with my name on and an incredible piece of cross-stich which had my finale look on from my season of *Drag Stars*.

That had made me cry and poor Colin had needed to hunt down a packet of tissues to carefully dab my make-up so it didn't run.

"You're amazing," I said as Colin pushed a sandwich into my hand. I had no idea what time it was. I took a huge bite and groaned because fuck, I'd needed that. "I love you so much."

"I love you too," he said. "Now eat that and then you need to go to the green room and get changed for the runway."

"Shit, is it that time already?"

"Yeah. You're doing great though."

"How's everyone else?"

"Good, we've organised breaks and everything. You don't need to worry about us, we're fine."

"I do though, because I love you and I'm so grateful for your help."

He smiled and pointed at my sandwich. "You can thank me later. For now, eat."

I grinned as shoved more of it into my mouth. I really wouldn't be able to do any of this without him.

It didn't take me long to finish eating and make my way to the green room to change, where I also found Maddi who looked equally exhausted but happy and we chatted quickly as we got dressed.

I was *so* glad I'd gone for cowboy boots over whacking great heels, because even though my feet were sore, I could still walk. And it meant I could put my big shoes on for the runway, along with the most incredible camped-up sixties ballgown and my giant crown.

I was serving queen, bitch, and kitsch glamour and I was living for it.

And as I walked out onto the glittering runway carpet to the thunderous cheers and applause of the watching fans, there was only one person I was looking for.

At the end of the runway, behind the metal barrier, in the space reserved for the attending artists special guests, was my Colin. His red hair shimmered under the lights, his Barbie Summers T-shirt and bell-bottom embroidered jeans making him look so fucking stunning I wanted to die, and his beautiful smile making me want to live instead.

I strutted down the carpet, my eyes fixed on him, unable to stop myself from smiling.

And when I reached the end, I struck a pose, waved, and then tottered over to the barrier and pulled him in for a kiss as everyone screamed and cameras flashed.

"Show off," Colin said with a grin, his mouth plastered in my cherry red lipstick.

"Yeah, but I'm Barbie fucking Summers," I said, throwing him a wink and a smile. "And I fucking love you."

"I fucking love you too."

I strode back down the runway riding emotions that were a million miles high.

I was a hot mess, queen of the motherfucking universe, and Colin's boyfriend. It didn't get any better than that.

ACKNOWLEDGMENTS

When I started writing The Court series, I knew I wanted to talk about some of the issues that drag artists, and creatives in general, face. And unfortunately, non-payment is one of those issues.

More than one drag artist has at least one story about not being paid, and often that amount of money is quite significant.

This book is another example of something I didn't set out to write but so many of us struggle with perfectionism, what-ifs, and blaming ourselves for things we're not responsible for, and although it was painful it was also freeing.

My thanks go out to Dr Rosie Fox for all their help and advice with the legal situation in this book. Any and all faults in the writing are completely my own.

Thanks to Charity for helping me along when I stumbled and convincing me to keep going, and to Noah for all your comments, feedback and advice.

To all my wonderful writer friends; Carly, Toby, Jodi, Lark, Willow, Kat, and more, I couldn't do this without your support.

To Jennifer, for helping me to make this story shine like a diamond and your endless patience with my abuse of the rules of grammar. And to Lori, for catching the things I've missed.

To Wander and Andrey for giving me the perfect Barbie Summers, and to Natasha for creating the most stunning covers for him.

To Linda, and her wonderful team, who's organisational skills leave me in awe.

To Dan, for bringing The Court to life in a way I never could.

To my husband, for his endless love, support, and being my sounding board.

And last, but never least, to you, my fabulous readers. Whether I'm new to you or you've been here since the start, I am grateful for you love and support.

If you enjoyed *Baby Queen*, please consider leaving a review. Reviews are invaluable for indie authors, and may help other readers find this book.

Until next time.

ALSO BY CHARLIE NOVAK

The Court
Drama Queen

Scene Queen

Baby Queen

Lincoln Knights
The Tighthead *(July 2024)*

Heather Bay
Like I Pictured

Like I Promised

Like I Wished

Like I Needed

Like I Pretended

Like I Wanted

Roll for Love
Natural Twenty

Charisma Check

Proficiency Bonus

Bonus Action: The Roll for Love Short Story Collection

Roll for Love: The Complete Collection (Boxset)

Forever Love

Always Eli

Finding Finn

Oh So Oscar

Kiss Me

Strawberry Kisses

Summer Kisses

Spiced Kisses

The Kiss Me Short Collection

Kiss Me: The Complete Collection (Boxset)

Off the Pitch

Breakaway

Extra Time

Final Score

The Off the Pitch Short Collection

Off the Pitch: The Complete Collection (Boxset)

Standalones

Screens Apart

Couture Crush

Up To Snow Good

Pole Position

Only Orlando: An MMM Romance

SHORT STORIES

One More Night

Twenty-Two Years (Newsletter Exclusive)

Snow Way In Hell

Audiobooks

Buy audiobooks directly from Charlie at charlienovakshop.com

Drama Queen

Scene Queen

Like I Promised

Like I Wished

Like I Needed

Like I Pretended

Like I Wanted

Natural Twenty

Charisma Check

Proficiency Bonus

Always Eli

Finding Finn

Oh So Oscar

Strawberry Kisses

Summer Kisses

Spiced Kisses

Up To Snow Good

Translations

ITALIAN

Qui Neve Ci Cova

For a regularly updated list, please visit:

charlienovak.com/books

charlienovak.com/audiobooks

CHARLIE NOVAK

Charlie lives in England with her husband and two cheeky dogs. She spends most of her days wrangling other people's words in her day job and then trying to force her own onto the page in the evening.

She loves cute stories with a healthy dollop of fluff, plenty of delicious sex, and happily ever afters — because the world needs more of them.

Charlie has very little spare time, but what she does have she fills with baking, Dungeons and Dragons, reading and many other nerdy pursuits. She also thinks that everyone should have at least one favourite dinosaur…

Website charlienovak.com
Shop charlienovakshop.com
Facebook Group Charlie's Angels
Sign up for her newsletter for bonus scenes, new releases and extras.
Or Patreon for early access chapters, flash fiction, first looks, and serial stories.

- facebook.com/charlienovakauthor
- instagram.com/charlienwrites
- bookbub.com/profile/charlie-novak
- amazon.com/author/charlienovak
- patreon.com/charlienovak

Printed in Great Britain
by Amazon